Dudesow: The Unlucky Dude

Christian R. Scrolls

Copyright © 2024 by Christian R. Scrolls

All rights reserved

The characters and events portrayed in this book are fictitious. Any similarity to real people, living or dead, undead, or the supernatural in any state or form is coincidental and is not intended by the author.

No part of this book may be reproduced, stored in a retrieval system, or transmitted in any form or by any means, electronic, mechanical, photocopying, recording, or otherwise, without express written permission of the publisher.

Image vectors are by creators CDJ, OpenClipart-Vectors, StarGladeVintage, StarGlade & b0red. Images are free for use via Pixabay. Pixabay images used are licensed for commercial use through Bookbrush.com

Final cover art design by artist Katarina @nskvsky

Final map design by artist Alec M @alecmck

Cover and map concept by Christian R Scrolls

I would like to thank my family, friends, and my love Jocelyn for their ongoing support. I'm glad that I can finally share a bit of my imagination with the world.

Chapter 1

P rince Dudesow is indisputably the least popular person in the entire Default kingdom. His parents found his company so unpleasant that they housed him at the far end of the castle grounds.

Visitors to the kingdom often hear from locals that Dudesow's unpopularity stems from a widely-held belief in a curse of misfortune associated with him. The closer one gets to the prince, the more likely they are to experience a day's worth of bad luck.

Whenever royal visitors inquired about the young prince's whereabouts, the King and Queen would respond with visible discomfort. They would somberly explain that their son had been cursed within an unshakable shroud of ill fortune. The King ordered the prince to remain locked in his room for his sake and the kingdom's safety.

Fortunately, the bad luck that shadowed Dudesow didn't seem to have any physical bearing on the young prince himself. The castle staff widely believed that the prince's misfortune would only extend to those who ventured too close to him. Because of this, Prince Dudesow grew accustomed to the castle staff maintaining a noticeable distance from him. Their interactions were slim to none. Dudesow would open the door slowly to grab his meal to see the staff peeking around the corner at the end of the hall. Dudesow had become accustomed to their averted gazes and expressions ranging between fear and hatred.

Whenever Dudesow ventured out of his room, a rare occurrence unless necessary, as he was ordered to to stay within his room. The few times he tried to leave, the King would order Sir Kerry to escort the prince back to his room. Eventually, by the age of six, Dudesow stopped trying to leave his room.

The castle staff attributed Sir Kerry's remarkable willpower and unimaginable courage as the driving force behind his willingness to visit the Prince. The gallant knight, Sir Kerry, Commander of the Default Kingdom brigade of knights, was blunt in his disbelief that Dudesow was cursed with bad luck. He openly derided those who propagated such superstitious beliefs. Few dared to challenge a renowned highly decorated war hero, except for the King and Queen themselves. When they caught wind of the knight's contrary views, they promptly instructed him to stop his outspoken beliefs on the matter. The King and Queen were the first to declare the boy's unfortunate condition, and it was prudent for Sir Kerry to refrain from questioning their words any further. Sir Kerry would've been swiftly reprimanded if he wasn't the only individual in the kingdom that the King and Queen could rely upon to conduct Prince Dudesow's health check-ins. To their chagrin, and with no other viable options available, the Queen assigned Sir Kerry to check in on the Prince's well-being at least once a week. Sir Kerry became the sole person to engage in weekly conversations with the Prince.

The reluctant scholars the Queen sent to tutor Dudesow would speak to the prince from the other side of his door. Dudesow gave up trying to remember the scholars' names, as they didn't show up for more than a few quick sessions. The Queen would often tire of getting replacement tutors. The queen's patience was thin due to the scholars constantly disappearing, and leaving without a formal resignation after a few short sessions. Eventually, the Queen gave up trying to find a reliable scholar for the prince, so she ordered a library installed in Dudesows' room, expecting the prince to study the academic material on his own preemptively.

Sir Kerry, had genuine concern for the young lonely prince and stopped by Dudesow's room for weekly well-being checkups. Sir Kerry, also conducted these visits purposefully, to impart essential knowledge to the prince, ranging from necessary academic fundamentals to self-defense techniques. The knight was often frustrated that the staff thought the prince carried some contagious affliction, they started to give Sir Kerry more than acceptable respectable distance when they crossed paths, others turned to try to avoid crossing his path. The knight felt sorrow for the prince for if it were not for his weekly health check-ins done, Dudesow might have remained utterly isolated for his entire childhood. Sir Kerry felt that a child who is ignored by his parents and is told that he brings misfortune to others is a considerable burden for a solitary child to bear alone. The knight asked Dudesow what made him happy, and the boy told him that his visits and his books brought him happiness.

The knight stood outside Prince Dudesow's room.

Knock knock

"You don't need to knock, Sir Knight. I already know it's you, it's only always you"
"It would be rude and dishonorable for a knight not to announce his arrival"
The knight slowly opened the door and scanned the room as he did. The prince was nowhere in sight.
"You've left the door unlocked, It would be ill-advised to continue on that bad habit."
The knight closed the door behind him, bringing in with him a bundle of cloth, wrapped tight with twine.
"No need; locking the door would keep you out and disrupt my project"
"It is always best to never let your guard down, especially in a room with no guard"
"You are the oldest knight, and you've never had a guard"
"I don't need a guardian following me around. For I can guard not only myself but also others who are of greater importance than I." He smiled, "If I, the one who leads an army into battle, needed a guard, then I wouldn't be that great of a knight."
The knight walked up to the prince's voice, hidden behind a stack of books. To Kerry, it appeared to be a fort made entirely out of books.
"Yes, that makes sense," the prince said, half listening.
"I see you built a fort, so you're not completely defenseless" The knight smirked.
The prince peaked over the tall stack of books. "I've decided to build a fort from all the books I've completed. I've read many books in my library, but not enough to build a solid impenetrable fort. It's an underwhelming fort so far"
The fort of books was at the boys' shoulder height in parameter.
The young prince sighed, "I have played with the idea of using books that I haven't read. But then it would bother me knowing that there are books within the fort's walls that have no right to belong within the wall of books I've read. I would feel guilty. My conundrum of no real importance. What will I be learning today?"
The knight shook his head, failing terribly to restrain his smile, "Today, we'll be putting the learning on hold. For we will focus on something of greater importance, celebrating your birthday."
Dudesow stood up, peeking his eyes over his wall of books, "Would it be rude for me to ask, did you bring me a gift? I hope it's more adventure books!"

"You'd be correct, but I'll let it pass now. Permission to enter this fort?"

"Ye may enter."

Sir Kerry overdramatically climbed over the wall of books and then sat cross-legged on the floor. He was careful not to bump into the fort walls. He handed the bundle of cloth over to Dudesow. "I bring you a gift, and...will I ask you to please be careful-"

Dudesow untied the leatherbound bundle, to reveal a scabbard, with a silver hilt glimmering in the light.

A smile rippled on Dudesow's face. "Is this what I think it is? My very own sword? Like yours?"

The Prince grabbed the gift and unwrapped it with anticipation.

Before the prince could even think about lifting the sword, the knight quickly placed a palm on the blunt side of the blade. "I appreciate the enthusiasm, but you must first remember what I've taught you."

Dudesow spoke the mantra as he admired the blade,

"Brace your mind, or you won't be slick, With every move, be sharp and quick. In battles fierce, make foes submit, Use your wisdom, or your body will end up split"

The knight nodded, "Treat the blade well, it is, after all, a gift from your father. Blessed from the court's holy man and forged by the best dwarven smith in the land"

The prince's smile faltered, "My father...doesn't care, I'm sure this is because of some-"

The prince's expression changed from sadness to anger, "Obligation"

Dudesow let the sword drop, standing up. His face scrunched up with anger, tears sliding down his cheeks before turning away from Sir Kerry.

Sir Kerry, laid a gentle hand on the boy's shoulder, "I know it's tough to believe ... that your father does care about you-"

The prince swiped the knight's hand away.

"Get out"

"I must insist that-"

"I said get out"

The knight stood up. Carefully went over the wall of the books. Straightened up and paused before heading to the door, "I'll leave you to your thoughts. I'm sure your father would've done things differently if he could. If you ever want to--"

"Get out now! Get out, get out. I command it!" The boy stood, pointing at the door, trying to hold back his tears with some composure.

The knight nodded, "Yes, your majesty"

Sir Kerry walked out, then slowly closed the door. The knight walked down the dim hall, with a stoic expression. He glanced back when he heard a loud clang, followed by the door slamming shut. The knight sighed, turning around to retrieve the blade. The blade lay on the ground, piercing a ripped book parchment.

Sir Kerry slid the parchment out and read the paper out loud, "Tell my father I despise him and that I don't want any more gifts"

He turned back and picked up the sword.

He sensed movement from the corner of his eye, someone was watching him.

Sir Kerry held onto the sword's hilt and then spun around, blade out front in a defensive stance.

Sir Archibald, strode forward from around the corner. He walked up confidently and stopped in front of Sir Kerry.

Sir Kerry arched a brow, "Brother, what brings you to this end of the castle?"

Archibald sneered and nodded toward Dudesow's door, "That royal stain gets more of your attention than the chivalric order that awaits you on the training grounds. I'm unsure why you care for the boy when he brings nothing but ill fortune to the Kingdom. I could take care of the problem for you. I'll make it look like an ill fortune has finally affected the boy himself. No one would question it or care. You can keep your hands clean, and I'll ensure it gets done"

Sir Kerry leaned forward, red-faced, "You're out of line. Speak no more of this or I'll cut you down right now for treason. Go back to the formation and await orders. I'll be there momentarily. You're lucky that you're family. I'll pretend just this once that you're joking"

Sir Archibald shrugged and averted his eyes, "You're in charge." Sir Archibald turned, he mumbled, "for now"

"What was the last word you spoke, repeat it"

Sir Archibald walked away, ignoring Sir Kerry's remark. Before reaching the end of the hall, he paused. "Brother, I wouldn't argue that you're great with the blade, nor that you're capable of leading, but sometimes you need to do what's best for the people of this kingdom. You'll never reach your full potential if you never clean questionable blood off your blade"

Sir Archibald walked away without looking back.

Sir Kerry sneered, "That is where you and I differ brother, for I am honorable. For I never question the blood on my blade"

Chapter 2

Dudesow had accepted that there wasn't a cure for his bad luck when the clerics, the medicine men, and the scholars stopped coming. Dudesow often asked his parents through handwritten letters how he ended up with such a curse, and the King and Queen failed to provide any answer as they weren't sure themselves. He once asked Sir Kerry, and the knight glanced around to make sure that no one was listening, and then bluntly whispered to the young prince that it was all bullshit. The knight couldn't provide any proof or reasoning, he just said it was his knight's intuition. A week later when Sir Kerry visited again, Dudesow pressed Sir Kerry to share more on his doubts. The knight's tone had changed and he kept speaking little of the matter. Sir Kerry promptly left the room stating he couldn't say any more on the matter as he had no right to question the King and Queen.

The King's court advisor was fired soon after Prince Dudesow's birth, due to failing to find the cause of the afflicted curse and a cure. The King and Queen had invited various scholars, clerics, and a wide assortment of power holders from within the Kingdom's borders and beyond to provide their input. The King and Queen listened to each one intently, regardless of whether the esteemed guests bothered to examine the young prince or not.

The King and Queen's patience grew thin as scholars advised safe theories. The King and Queen listened to each person who offered their knowledge, but they had yet to provide valuable or worthwhile information. The King had thrown one scholar in the dungeon for assuming that there was nothing wrong with the child and had warned the court that anyone else who was naive enough to believe there was nothing wrong with the prince would end up in the dungeon as well.

The King and Queen proceeded to listen to each guest's wild guess. The theory of what started the curse range from ridiculous theories of "it was a curse put on him from a spiteful sorceress who wasn't invited to the Queen's baby shower", to more divine theories such as "maybe it was a nefarious god who observed the kingdom, and had made the decision to send divine punishment onto the Kingdom's heir." The Queen did raise an eyebrow at a theory that a god was jealous and had brought the curse onto the child as an obstruction towards potential greatness. The King momentarily pondered on this theory before waving away the idea and the scholar.

The next individual walked up and bowed towards the throne. He dressed like a wealthy merchant, "King, Queen, I may not be a scholar, but I request that I may speak freely. As my theory may lean more towards the controversial side"

The King, rolling his eyes, leaned forward.

The man cleared his throat, "I believe that perhaps the gods may have seen the Prince, having a less than palatable appearance and an ear missing..." The man glanced down, averting his eyes. The sudden look of fear on the man's face was apparent, as the man now realized the potential consequences of what he said, and it was too late to retreat. "I believe the Gods may have felt insulted by the sight of the child, that they added additional misfortune onto the child for its mere existence."

The Queen stood, glaring at the man, "Did you just call my child grotesque?"

The face of the King turned red, but before he could speak-

Dudesow, hiding nearby and listening in from behind a pillar, had an emotional breakdown and ran from the room. The King and Queen were startled, unaware of his presence. They heard his wailing as the young prince ran down the hall.

The King ordered the three court clerics of different religious faiths, to immediately pray to their gods and beg to receive protection from ill fates.

It was too late, as a candle chandelier above broke free from its support chain, hitting the ground, crashing down hard, landing in front of a crowd of court officials. A candle ricocheted off the shattered chandelier and hit a tax collector in the face, who then shrieked in pain.

The Queen ordered the immediate execution of the wealthy man. Guards grabbed the noble by the arms and dragged him away. The others in the audience remained silent as the wealthy man pleaded loudly as he was dragged out of the throne room. The other scholars in line found themselves shaken from witnessing such an act. They've all proceeded to provide more mundane, safe, and unalarming theories.

Dudesow slammed the door to his room and plopped onto the bed facedown. His eyes were draining. He was fed up with their theories and his curse. Dudesow was born with an entire kingdom, despising him for having a curse. He sat up and wiped his eyes. Dudesow was done. He was done with people who treated him with fear and disgust. He grabbed a small paper volume from a shelf and immediately calmed down. He found his quick escape in the pages, a satisfying distraction from reality, even if he couldn't escape from this reality for very long.

Chapter 3

Nine years ago, King Hubar and Queen Stace never forgot the peculiar events of Prince Dudesow's birth, as they constantly shared the tale with esteemed guests. The misfortune started when the midwife was about to hand over the young baby to the Queen, she lost her footing and slipped. Prince Dudesow flew out of the midwife's hands, flying a short distance, feet first into the King's face. The Queen, exhausted, used her remaining energy to catch the child, but ended up sliding off the side of the bed, clumsily onto her husband's feet. The King, disoriented, couldn't get a firm grip on the infant in time, causing the baby to slip once again to land smack bottom first onto the Queen's head. The court healer and the midwife stood in shock. After pausing to take in what had happened, they immediately rushed over. The court healer quickly handed the now irritated baby over to the midwife, to focus care on the queen. The King turned and glared at the chambermaid, who was rocking the infant. He gave them an intimidating scowl, lifting his hand and pointing at the midwife. The King was about to start a storm of scolding but the entry door swung open, striking the King hard in the face.

The door swung open hard.

The young soldier stood at the door, panting. He looked around the age of fifteen. He positioned himself to make an announcement but hesitated. He felt the eyes of everyone glancing between him and in the King's direction in disbelief. They were holding their breaths, in anticipation of the King's reaction. Even the young infant stopped wailing and just stared at him in shock.

The guard blinked twice and stood up straight, realizing his error by barging into the royal quarters unannounced, not yet realizing that there was a King with pent-up rage on the other side of the door.

King Hubar shoved the door out of his way. The door smacked the guard hard, causing him to almost fall off balance before his collar was grabbed by the King. The guard gulped and quickly remembered his task.

"Your...your Majesty, I have word from the lookout east tower that enemy troops crossed the border and are on route, expected to strike as soon as tonight-"

"Silence!" King Hubar snapped, wiping his hand under his nose. The soldier grimaced as he saw the blood on the King's hand. The King continued,

"If we win this battle and you somehow survive combat, I'll have you severely reprimanded for such incompetence. Hurry and take me to Commander Kerry"

The King shoved the guard away from him and strode down the hall.

The guard fell to the ground hard but quickly got back up on his feet, "Yes, my King". The guard rushed after the King, accidentally slamming the door closed behind him. The baby Prince then started crying at the abrupt sound. Queen Stace reached out to the midwife to transfer the task of comforting the baby, with gentle pats on the little one's back.

The guard, peeking back into the room with a worried expression, smiled and turned towards them, "Oh I'm so sorry for the noise, please excuse us, I mean me. My deepest apologies my Queen and oh the little Prince is adorable-"

"Hurry up, you incompetent fool! You're testing my patience" The King snapped from down the hall.

"Yes, King Huber", The guard squealed, gently closing the door on the way out.

The queen, lying back on the bed, patting the infant's back more slowly with each pat, eventually passing out from exhaustion. The baby Prince was asleep in her arms.

The castle staff glanced at one another, and they all quietly left the room.

Several hours later, the Queen woke and finally noticed the Prince was born without his left ear.

The Kingdom was defending the castle from intruders who charged into the kingdom later the night of Prince Dudesow's birth. The kingdom won but at a severe cost. The rain fell the moment swords clashed. After two hours of muddy bloodshed, the unstable footing ground caused a disadvantage to both sides as troops struggled to stand. The King's troops found stable footing by standing on the fallen. Lightning was bright and frequent. Aiding the battle more than the dim moonlight, covered by hellish yellow clouds. Fighters paused as the ground started to shake, causing many to lose their balance. The horses neighed and reared back as the adjacent mountain shook. Battle shouts translated to cries as the sky flashed white, and It was too late for the troops to react, as the mudslide nearly wiped out most of the trained infantry.

The few survivors retreated to the castle to alert the commander Kerry. The Kingdom was not prepared and was barely keeping the intruders outside the Kingdom gates. Scouts used lightning flashes to their advantage as they provided visual updates. Kerry had to make a tough call as a second wave of enemy troops was intermittently seen advancing on the horizon; there weren't enough castle guards stationed inside the gates to head out to support. Commander Kerry demanded all retired knights and able-bodied to assist in the conflict, drafting those who appeared strong enough to carry a sword.

Commander Kerry was in the meeting room, a map on a table in front of him. Kerry was discussing plans with his subordinates. King Hubar barged into the room, a young guard tailing behind him, trying to catch up. The King demanded that Kerry initiate the order of drafting untrained Townsfolk to partake in battle, with the sole criteria being "anyone who can hold a weapon"

The King pointed at the young man behind the commander, "Send that young man out to battle with the next batch." The young man's face went pale. The King continued, "Find more able bodies, I want this battle over by morning"

※※※

The final raindrop descended just before sunrise, leaving the Kingdom's survivors with enduring scars. As the somber troops retreated behind the castle walls to safety, each step they took resonated with a faint echo.

For the next two days, the people stayed in their homes to rest before going back to routine. The townsfolk held a grudge against the King for the rash decision. Many children were now orphans as their parents were given orders to go to the front lines or be executed for rejecting the King's orders. The Kingdom had suffered a major shortage of farmers and skilled laborers. Tensions rose amongst the commoners, guards, and royal officials.

The King sent out messengers to announce that he was deeply saddened by the decision to call for the draft order and offered a sincere apology to those who had lost loved ones in the battle. In addition, the King has unfortunately declared that compensation cannot be provided at this time due to budgetary reasons.

Most messengers soon returned bruised and beaten.

A few didn't return.

The price of goods had increased drastically since the battle. The townsfolk pleaded for a tax break, any type of solution to ease their suffering, but King Hubar ignored the pleas.

A year passed. Food and supplies became more scarce and crime rose. King Hubar and Queen Stace felt the tensions gradually rise from not only the townsfolk but even the royal staff within their castle walls. Word had spread far out enough that adjacent Kingdoms were tempted to move in to conquer the land. The only restraint holding them back was the curiosity to see if the Kingdom's situation could fare any worse to call in a quick sweep instead of an expensive and timely calculated move. The King went on a long exasperated rant one night. The King paced while the Queen stared out the window, deep in thought. The King goes on and on about how their little Prince Dudesow brought nothing but misfortune to their once-prosperous Kingdom.

The Queen reluctantly agreed.

Chapter 4

Two years have passed. The Prince had long ago given up trying to figure out the reasons why he was stuck with such an unfair curse. Even with a so-called "Bad luck" curse, Dudesow was far more frustrated lately that he was confined to his room most of his days. Having read every book in his room (and probably the entire kingdom)…..Dudesow was bored. Sir. Kerry had reduced the routine checkups due to King Hubar's demands to build a larger militia. He was sitting sideways on a chair, staring at the ceiling.

There was a light knock at the door, followed by a scurry of footsteps. The King and Queen agreed it would be best to order a decree that all castle staff who deliver food to Dudesow quarters, must leave it outside his bedroom door. Knock and then sprint a safe distance away from his door. This was not only for the safety of the staff but also to prevent the fear that the bad luck curse may somehow be transferable.

The kitchen aid who just sprinted away from Dudesow's door, turned a corner and reduced their steps to a brisk walk. They turned and swung by the kitchen area next, grabbing onto the serving cart that contained the King and Queen's food. The Kitchen aid pushed it along to the royal couple's bedroom. Standing outside their door, the kitchen aid firmly knocked, "Your majesty, food is delivered and waiting for the both of you".

"Leave it outside, and leave us be" The Queen barked.

"Yes, Your Majesty." The kitchen aid had stepped back, turned, and left.

✲✲✲

The Kingdom rulers, King Hubar and Queen Stace were constantly on edge, tired, and bitter following the day of Dudesow's birth. They were both lying on the floor, arms crossed behind their head, staring at the ceiling. The ceiling held a mural of the stars. King Hubar sat up and walked over to the open window. There was a restless crowd, protesting in front of the castle gates. The King's guards prevented the mob from getting to a considerable distance, but the crowd gradually increased in size each day.

The King sighed, "All these years and the people still are restless, persistent, and fuming. We....we may need to...no, we have to resort to our final option. The guards can't keep them away indefinitely, especially when they figure out they outnumber the Knights 10 to 1"

The Queen closed her eyes for a while and began to pinch the glabella with her thumb and finger in frustration. After a moment, she turned to face her husband, "I loathe this just as much as you do my love, but we need to act now. We can't pretend our lives won't end abruptly soon if we don't find a solution by the next tax collection. We're lucky they haven't had a full-on revolt towards the castle yet, and the protests are getting worse out there each day. I tire of the staff constantly tasting our food for poison, guards missing or guards leaving their posts, I don't feel safe here anymore. A Queen should feel safe in her kingdom"

The Queen stood up and walked up next to her husband. She continued, a weariness was now evident in her expression as she spoke, "We've stretched ourselves thin by enduring hatred, averting wars, and bearing witness to our Kingdom's suffering. Deep down, we find ourselves laying the blame on our son. Despite my unwavering love for him, it's clear that we've neglected to nurture a true bond with him in these past years. Our fear... no, our trepidation stems from his curse. We've let this fear distance us, preventing any emotional closeness. Can you remember the last time you held him in a warm, caring embrace? I certainly cannot. This is a truth we must confront: Do we genuinely love him, or are we more concerned about our well-being? We've sequestered him in his chamber for all these years, desperately seeking a solution. Yet, the answer has been before us for a year now, though we keep pushing it aside. Regrettably, we're left with no alternatives... we must take action"

The King placed a gentle hand on her shoulder. "Remember this, I'll be by your side, we'll be both sharing this pain until the end of our days"

The King turned her way, crinkling his eyes. "I'll summon the executioner"

Before the King wandered off, the Queen pulled in the King for an embrace from behind. tears streaming down her face. After a moment of shared silence, the King spoke again. "I can only pray that this will dampen the heated flame of anger that grew that has grown these last few years"

King Hubar, kissed his queen on the forehead and stormed out.

Hubar was unable to contain a smirk for much longer.

✵✵✵

It was late in the evening, and Dudesow was peeking through a crack in the boarded-off tower window, watching the protesting crowd nearby with passive interest.

The knock at the door startled him. Dudesow, a mix of eagerness for news and the prospect of training, hurried toward the door. Typically, Sir Kerry awaited him there outside the door with a fatigued but kindly smile.

Yet, now, weariness marred his features, replaced by a somber expression.

Sir Kerry entered swiftly, his eyes scanning the room before his hand settled on the sword hilt at his side. With a brisk motion, he flung a substantial bag to Dudesow.

"Pack your belongings and anything essential, cram it all into that bag. We'll be departing shortly. If it doesn't fit, then it's not crucial," Sir Kerry's tone was decisive.

Dudesow's brow furrowed with confusion. "But why? Can I not—"

"No exceptions, no time for queries. I'll be posted outside, guarding your door. Don't dawdle." The commander turned, and his forehead smacked into the door frame. The commander grimaced momentarily before he recomposed himself, exiting with an air of dignity and closing the door behind him.

Dudesow feared this day would come. From a young age, Sir Kerry had imparted the harsh reality to him: That townspeople would readily hold the King and Queen accountable for common grievances like taxes and impractical royal decrees when it came to graver matters beyond anyone's control – failed crops, illnesses, or even inclement weather – Dudesow was the chosen scapegoat. It was a realization he had come to terms with early on, understanding that he would forever shoulder the blame for the town's misfortunes.

Compounding his burden, the King had not hesitated to confirm suspicions or even redirect blame, attributing misfortunes to his son's supposed ill luck. Dudesow had long known the futility of attempting to alter the townsfolk's perception. He sought to deflect the onslaught of negativity that would surge within him if he dwelled on it for too long.

At times, he couldn't help but wonder: could he assert with absolute certainty that his curse bore no influence on the town at large?

The notion of the scope of his curse's reach had never been explored, and this realization weighed heavily on the shoulders of the twelve-year-old child. An unsettling unease took hold as he began to realize: was his very presence causing the kingdom's collective suffering? Had matters escalated to the point where his death or exile would resolve the Kingdom's problems? Interrupting his tumultuous thoughts, Kerry's head appeared at the door. "Time is short. We must move swiftly to slip you out of the castle unnoticed"

✱✱✱

King Hubar ascended the stairs with a slight spring in his step. As he reached the ledge of the wall, he peered down and beheld a substantial gathering. The crowd pressed close to the wall, with townsfolk continually maneuvering to secure a solid vantage point, eagerly straining to catch every word from their sovereign.

Amidst the crowd, a low hum of conversation persisted. The evening had descended, the moon's glow not yet illuminating the scene, compelling many townsfolk to rely on the flickering torchlight. Guards stationed around the assembly were vigilant, and steadfast in their resolve to maintain order and be prepared to act if the crowd were to deviate from civility.

A knight, arms crossed in front of him, approached and stood beside King Hubar. The King acknowledged him with a nod, and in response, the knight returned the gesture. The King returned his attention to the crowd, raising his hands high in the air. The murmurs in the crowd were immediately silenced.

"My people, I bear grave tidings to share with you today," King Hubar began with a heavy heart. "Earlier this day, our beloved Prince, my dear son, Dudesow... he was attacked in his slumber and tragically lost his life"

A collective gasp swept through the townsfolk, followed by a few callous cheers that quickly withered under the frigid gazes of the guards.

The King's brow twitched, but he composed himself, drawing in a deep breath to continue, "The assailant, an outsider, was swiftly dispatched by our valiant Commander Sir Kerry. He displayed exceptional bravery in confronting the intruder. By the time our reinforcements arrived, the assailant lay lifeless at Commander Kerry's feet, his sword having served as the instrument of justice. The knights discovered Commander Kerry, heroically pinning the intruder to the ground with his fine blade. It brings me sorrow to relay this news. As our healers were unable to save Sir Kerry, who later succumbed to his wounds"

The King paused, his voice filled with deep respect, "Sir Kerry met his end as a hero, and his honor shall never fade from memory. I pledge that his intermediate family will receive the utmost care and rewards for as long as I draw breath. As for the vile remains of the intruder who trespassed upon our kingdom… they shall be cast to be fed to the swine!"

The crowd roared in cheer, and even the guards joined in on the celebration. From the shadows of the battlements, Sir Kerry and Dudesow snuck traveled along the castle's shadows, trying to avoid detection as they made their way to the stables. The two of them were wearing dark cloaks and were slow at making progress. Sir Kerry, cautious in avoiding detection. While Dudesow, with cautious paranoia that his curse would somehow end up getting them noticed. They were halfway to the door that would lead them to the stables. Dudesow could vaguely hear the King's speech, but he could hear the crowd cheering outside the castle loud and clear.

After a few more moments of the townsfolk yelling with cheer, the King raised his hands again. Instantly silencing the crowd.

"I would also like to take a moment to acknowledge a rumor spreading along the kingdom walls for quite some time. It has been tough…for a father to accept the facts, but the coincidences and the ill timing. I can't turn my back any longer away from the truth. My son's birth and the Kingdom's misfortunes are correlated. I've been in denial for far too long."

The crowd started to mumble quietly. The King let it slide. Prince Dudesow stopped a moment and turned his head. In the distance, Dudesow can see the back of his father's head, addressing the crowd. Dudesow grabbed Sir Kerry by the shoulder and halted. Dudesow needed to hear this.

The King pressed on, his voice unwavering. "I must emphasize a fundamental truth - I love my son dearly, and this revelation does not leave me untouched. It is time to address the rumors that have lingered for far too long. His passing, while heartbreaking, brings tranquility to our realm. It is bitter when I say that we ought to move forward. We can finally embark on a new chapter, free from the shackles of death, adversity, and ill fortune that have gripped us for so long. I believe that brighter days await us"

His gaze steady, the King continued, "In light of these circumstances, it has become clear that our Kingdom requires a leader of unwavering strength and wisdom to guide our formidable military"

Dudesow stared in disbelief, his heart heavy with shock at how swiftly the King appeared to seemingly move on with ease regarding the loss of his recent son. Dudesow knew he was never close with his father, but this still felt wrong. His eyes began to well up with tears. Kerry grasped his arm urgently and whispered, "We must leave, now"

Dudesow realized that his escape was probably orchestrated by his father, and the assassination story served as a mere facade. It marked one of the kindest gestures his father had ever made towards him. A smile crept across his face as he wiped away a tear from his eye and fell in step behind Sir Kerry.

Dudesow and Sir Kerry swiftly slipped through the door, closing it behind them. Dudesow is unable to hear any more of the King's speech from the other side of the door. They moved on.

✳✳✳

The King gestured toward the knight who stood at his side. "In my company, we have the valiant Knight Sir Archibald. He shall take Sir Kerry's place as the new commanding Knight."

Sir Archibald stepped forward, drew his sword, and raised it high into the air. The crowd erupted in applause, while the guards, in acknowledgment of their new leader, raised their swords skyward.

The King waited for a moment before raising his hands once more to silence the crowd. With a nod from the King, Sir Archibald sheathed his sword, crossed his arms, and took his place beside the King.

"In memory of my beloved son, whose untimely departure from this world has left a void in our hearts. He was a noble lad, whose destiny cruelly bound him to an unspeakable curse. From this moment until the next two days pass, I decree a period of solemn silence in honor of my innocent child. Prince Dudesow deserved a far kinder fate. May the Gods bless him in the beyond. Additionally, I order a day of quiet reflection for our late Commander, Sir Kerry, who served with unwavering honor, dignity, and a valor that will echo in legends. I extend my gratitude to him and all of you. You are hereby dismissed"

The crowd dispersed, and light murmurs could be heard as they walked away. Archibald leaned and whispered into Hubar's ear. "If I may, my sire, why so many days of silent reflection?"

The King sighed, "I had to, I didn't want the town to loudly cheer over my son's death"

Archibald stood silent momentarily, "That was a wise move, Your Majesty. I'm sorry the townsfolk blame their misfortunes on your son."

The King remained stoic. He gave the knight a slight nod before walking away, quietly mumbling to himself.

※※※

Former Commander Kerry and Dudesow made it to the stables.

Dudesow was nervous about riding a horse for the first time on his own. So Kerry decided it wasn't worth the risk of compromising their escape with Dudesow's unfamiliarity with how to properly direct a horse. Sir Kerry lent out a hand, pulling Dudesow up to ride as a passenger. Kerry can tell that Dudesow needed some time to process the King's speech, so he kept silent.

Kerry led the horse out of the stable yard and nudged the horse with his foot to speed up. They made it out of the castle grounds and were riding through the village. Going at a casual pace to avoid attention.

Guards they passed had not noticed them in the crowd. The two of them wore cloaks, hoods drawn low to cover their faces. The roads were crowded with people headed home after listening in on the King's speech.

Dudesow was uncomfortable, he was not used to being surrounded by groups of people, being on a horse, and the bulky bag strapped to his back, which was smacking into his back repeatedly, his hands were hanging onto Kerry with his dear life and the cloaks were itchy. Regardless, Dudesow stayed silent.

Once they had left the city, Kerry gave a gentle kick, and the horse bolted to full speed. Dudesow glanced back and wiped a tear from his eye, watching as the castle grew smaller in the distance.

Chapter 5

Kerry and Dudesow entered the forest weary.

They have finally made it to the Troubled Woods.

No one was on their tail, Kerry reassured Dudesow.

"How safe are these woods? I'm hoping my father named these woods that concern the name as a deterrent to any opposing kingdoms"

"I wish that were the case," Kerry said grimly.

The Troubled woods were dense, with little to no moonlight. Kerry lit a torch and handed it to Dudesow.

Kerry slowly guided the horse around the shrubs and thick roots that crowded the ground.

Dudesow whispered, "Why is it called the Troubled Woods"

Kerry spoke in a lower tone, but not quite a whisper, "Woods can provide shelter and resources to those seeking it, including predators. From bands of thieves to the supernatural. As time passes, so do the troubling stories that originate in these woods. It would be best to be cautious."

They continued in silence. Kerry pulled the reins suddenly as a river appeared to Dudesow's surprise. He didn't notice the river before.

The river was dead calm, appearing stagnant.

Kerry peaked over Dudesow's shoulder, "Stay here and don't make a sound"

Kerry unmounted. He walked to the side of the horse and opened the supply pack. He carefully placed his sheathed sword into the bag. He then removed a leatherbound bundle.

Kerry walked three paces towards the river before leaning down to pick up a pebble. Kerry examined the pebble. Satisfied, he tossed the pebble into the river.

The pebble dropped into the river without a sound.

Kerry went down on one knee and held out the bundle of cloth. Dudesow recognized that it was the same leather-bound bundle that contained the blade he rejected from his father.

Slowly two heads ascended from the river. They climbed onto the riverbank. The two that appeared were undead humans, with a blue glow. Once they found their footing, they stood at attention. There was a loud eruption, as water sprayed in all directions. A massive serpent made a grand entrance. It was as tall as the trees. Its scales shimmered a shade of teal. It loomed over the riverbank, moving right above them all. The serpent, with piercing white eyes, stared at them intently. Extending out of the water, it had two arms and placed one of its scaly claws onto one of the undead human shoulders.

Kerry kept his head down in respect.

The eyes of the undead human with the serpent's arm on his shoulder spoke. The human eyes glowed a bright blue. It spoke, "Provide tribute to cross the Teal River"

With his head still down, Kerry spoke, "I offer this finely crafted blade as a tribute for our safe crossing"

The other undead human walked over, took the blade, and took the blade at a deadman's pace. The undead minion tossed the blade into the river. Kerry failed to hide a grimace.

The serpent spoke, "That provides passage for one. I assume the other human behind you requires passage as well or will they suffer the consequences of providing no sufficient tribute?"

Kerry glanced up, "I can pay for their tribute as well. I was unaware that the price of passage had changed. My apologies." After a moment, Kerry sighed, "Does the horse crossing require tribute as well?"

The serpent flared its nostrils, and it spoke, with a deep raspy voice, "My master has increased the cost of passage to cross the Teal River. No longer is it acceptable for one tribute to be covered for group passage. The toll for passage is now one tribute per person, per animal. No exceptions"

Kerry sighed, "I understand. Everything is going up in price"

The serpent let out a deep sigh, "Thank you for not making this more difficult than it needs to be. I just cursed to work here for all eternity, and it's been a long, busy day."

The serpent paused, glancing to the side, "Please be quick, I sense more trying to cross elsewhere on the King's river"

"I can offer my armor, my shield, and this weapon as tribute"

The river serpent nodded, "that will suffice. You and the child may pass. The undead minions took the armor and sword from him and returned to the river's depths.

The serpent observed Kerry, "I'll turn this part of the river on my right into shallow water for an easier crossing experience. Alternatively, for an additional tribute, I can create a temporary bridge to create a dry crossing experience"

The serpent let out a deep growl, and the river adjusted, water separating just enough to create a more shallow passage across.

Kerry bowed, "Thank you and with absolute respect, no thank you". Kerry mounted the house and guided it through the magically adjusted part of the river. Once they crossed, the serpent growled, the river water rushing back into place. The serpent drove into the river.

Dudesow shook his head in disbelief, "Is that why it's called the Troubled Woods? Because I found that experience quite troubling"

Kerry grinned, "I don't know what you mean, because that was no trouble at all"

✳✳✳

Dudesow wasn't sure if an hour or hours had passed; he had fallen asleep earlier when the sun started to set. Dudesow slowly opened his eyes, he saw a cloudless sky, adorned with a multitude of stars. The horse was no longer galloping but moved at a steady trot. The horse slowly trotted along an embankment.

Without warning, Kerry pulled the reins and climbed off the horse. Startling Dudesow, who'd almost lost his balance. Kerry put his hand on Dudesow's shoulder to stabilize him, "Careful my prince"

Dudesow responded with a wry smile, "Sir Kerry, my noggin remains bump-free, and I intend to keep it that way tonight"

Kerry assisted Dudesow down from the horse, apologizing, "I must beg your pardon, my Prince, for I am not accustomed to riding with a passenger"

Yawning from exhaustion, Kerry added, "I confess, I am growing old and weary. We've been on the move for hours, and I am thankful that your unusually loud snores have kept both me and our trusty steed awake." Kerry chuckled lightly.

The horse neighed in agreement. Dudesow felt immediately embarrassed and was about to deny it but then decided against it. Dudesow couldn't prove he didn't snore, so he figured, what's the point of denying it? It didn't matter.

Dudesow took a moment to survey his surroundings. In the distant backdrop, a wall of pine trees stretched as far as the eye could see. The spaces between them were swallowed by an impenetrable darkness, leaving only the eerie silhouettes of treetops. Grateful for the moonlight's faint illumination, he couldn't shake the unease that gnawed at him. This was the first time in the wilderness. The moonlight, though helpful, remained insufficient to reveal the lurking creatures concealed within the depths of the dark forest. Dudesow resolved to put these unsettling thoughts aside, feeling a growing internal fear as the reality of the more concerning situation sank in.

Dudesow wondered where they were going and what the plan was. Dudesow waited for Kerry to say something. The knight was staring out into the ocean, deep in thought.

Dudesow was about to say something until the distant howls of wolves sang. Dudesow stood close to Kerry's side, clutching his bag of belongings extra tight. Kerry turned and guided the horse toward a grassy patch. Not far ahead, the shoreline of the ocean sprawled out. To their right, an abandoned fisherman's vessel rested on a dilapidated dock. The ship was slightly compact and was suitable for small crews going on long-distance journeys. It featured a hut for shelter, packed with nets, fishing rods, barrels, and crates. Dudesow couldn't help but feel a sense of concern; the boat seemed a little rundown, and there wasn't enough room for their horse.

With a yawn, Dudesow gently tapped Kerry's shoulder, concern in his voice, "Sir Kerry..."

"It's just Kerry now," Kerry interjected.

"Oh, right, sorry," Dudesow continued, now stammering with embarrassment, "Kerry, I was wondering—how are we going to accommodate this old horse onto the boat with us?"

Kerry paused, his gaze fixed yet again focused on the expanse of the ocean, wearing a somber expression. "The horse won't be joining us; it will remain here with you".

Dudesow stared at him in shock and disbelief, "What do you mean, aren't we taking the boat? Please tell me we're just resting on this vessel tonight and carrying on the horse together tomorrow?"

"I'm sorry Dudesow, but this is where we must part ways"

The realization struck Dudesow hard.

Dudesow's voice trembled as he protested, "What do you mean? You can't leave me alone here, in the middle of nowhere. I'm just a child. I—"

Kerry raised a finger to silence him, his tone firm but reassuring. "You're well old enough now to take care of yourself. You've done well on your own, you've done so your whole life within your confined space at the corner of the castle, I've helped guide you and taught you life's essentials, but you've done most of the work"

Before Dudesow could speak, Kerry continued, "Over the years, I've trained you to think tactically, use hand-to-hand combat, be an expert with the swords, and use self-defense. I'm confident that the books in your library, which you've read at least twice over, have equipped you with everything else you'll need to know. You'll have to fend for yourself from now on, but—"

Kerry paused, retrieving something from his pocket. "You misspoke about one thing, young prince. You won't be alone. This horse will be your protector... come morning, she'll be your steadfast and noble guardian"

Kerry produced a small vial and a carrot, pouring the vial's contents over the carrot. He approached the front of the horse, which eyed the tempting treat with anticipation but held back from taking a bite. Kerry tenderly petted the horse's mane, whispering soothing words. The horse neighed, its gaze fixed on the carrot.

Dudesow just gawked in disbelief at him. Kerry fed the carrot to the horse. The horse gleefully munched away at the carrot. Kerry then handed Dudesow the reins, "You're old enough to make your own choices now"

Before Dudesow could ask, Kerry grabbed his shoulder and pointed to the distance behind Dudesow, "Now, look over there at that incline near the shore"

Dudesow turned around and focused on what was ahead. A short distance away, the shore started to incline up to form a hillside cliff. The hillside facing the ocean had a sharp jagged cliff, with rocks below that shot out like teeth emerging from the water. Most of the hilltop had brick walls that surrounded a lone tower. Dudesow stared at the dark castle in dismay. Even in the late hours, Dudesow could see the keep appeared abandoned. Shrubs and long vines were deeply embedded into the walls. Parts of the walls around the keep had crumbled away. The tower itself had a few holes from missing bricks.

Kerry's voice remained steady as he continued, but Dudesow heard a hint of emotion in his tone, "That is a keep that was given to me for winning the great battle the day of your birth. The King had been cutting costs. That included my pay. I wasn't able to afford maintenance. Nature and local delinquents had their way with the keep. I stocked it recently and fixed it up all I could in my free time"

Dudesow eyed the castle skeptically.

Kerry continued, "Don't be deterred, Inside the castle walls is a lone tower, you'll discover enough preserved rations to sustain you for two seasons. I've been preparing for this day, fortifying it and stocking it whenever I'm able. The tower is locked. Here," He handed a key to Dudesow, "That's the key to the tower entrance door. You'll find in your room a farming guide and a crate of seeds to assist you in self-sufficiency. I hope it won't be gone long but just in case…"

Kerry sighed, "I hope to return soon, and when I do, I'll explain everything. Most importantly, I have a lead on what caused your curse, and time is of the essence. It may take me a while to pursue who or what I seek. You'll have more than enough supplies one would require to start anew. You needn't confine yourself just here, but this location is a resource at your disposal. If you do leave, leave a note so I can find you on my return. If I find the info I seek, I shall return. I urge you to remain safe and seize this chance to live a life far removed from those who hold disdain for you. Embrace this opportunity"

Tears poured from Dudesows' eyes. He was unable to fully wipe the tears away, "please stay, I need you. You're like a father to me"

Kerry's countenance betrayed the pain he felt, struggling to contain the overwhelming emotions within. He released a slow, heavy sigh before speaking with a heavy heart, "It pains me deeply to be parting ways. You can't be seen with me, people recognize me, and very few have seen the looks of you"

Kerry deftly steered the conversation in a different direction, to maintain his stoic military demeanor. "Bear in mind, starting now, you must relinquish your identity as Prince Dudesow. It's of paramount importance that you adopt a new persona, as revealing your true name and lineage could pose a grave risk. If I accomplish my quest, survive, and return—rest assured, I will leave no stone unturned to locate you. While I won't make promises I cannot keep, understand that my concern for your well-being is genuine. Perhaps in the future, circumstances will allow for a more comprehensive explanation of why this course of action was necessary"

Desperation clung to Dudesow as he clutched Kerry's arm, his voice wavering, "Are you sure you cannot stay a while longer?"

Kerry averted his gaze, gently but firmly disengaging Dudesow's grip. "I know this is difficult to accept, but I believe deep down…you sensed this day would come"

Kerry gently released Dudesow's grasp and headed to the pier, Dudesow followed.

Kerry continued, "Earlier today, I found an assassin attempting to take your life. I put a stop to it, but before ending the wretched man's life, I was able to extract the name of the man who hired him. After the dead man's dying breath told me the individual's name, I confronted the individual who hired him, who then tried to have me killed"

Kerry took a moment, inhaling deeply before continuing, "Your mother, the Queen, deemed the Kingdom too perilous for your continued presence. So, we reached a consensus that it would be safest if you and I both departed from the castle grounds, with the Queen providing the King a fabricated account of your death. That's the reason behind the King's announcement on how we met our demise. Thanks to your mother's quick thinking, we find ourselves in a temporary state of safety. However, we cannot remain together for an extended period, as the risk of someone recognizing me within the Kingdom is too great. Let a few years pass, and then perhaps we can arrange a rendezvous. Notably, most people in the Kingdom are familiar with my face, but your visage remains unfamiliar to the majority. Even among the castle staff who may have caught a glimpse of you, none have had the opportunity to scrutinize you closely enough for recognition"

Kerry untied the rope that kept the boat in place, then hopped onto the boat before it drifted away. Kerry smiled, but it did not reach his eyes, "I can finally retire, and you can live a normal life if you choose to stay here or find a new town. Your choice. Farewell my friend, I'll be sailing my ship far from here. Remember, your mother loves you. Our new freedom will also bring calm to the Kingdom. This will mean your parents will most likely be safe, now that the townspeople will rest easy. Remember, you can do this, because curse or not, there's no room for failure when you're on your own"

Dudesow watched as the boat sailed away. He stood there long before he could no longer see the boat in the distance. He turned and returned to his noble steed, guiding the horse to the castle up the hill.

The castle gate stood ajar as Dudesow entered. He surveyed the nearly empty courtyard with weary eyes. Exhaustion weighed heavily on him; his legs throbbed from the arduous horse ride, a migraine pulsed at his temples, and his eyes constantly welled up with tears. Grateful for the bright moon that cast its glow on the area, he was determined to secure a place for the horse and then find respite for himself.

After a brief search, Dudesow discovered what seemed to be a stable, now a mere shell of its former self. Leading the horse inside, he noticed a pile of straw already prepared for the animal. He considered resting there but the horse reached the straw pile first, leaving no space for him to lay. Sighing, Dudesow made his way toward the tower.

Within the tower, darkness enveloped Dudesow. To combat the obscurity, he yanked the door open, beckoning in as much moonlight as possible to illuminate his path. Tentatively, he ventured inside and his knee immediately encountered a crate. His startled cry of pain sent an echo up the tower. He extended his hands, using touch alone to guide him up the stairs, occasionally brushing against crates and barrels, navigating with caution to avert any potential stumbles or falls.

As he climbed, intermittent gaps in the brick tower's walls allowed slender beams of moonlight to penetrate through missing bricks, casting periodic light on the steps. These modest slivers of light offered a measure of comfort.

Upon reaching the summit, the area was bathed in moonlight, thanks to a wide window and few gaps within the walls. Dudesow's eyes fell upon a straw bed beside a small fireplace and a stack of crates. A fleeting thought about the castle's gate and tower door being open for bandits crossed his mind, but fatigue and exhaustion overcame his concern. He collapsed onto the straw bed and was quickly overtaken by sleep.

The morning sun was unforgiving with a sunbeam from the sole window hitting him directly in the eyes. Pressing his hands against his eyes in frustration. He groaned in frustration and slowly walked over to the window. Disappointed with the lack of curtains. Slowly, he approached the window, squinting at the unwelcome brightness outside. His eyes located the horse stable. His horse was nowhere to be seen.

Panic surged through him like a bolt of lightning.

Without hesitation, he bolted from the room, thudding down the stairway in a frantic rush. Bursting into the courtyard, he shouted, "Horse! Where are you?" Regret washed over him as he wished he knew the horse's name.

He jogged around the courtyard, calling out for the horse.

Then, it struck him—last night, he had been too weary to close the entrance gate. Anxiety turned to panic as he dashed beyond the castle gate, realizing he might have lost his only companion.

He glanced around the field and the shore.

His eyes darted across the fields and shoreline, the horse was nowhere in sight. A tremor overtook Dudesow, and he forced himself to take a deep breath in, an attempt to regain his composure. With closed eyes, he tilted his face to the sky and bellowed, "Horse!" in one final, resounding cry, loud and clear.

A wooden cart plummeted from the sky, landing with a resounding thud right before Dudesow. The sudden spectacle sent him stumbling backward in sheer shock. He lost his footing and fell onto the ground. Instinctively, he scrambled back to his feet and dashed away, taking refuge behind the gate entrance wall, where he cautiously peered around.

The fallen cart, now strewn with an abundance of carrots, showed no signs of threats surrounding it.

Dudesow turned his attention towards the sky, the color drained from his face.

A massive white dragon descended with an almost clumsy grace, displaying signs of either injury or a struggle to master its flight. Its colossal form towered over the cart, and it bent its head to examine the contents. Perhaps, Dudesow mused, the dragon was searching for the merchant to whom the cart belonged.

Rapidly the dragon plunged its head into the cart, enthusiastically devouring the carrots.

Dudesow blinked twice, his eyes widening in a blend of amazement and disbelief. "Horse?..." he stammered.

The dragon responded with a low grunt.

With measured steps, Dudesow approached the dragon.

The dragon was nearly as tall as the tower.

The former horse made no reaction to the former prince's approach.

Reaching out, Dudesow placed one hand on the dragon's wing. The dragon gave no notice and kept munching away.

"I shall call you.....Horse"

The dragon's head turned and spat a single carrot directly at Dudesow like a human would spit out a sunflower seed. The carrot bounced off Dudesow's chest, leaving a glob of saliva on his shirt.

Frowning, "You know what, Carrot would be a more fitting name"

The dragon grunted in approval and licked the cart of any remaining carrots.

Dudesow realized the dragon must've been the result of the mysterious vial liquid that Kerry poured onto the carrot that the horse consumed last night.

For a moment, he felt a pang of sympathy for the merchant whose cart had become a dragon's meal, imagining the poor soul who must have been terrified beyond words. He waved that thought away, as he was more concerned about figuring out how to keep his noble steed well-fed.

✳✳✳

Dudesow sat down on the end of his bed, feeling refreshed after a much-needed bath. He reached over to grab the book off the nightstand. He glanced over a few random pages. Information ranging from farming. He had other books in arms reach, ranging from hunting and first aid. Dudesow tossed the book back. The book hit the edge and fell to the floor. Dudesow sighed and lay down, staring at the ceiling.

Dudesow pondered aloud, "I must come to terms with the fact that none of the royal staff will be delivering my regular meals, let alone anything else. It seems I'll have to rely on my resources. It will be just me and my horse—well, I suppose it's more of a dragon now. Is the transformation permanent? Who knows. From this point onward, I am embarking on a new chapter of my life with a fresh identity. Henceforth, I shall go by the name 'Dude.'"

✳✳✳

A year had come and gone, and Dude found himself gazing out of the open window at the tower's summit, his attention drawn to his modest vegetable and fruit garden below. His excitement was palpable. A year ago, he had stumbled upon a crate of potatoes. On the crate's lid, someone had etched a message onto the lid "READ BOOK BEFORE EAT." Dude opened the crate, inside a small handbook lay on top of the potatoes, described in the pages, there were clear instructions explaining that if he left the potatoes untouched in the crate for a month, they'd sprout roots. They then would be ready to be cut into thirds and set for planting. The thought of having a reliable, everlasting supply of potatoes had filled Dude with joy.

✳✳✳

A year later, Dude couldn't bear the sight of another potato and eagerly anticipated the moment his fruits and vegetables would be ripe for consumption.

Dude's attention shifted as he glanced up and saw Carrot, peacefully grazing on the grass outside the castle walls. Thankfully, the frequent rain in the area helped the grass grow back quickly. Dude had tried to convey to Carrot not to seek out more food carts to raid, but whether the message went unheard or Carrot simply didn't care, Dude would never know. It's been a month since the last merchant cart dropped.

In front of the castle lay several dozen empty food merchant carts, some stacked atop one another. Dude remained perplexed about the origins of Carrot''s consistent supply of merchant carts. The sight resembled a raided caravan, long abandoned. The thought gnawed at him—someday, there might be a possibility of a horde of irate merchants descending upon his castle gate, brandishing torches and pitchforks.

Perhaps, he mused, there was no need to worry about such a scenario. It was entirely possible that people were aware of the dragon's presence but deliberately maintained a safe distance. Dude had come to accept this as the truth, explaining why he had never encountered travelers or received visitors at the castle during all this time. It felt as though the land was his, yet the world perceived it as the dragon's territory.

***

A few more years passed. Dude glanced at a cracked mirror and patches of peach fuzz growing on parts of his jawline. He was excited to have his first beard grow out any day now, as it was still stuck in the peach fuzz phase. Dude went to his window to observe the scenery from the tower. Carrot has gone to who knows where. He noticed something in the distance. Was that Carrot galloping in the distance? It was far on the horizon, difficult to see. Dude wouldn't say he'd be surprised if it were Carrot. Yes, Carrot can fly anytime he wants, but sometimes his noble steed did gallop around the field. The dragon did have the mind of a horse after all.

Dude was thankful to have a dragon as his protector, but sometimes his noble steed gave Dude a headache. Carrot would fall asleep too close to the castle, and its tail would hit the castle wall, knocking bricks down. It wouldn't wake up the dragon, but it sure jolted Dude awake from his sleep when it happened, causing Dude to have a minor panic attack.

Dude, carrying buckets of water he got from the well, had to catch his bearings when he heard the galloping. It wasn't the loud and ground-shaking galloping sounds he was used to hearing from his dragon but galloping sounds from actual horses. He dropped the buckets and ran into the tower. Closing the lone door, locking it up. He rushed to the top of the tower. Out of breath, he carefully peeked out the window.

There were four men on horses, making their way into this castle yard. The men dismounted from their horses and spread out. Three had swords drawn and one had a bow and arrow, latched and ready. He ducked the moment the archer's sights aimed at the tower.

Dude overheard them below.

"Looks like someone has been living here"

"Perfect location"

"Search the premises, anyone you find, bring them to me. kill them if they cause trouble"

Dude didn't have a weapon on him.

Dude was annoyed at himself for not asking Kerry for a weapon before he left long ago. To be fair, it was late at night, and he was tired. Weapons were the last thing on his mind. Where was Carrot? She was nowhere in sight.

Dude got up and once again carefully peeked out the window. One of the men was eating his tomatoes. He bit his tongue to reframe himself from cursing out the man. He felt the irritation gnawing at him. he put so many hours into that garden each day. Now some degenerate was eating up his precious supply of food.

There was a shout outside, "Hey, someone help me open this door"

Dude felt tense, and he glanced around the room, looking for something to defend himself with. Dude thought about using one of the loose bricks in the walls. Contemplating about dropping several bricks on the heads of the intruders. Dude decided against it, it would either knock them out or just make them angry. Dude thought about these men eating his harvest and decided it would be worth every drop of brick that hit their head. He pulled out some loose bricks from the walls, went to the window, and leaned over. Two men down below were slamming their shoulders into the tower door. Dude aimed the brick directly above one of the men's heads and dropped it. It landed with a loud crack. The man fell over.

He didn't move.

By the time the other man comprehended what happened, he looked up to instantly catch a brick with his face. This man fell to the ground as well. The man who was eating the tomatoes stopped and turned toward the tower, spotting Dude's head before Dude ducked down below the window sill.

"Terry, aim for the lad in the tower. Kill him now!"

Dude didn't see where Terry went so he ducked. An arrow grazed past and struck the back wall. Dude was trapped.

Dude knew he would've been saved by now if his dragon had been here. Carrot would be gone sometimes for hours at a time.

"Some protector she is", Dude grumbled.

The man near the garden, who held a sword, dropped it onto the ground, "Lad, we mean you no harm. Just exit the tower and no one else gets hurt. If you agree, I'll ask my friend Terry here to un-notch his arrow, put it away, and we can pretend this didn't happen." The man, whom Dude assumed to be the leader, gave a moment for Dude to respond.

The leader continued, "I'm giving you one more chance to surrender, or Terry and I will burn you out"

Dude did not like the sound of that one bit. Dude crouched down next to the window and cupped his mouth with his hands. "Carrot! Carrot! CARROOOOT!'

The gang leader, and the archer both exchanged confused glances.

"What is this about carrots, Lad? Enough of your games. Get down here and-"

The gang leader didn't have a chance to finish as a white dragon dropped down in front of him. The dragon's back facing him. The three unmanned horses sprinted off as the Dragon leaned forward and used its hind legs to kick the gang leader. The man screamed and he flew high and far...over the castle walls and fell into the ocean.

The archer notched an arrow and then aimed at the dragon.

Carrot blew hot steam from her nostrils, glaring orange intimidating eyes directly at the archer.

The archer wisely dropped the bow and arrow, hopped onto his horse, and retreated away.

Dude leaned out the tower window and yelled praise, "That's a good Carrot!"

Carrot picked up the two remaining unresponsive men with his teeth and flung them into the ocean. Dude yelled, "Yeet!" with excitement. He vowed to never doubt his noble protector ever again.

Dude went to the courtyard and picked up the swords and the one bow. Well, Dude thought, I've solved the weapon shortage problem. Excitement grew as Dude knew exactly how he was going to spend the remainder of this day, refreshing himself on how to use a weapon.

Later at night, Dude read the sections in the book on how to master the sword, and how to use a bow. Hoping to learn anything new that Kerry missed in his lessons when he was a child. Dude was determined to master these, for he was determined to no longer solely rely on his protector.

✳✳✳

In the nearby town of Wetmore, an exhausted archer stumbled through the tavern's door of The Troubled Ale, collapsing into a seat at the bar.

"I need a drink"

The barkeep cast a cynical eye at the disheveled archer. "Do you intend to pay this time?" the barkeep retorted.

The archer slumped, his demeanor defeated. "I don't have a coin to my name, but I offer you a tale of a dragon and a boy at the cliffside castle. Grant me one drink in exchange, for I've just survived the encounter, and I assure you this story is well worth your time"

The barkeep regarded the man for a moment, then grunted, "Half a drink. Can't tell if you're fibbing. I'll pour the other half if I find your story genuine and worth my time."

"Fair enough, and I promise you this tale is true," the archer conceded. The barkeep poured half a glass of ale, which the archer eagerly downed.

As the archer began recounting his tale, the tavern gradually fell into a hushed silence, the patrons hanging on every word. His narrative stirred curiosity and interest among those who listened, and the archer found himself rewarded with more ale that night. Others in the tavern were eager to buy him drinks in exchange for further details of his captivating story.

Many who were there that night, passed the story along to others. As the tale passed along, the story diluted further from the truth. As people do when sharing stories, exaggerated events and circumstances that never happened were added to the tale. Years passed, and eventually, the story changed to a damsel stuck in a tower, with a dragon guarding the castle and consuming all who dared step too close. Tales of caravan carts in front of the castle are evidence of the many victims who have fallen to the dragon's wrath. Many heard untold riches and a lonely damsel was waiting for those brave enough to slay the dragon.

Most shrug the tale off as a mere tale to tell the children, to get them to bed. Others, however, prepared to see if the tale was true. What prevented most from seeing if the tale was true was not only the dragon but the journey to get there. One who dares travel to the direction of the tower will find themselves surrounded by bandits hidden in the Troubled Woods. North of those woods is a river of death. Patrons of the tavern, The Troubled Ale, shared tales of the serpent who resides in the river, put there by the King's orders to deter invaders from crossing. There's a rumor of a hidden bridge to cross this deadly river, but no one can confirm ever seeing it. A bandit-ridden forest, a deadly river, and a dragon are more than enough to deter most from considering embarking on such a foolhardy quest.

Chapter 6

Dude, now in his early 20s, was currently swinging a blade at a straw dummy that was tied to a makeshift pole in front of the castle. Dude found himself quite skillful with the blade, even confident enough to shave with it a few times. Lately, though, he has let his beard grow out. It has grown to be a strong and respectable beard. He has grown stronger and toned, looking nothing like his weak longer self. Dudesow smiled and gave the straw dummy a satisfactory stab.

About two months ago, Dude had stumbled upon a book wedged behind the bed and the wall, intriguingly titled "How to Ride and Train a Horse." To his surprise, he found that much of the knowledge in the book could be applied to his dragon. Initially, he approached the idea with a sense of humor, proclaiming that "if you can ride a horse, then you could probably ride a dragon." However, the more he practiced, this humorous statement morphed into a genuine boost of confidence to keep him from giving up.

He began his training with the dragon, practicing balance and using the reins as she galloped across the land. Dude was growing confident in preparing to travel out with Carrot someday...by land. For they had yet to venture into the skies together. The thought of being high in the sky made Dude feel uneasy.

Dude promised himself that he'd save airborne training for last, for now, he wanted to practice something he's been meaning to do.

Dudesow jumped out the castle window.

He landed awkwardly onto Carrot's back, missing the saddle entirely.

Dudesow, the last few days has been practicing jumping out of the tower window a few times, attempting to land onto the saddle onto Carrot's back. He was determined to practice, just in case he needed to make a quick escape one day. While he had come close calls to missing the dragon back entirely due to Carrot getting distracted or tripping off the window sill, he had placed some hay piles on the side of the dragon as makeshift cushions, just in case of a less-than-graceful landing. He promised himself that once he's mastered this, he'll feel ready to try going airborne, but not today.

✲✲✲

Carrot currently lay bored on the beach shore, listening to the calm sound of ocean waves.

Dude left the sword in the straw dummy and walked out of the castle entrance towards Carrot. He made his way down the slope, swiftly kicking off his shoes before stepping onto the warm sand.

Carrot grunted and blew out steam from his nostrils in acknowledgment.

He petted Carrot's mane. It was one odd thing that stayed with Carrot after he transformed from a horse to a dragon. He was a dragon with a horse's mane.

Dude grabbed the bow and quiver full of arrows on the ground, lying next to a pile of wood. The pile of boards was pulled from some of the years of accumulated merchant carts. The arrows were made from the accumulated wood as well. Dude, notching an arrow, he side glanced and nodded towards the stack of boards and sternly stated, "Carrot, throw". Carrot knew what that meant, as the dragon walked over, grabbed a handful of planks with its talons, and flew up into the air.

Carrot dropped planks, a few at a time.

Dude released the arrow, striking a board. He quickly notched another arrow, released to hit another plank of wood. Dude quickly repeated the process.

Carrot flew down to restock but halted when Dude held up one hand.

"That will be all for today Carrot, thank you". Dude reached out behind him and tossed a carrot, "A carrot for my carrot"

The dragon easily caught it with its jaws.

Dude walked around the field, to examine the fallen planks, and admired his marks. He had painted circles onto targets. He smiled as he observed that the majority of planks that were dropped, were hit successfully. Dude knew he was getting better at targeting practice, but he still had a ways to go. He felt more confident in his ability with a sword, but he felt it wise to expand his talents and knowledge, for it would only benefit him. Dude only had time and lots of it. So he might as well use it.

***

A few days later. Dude sat on the open window of the tower, lazily making another arrow with a pocket knife he found a while ago in one of the merchant carts. He had a leg dangling off the edge, he whistled a tune of his creation.

Dude turned his head at the sound of Carrot getting up and flying off into the distance. Dude's gaze followed the dragon to see her flying towards a group of men on horseback who rode steadfastly towards the castle.

A dragon was flying full speed towards the men. Some of the men on horseback had pulled the reins and began to turn around. The men who were foolish enough to stay halted and pulled out their crossbows. They've begun firing at the Dragon. The arrows had harmlessly bounced off Carrot's scales. Carrot landed in front of the gang of intruders. The horses reared back. The men slid off their backs, their horses wisely retreating. The Dragon glowered, fierce eyes glancing at the men. The men trembled in fear. The Dragon pulled back its head and then whipped it forward. Opening its mouth, it neighed.

The loudest neigh.

The men were confused and sat on the ground speechless for a moment.

They sat there, unsure of what to do until the dragon flashed its teeth.

One man fainted, and the others ran away.

Carrot, neighed in laughter as the men fled screaming. Some of them dropped their gear on the way out. Dude smiled, eager to loot the new supply drop. He hopped off the windows ledge. His boots hit the wood flooring hard before he ran down the stone steps to head over to the field.

Several times a moment month, there have been ambushes of different groups trying to raid the castle. They fail every time, thanks to Carrot. They usually leave something behind: money, food, and sometimes weapons. Carrot was starting to lean forward in preparation to yeet the one man who fainted into the ocean. Carrot paused when she heard a shrill "Wait!" from Dude.

Dude ran up beside Carrot, heavily panting, hands on his knees. He held up one hand, trying to catch his breath, "I'mma gonna question him"

***

The stranger woke up wearily, finding himself tied to a pole, a straw dummy lying limp by his side. It was late evening. A bonfire burned a few feet ahead of the man. The man quickly glanced around. Dude was walking up carrying a bucket of water and a tin cup, not yet in the man's peripheral vision.

The man, realizing he was securely bound to a pole in front of the castle's lone tower, started squirming to break free, then paused when his eyes noticed Dude walking up to his side. A desperate look overtook his features as he stammered, "Please, don't offer me as a sacrifice to the beast. I'll do anything. I don't deserve such a fate. Show mercy. I—"

"Enough, cease," Dude interjected sternly. "Now, listen to me carefully. The dragon IS my noble steed. He guards me and follows my commands, to an extent. I strongly advise against any foolish attempts, or else I'll—"

Carrot flew down low, circling the castle before landing on the other side of the bonfire.

"You'll get no trouble from me"

Dude put the bucket down, then lowered a cup into the bucket to fill it with water. Dude raised the cup and offered the cup to the man. The man nodded. Dude tipped the cup slightly, the man eagerly drank the water.

Dude stayed crouched next to the man, looking the stranger directly in the eyes, "I have some questions for you"

The stranger glanced around for the dragon, "ok, hurry and ask, then set me free before the dragon returns". The man's eyes frantically searched the sky.

"Why were you and the other men trying to ambush this castle?"

"The gold, and the fair maiden trapped in the castle. I, for one, only wanted the gold. Now, if that was all, please set me free, you can have both for all I care"

"There is no gold, and there's certainly no fair maiden. I'll repeat, there's no gold, no ladies, just me and my noble steed—"

"Fine, release me! I'll tell others if that is what you desire," the man exclaimed, his voice quivering with fear, "Or I can remain silent, whichever you prefer"

Dude placed a reassuring hand on the man's shoulder and spoke in a calming tone. "Calm down," he said, "I just want to know where you heard this absurd idea of gold and fair maidens being hidden here. I can assure you with absolute certainty that there is no gold and no damsel within this castle. I assure you, I hold no grudge. Just answer the question and I'll let you go"

The man fell silent for a moment, then let out a deep breath before continuing, "You have to understand, I meant no harm. I'm just a homeless man down on his luck. I was a mason for hire in the town of Wetmore. As demand for work started to decrease due to people leaving town and bandits starting to move in, I was desperate, desperate enough to consider some questionable work for a bit of gold. I was sitting at my usual tavern, The Troubled Ale, nursing an empty glass, when I overheard a fellow drunkard. He was recruiting, seeking volunteers to mount an assault on this tower keep. He said something about having heard something from someone of importance at a tavern at Default Kingdom. Times are rough in the kingdom, and many, myself included, are willing to take significant risks for a chance at a better life. We all knew the odds were stacked against us and that we might meet our end...but what other options did a man like myself have? I was down to my last coin. The leader's plan was simple: gather enough people, overwhelm the dragon through sheer numbers, claim and split the wealth, and then we each go on our way. Our ostentatious leader, however, said he didn't want any coin because he had set his sights on saving the damsel in distress. He led us into battle, only to be the first to flee when confronted by the dragon"

"I assure you, there's no coin to be found here," Dude stated firmly. "In a moment, I'll release you, and you can explore for yourself. There's no gold here. In return, I ask that you dissuade anyone else you encounter who might have thoughts of storming my home"

"You have a deal," the man agreed.

Dude hesitated briefly before untying the man. "Just a friendly reminder," Dude cautioned, "all it takes is a whistle"

The man nodded earnestly. "I understand, I'm no troublemaker"

As Dude untied the man, the man quickly sprang to his feet and assumed a defensive stance. Dude, momentarily caught off guard, assumed a fighting posture. The two stared at each other for a moment until the man started laughing, then quickly put his fists down. He then casually walked closer to the campfire, sat down, and put his hands out for warmth, "Ah, that's a nice set of flames."

Dude walked over to the bonfire and crossed his arms. "That wasn't amusing, I could've called over the dragon to feast upon what little meat there is on those bones of yours"

The man scoffed, "Doubt it. Your face is easy to read, you had no intention of feeding me to the dragon. When I put up my fist, you didn't whistle. Instead, you held your ground and prepared to defend yourself. I can respect that. I did tell you I cause any trouble."

"If you're not going to confirm there's no treasure here, you best be going on your way. For you are still in danger of receiving misfortune. For I have a curse. Those who are near me and linger around me too long will receive bad luck"

"That sounds like you're being honest with me. Ok, when?"

"What do you mean when? I can't control a curse. It just happens"

"Sounds like dragon's shit to me". The man patted himself in exaggeration, "Here I am, feeling just fine.

Dude shrugged. "Don't say I didn't warn you"

"So far, since I woke, I've received clean water and warmth. You have untied me and have kept the dragon from harming me. I feel like I'm experiencing good fortune. I feel blessed to be alive, warm, and on the dragon's good side right now. Now if you don't mind. I'll be preparing to rest up before I trail off In the morning"

Dude simply gazed at the man, unable to find words. In silence, he turned and walked back to the tower. Once inside, he secured the door and made his way to bed. His thoughts were a tumultuous storm; he couldn't decide how to feel. Dude's mind was racing, his thoughts nagging at him: Was the man outside somehow immune to his curse, or was the curse gone? Was it even real in the first place? It had been so long since anyone had come close enough to test it. These questions and the overwhelming aura of uncertainty gnawed at him.

He stared up at the ceiling, thinking about his youth. Many of his days of youth were a blur. Confined to his room. He treasured the days that Kerry would visit to check up on him and teach him valuable life lessons. He never seemed affected by my curse. Why was everyone else in the Kingdom so scared to get close to him? Was it safe to finally leave this castle and explore the world? He needed to know.

Curious in his resolve to find out more, Dude decided to check on the man in the morning. He needed to see if misfortune befell him, if at all.

Chapter 7

Kerry was lying down on the floor of his boat. He was looking worn down, skin was turning leathery from the many years at sea.

His eyes closed, relaxing under the boat's canopy. Listening for movement from his fishing line.

When he wasn't fishing for food, he was fishing for a particular mermaid.

A Sorceress.

He had tied a pair of shears at the fishing line. The shears themselves were melted shut. He hoped his target didn't notice that, and instead would try to pull the shears off the line.

Years ago, the night before he went on the run with Dudesow. Kerry was peeking out a window in one of the guest room suites. He observed the protesting crowd with a frown. The crowd was starting to throw rocks at the guards. The guards fell in and steadily made their way back towards the castle's entry gate, using their shields for cover against the raining stones and bricks. Kerry had set strict orders for the guards not to use excessive force to prevent the riots from further escalation. Kerry knew the real reason the King wouldn't allow more guards outside to assist with the riots was due to the abysmally small total of guards left within the castle defending the King and Queen. Kerry worked hard to make sure that the people didn't know that or they'd overrun the place. So he placed most of the guards out in the open, to create the illusion of superior numbers.

There was a knock at the door.

"Come in", he yelled over his shoulder, his eyes still focused on the retreating guards. They made it safely towards the other side of the gate as it sluggishly lowered down into place. The arms of peasants went through the openings of the gate, shaking fists and making obscene gestures.

The Queen tapped his shoulder. He turned and provided a weary smile.

Kerry closed the window, "is…?"

The Queen smiled but it didn't reach her eyes, "yes the door is locked, we have some time alone"

They held each other in a tight embrace.

Tears went down Queen Stace's eyes.

Kerry eased the embrace and lifted Stace's chin.

Their eyes locked.

Kerry went in for a kiss but the queen put her finger on his lips.

"This is urgent. My husband put the order in. He's done waiting"

Kerry's eyes went wide, he put one hand on the hilt of his blade and started to make his way towards the door.

Stace put her hand on his shoulder, and Kerry froze in place, "Kerry, wait"

"What is it? I must make haste. I can save him"

"There is time, the King has ordered one of the kitchen staff to carry out the task. Dinner tonight. When the staff member knocks on the door, instead of retreating, he will wait outside the door. When the door opens, the kitchen will use a blade to leave a fatal mark on the young prince, I-" The queen's eyes teared up once again, and she fell to her knees, "I can't keep this up, this facade. I don't want my son to die. I want to see him, to hold him, to love him. Not kill him".

"I'll make sure he will live another night. I'll take him away far from here. He'll be safe at my family's estate. It's a safe house, I've prepared for this day. We could leave together, the three of us-"

"No", Stace said firmly. She stood up and wiped her eyes, a look of resolve on her face, "my husband would spend every resource to hunt me down. He wouldn't put near enough effort to find you and my son. Leave me."

Kerry reached out and Stace gently pushed it away. Stace looked away, "You know as well as I that what we have isn't meant to be. If it were, then fate would have made this, us, be together."

"Screw fate, we could still try"

"No, it wouldn't work and you know it wouldn't" "I'll dream at night, at the lifetime of what could've been if it did work"

Stace went up to Kerry to give him a tight embrace.

Moments passed, and a heavy silence lingered in the air.

They were both pondering deeply, on how to proceed.

Stace let go and sighed. She reached into a concealed pocket at her hip and pulled out a necklace, hanging limp at the end of it, was a key.

"Leave Dudesow somewhere safe. If you truly believe this estate of yours that I'm now aware of is safe, then so be it. I trust your word. After you know he's safe, I need you to find the sorceress Ari Feirune. She'll give you the truth regarding the curse. She is out hidden within the Copper Sea. I believe you can get her attention with a pair of shears. You will find out what I mean when you see her"

She pulled out a vial as well, "Also, take these. I took it from a cabinet while exploring Hubar's experiment chamber room. He's been finding humor lately by giving these to dogs. The dogs transform into random creatures when they consume this liquid, but their mind remains one of the dogs. Use this vial wisely. If you have time, swing by Hubar's experiment room to grab more vials. Grab the ones that are labeled, unlike the ones I gave you. For I imagine they do have various effects. Perhaps they will help. I need you to stay alive…my knight, please keep my Dudesow safe."

She pulled him in for a kiss and then shoved him away.

"Go, and please promise me Kerry…you won't return"

✳✳✳

Kerry had decided long ago that the shears he used as bait needed to be unusable. They were sealed shut permanently. Because If they were operable, the mermaid would use them to cut them off the line. He couldn't risk that happening.

After all these years, of trying different locations across the sea with no success. Kerry was starting to lose hope. Internal turmoil that he should be at his estate, being there with Dudesow.

He did raise the prince the essentials to defend himself, so he felt confident that-

The fishing line moved.

Kerry got up and rushed over and put both hands on the fishing rod.

The rod lurched forward from a mighty pull from somewhere down below.

Kerry knew better than to try to reel in a mermaid, he had a plan.

The pull on the line was straining the pool. He used all his strength to pull the rod with him as he walked around the mast of the sailboat. He then placed the rod against the mast, and tied rope around it quickly. Then shoved a crate against the rod.

He sat down. Panting.

He overexerted himself in his old age, but he needed this to succeed, he wasn't taking any chances.

The ship started to tilt at its side, as the line pulled.

The boat gradually tilted more severely, and items on the boat slid down the deck.

Small tools and supplies started to fall overboard.

He knew if she kept swimming down, it would tilt the boat over.

"Please, please Ari Feirune, just rise up from the ocean water and talk to me-"

The ship jolted.

The crate, acting as a redundancy, started to slide away from the mast.

The rod started to bend.

The mast started to creak.

Small cracks started to show along the mast.

Kerry started to slide down.

Then there was a loud crack, as the rod broke in half. The boat landed hard, wobbling back and forth, slowly regaining its balance.

Kerry lay down on the boat, facing the sky. He stared through a tear on the makeshift canopy.

His only plan failed and his only fishing rod was gone.

He failed.

Chapter 8

Dude opened the unlocked and opened tower door and stepped out into the courtyard. His fruits and vegetable garden was still in good shape, his supplies were still around the walls of the courtyard. Happy that the guest did not steal his food and supplies, he headed outside the castle walls to check up on the man. He really should've asked for the man's name earlier.

As he walked towards the castle entrance, he smelled something cooking. It smelled delicious, so he picked up the pace.

Dudesow saw the man, crouched over the first pit. He set up a makeshift grill over the pit. Fish were cooking over the fire, and a fat stack of wood kept the fire strong.

The man looked up and nodded towards Dudesow, "Morning, your dragon has been kind enough to keep the fire going and to retrieve our breakfast"

"Breakfast?"

"Aye, the dragon lay next to me while I cooked some fish. I was startled at first but then I noticed his hungry eyes were on my meal, and not I. That's when I offered to season some fish for her, too, if she retrieved some fish. He's out right now to grab some fish, how? I'm not sure. She said she'll find a way.

The man pointed at the wood pile behind him, "I figured that pile would cook a lot of fish, real fast. I imagine that dragon of yours has a mighty appetite"

The fish landed on the Dude's head. They both glanced up to see Carrot descending onto the ground.

Carrot leaned over the large pile of planks and opened her mouth.

Dozens of fish fell out of the mouth and onto the planks, some still flapping around.

The man stood up and walked over to the pile, "Now, aim your flame toward the bottom of the pile; this way, you don't burn the fish"

Carrot reared her head back and then shot a fireball at the bottom of the stack.

The man smiled, "now that was a mighty haul. Give it a few minutes, and the fish should be ready to consume; that's some intense heat right there"

Carrot stared at the man, not blinking.

Dude stared at both of them, speechless. Unsure if he was still dreaming.

The man ran his hand through his hair, "I just realized I should've seasoned it first"

Carrot nodded and blew some steam towards the man.

The man gave a weary smile, "You could always add some hay and carrots to the top"

The dragon sprang up and headed towards the castle.

Dude ran towards the castle, "Carrot, no! I've told you not to mess with my food! Don't!"

It was too late now, Carrot swooped down and gathered up most of the carrots section of the garden in the mouth, taking some of the soil with her. She flew back to the pile and spit the harvest onto the pile. Dude stared at the damaged garden. Perhaps he's the unlucky one.

Dude stomped back to the firepit. His face radiated red with frustration, as his mind was blaring the question: who is this man who has the sheer audacity to just show up in his home, act like everything is forgiven, and make himself at home? What irked him was that his very own steed quickly became fond of the newcomer in such a short amount of time.

The stranger and Carrot were staring at the sizzling fire. The man pointed at the fish cooking over the fire, "Give it about fifty heartbeats worth of your time, and it should be done". The man turned his attention towards the dragon, and then at Dude, "You're right Carrot, Dude looks pissed"

"What is your problem, I..." Dudesow paused, he blinked a few times before continuing, "How do you know his name? How did you know my name?"

The man shrugged, "I probably should've mentioned, I do have a unique ability to converse with animals using my mind. It's not a skill that can provide a reliable job, but it can be useful to have at times."

The man pointed at the makeshift grill, the flame starting to die out. "Your fish is ready," he said.

Dude stared at the man in disbelief and then at Carrot, "You trust this man?"

Carrot started to eat the fish off the top of the wood fire.

The man spoke, "Carrot says that he integrated me earlier this morning and found me to not be a threat. He said he'd tell you more later once he's finished his breakfast".

Dude stared at his dragon, shook his head, and shrugged, "Ok, fine, I have no real way to tell if you're telling the truth, so I'll take your word for it. What's your name? You already know mine, thanks to my noble steed Carrot who decided to spill all my name and perhaps all my secrets"

The man smirked back at Dude, noticing the irritation in Dude's tone, "How rude of me, I should've introduced myself at an earlier time. I should've done so the moment I woke up tied to a pole at the center of this dragon's lair"

"To be fair, I didn't expect to see you long enough to care for a name. I assumed you'd be a coward and run away in fear the moment I untied you. I thought you'd be soiling yourself in terror last night, not here the next morning, interrogating my dragon"

Carrot neighed loudly.

The man raised his eyebrows, staring directly at Dude, before turning to face the dragon with a smirk, "Interrogating your dragon, he says? I have you know that I'm having a lovely conversation with Carrot here." The man let out a chuckle, "You're right Carrot, this young man is acting like someone defecated onto this haystack this morning."

Dude glared at the man.

The man put his hands up in the air and took a step back, "Hey now, I see daggers in those eyes. Let's put this all behind us and start fresh, if I were a threat, your friend here would've probably munched or crunched me to mush by now"

Dude averted his eyes, stared at Carrot for a moment disapprovingly, and then sighed. He closed his eyes and exhaled."Fine", Dude put out his hand, "I'm Dude"

The man put his hand out and firmly shook Dude's hand, "I'm Adam Yutae, and your noble steed here just told me to tell you this, 'don't be rude to Adam, he's a guest. Plus, he can speak for me"

Dude shook his head in disbelief, "You expect me to believe that? How can I tell you're not lying? Ask him to share something that only she and I would know"

Adam smiled, "She told me that sometimes you like to have evening conversations with your vegetables. Sometimes you sweet talk and dance with a broom-"

Dude waved his hands, "Ok ok, that's enough"

The dragon opened its maw and started to make a series of strange sounds. Adam started to laugh.

Dude realized that Carrot was laughing.

Adam smirked, leaning towards Dude, giving him a playful nudge with his elbow, "So...a little dragon told me that you like to read books naked? Can you not do that, while I'm here?"

Dude sighed.

✴✴✴

In the afternoon, Adam offered to help by tending to the garden, doing his best to repair the area that was damaged by Carrot. Adam told Dude he was sorry, but Dude told him it was okay and then stomped out of the castle gate.

Dude walked over towards the ocean shore and sat. He knew he was acting childish. He had some growing up to do and had a lot of questions left unanswered in his mind.

Was he feeling this way because he was still adjusting to social interactions?

Was the curse still active and did it transfer to Adam? Because to Dude, it felt like he was feeling the side effects of the curse today.

A part of Dude, aching at the back of his mind, told him there wasn't a curse at all.

Dude stared out into the horizon, he wished Kerry would return.

Adam made his way down the slope and walked up to shore, kicking off his shoes and plopping down onto the sand next to Dude.

Dude and Adam both sighed at the same time.

It was awkward.

Adam stared out at the horizon for a few moments before speaking, "I did my best to get the garden tidied up. I'll be honest with you, it may take some time to get the carrot portion of your vegetable garden back into its prime. The good news is the other parts of your fruit and veggie sections were left unscathed"

Dude nodded, "thanks"

They both stared out into the horizon.

Dude broke the silence by throwing a rock. It skipped over the top of the water.

"That was impressive; you were able to get it over the shore waves to the calmer part of the water. You got in some solid skips"

"Thanks, it was really nothing. It just takes practice and a lot of free time"

Adam picked up a shell and flung it. It was engulfed in a wave, "well, I'll keep at it. Maybe I'll master it someday"

"Ideally with rocks"

"Yeah, I'll stick with rocks next time"

"Maybe next time I'll rock with some sticks too, just to see what happens"

Adam smiled, "hey, you do have a sense of humor. I couldn't tell with that stoic expression stuck on that face of yours all the time"

Dude cracked a smile, a bit embarrassed, "I believe I can finally ease up a bit"

"I've convinced you not to feed me to your dragon; I've instead fed your dragon. I tended to your carrot garden. I feel less guilty for storming your home. As a bonus, I got you to loosen up that stoic expression a bit. I believe my work here is done"

Adam began to walk away. Dude quickly followed, "You're leaving?"

"It's time I head out before I overstay my welcome. I'm sure you want me to share with the others in town that there's nothing here so they can stop storming the place. Hopefully, that's enough. I can't stop the dreamers, but I can certainly try on your behalf"

"Oh, yeah. That would probably that would be for the best"

Dude and Adam back headed towards the castle in silence.

Chapter 9

Nails dug deep into Kerry's leg.

Kerry awoke, letting out a yelp.

Sitting up, a mermaid sat on the ledge of the boat.

Her fierce eyes glared at him.

Kerry observed the bruise on his leg, the nails didn't pierce his skin.

The mermaid was pointing at her mouth. Her lips were stitched shut.

Kerry stared at the stitched lips, he looked repulsed.

She dug her nails into Kerry's leg again.

Kerry retracted and shouted, "What was that for?"

A look of impatience was blatant on the mermaid's face. Eyes piercingly staring back at him.

She pointed at her mouth in frustration.

Kerry nodded in realization, "Aw, I see. One moment"

He slid across the boat deck, opening a chest that was built into the boat. He pulled out a pair of shears.

The mermaid slid onto the desk, awkwardly and eagerly sliding across the desk, arms reaching out desperately to the shears.

Kerry spoke, keeping the shears out of her reach, "I believe it's safe to assume that you're...Ari Feirune?"

Ari rolled her eyes and nodded, eagerly reaching for the shears.

"Now, promise me that you won't leave until you hear me out, if you can do that, I'll give you these shears"

Ari nodded frantically, her hand moving in a motion that indicated for him to hurry.

Kerry tossed the shears to her.

The mermaid slowly cut the stitching.

As Ari cut the wire that kept her mouth closed, a blue mist evaporated around her mouth.

When the mermaid finished cutting the wire, she began stretching and moving her jaw. She then placed a finger over her lips and whispered an incantation. She pulled the wire from the skin around the lips slowly out, and the holes from the stitches around her lips slowly healed. The deep scars slowly closed up. Faint reminders of the scars remained.

She then turned her attention to Kerry, she smiled as she moved her jaw for a moment and then spoke with a raspy voice, "Thank you, but please now ask what you need to ask. Being out of water for too long can get uncomfortable real fast. Nothings worse than dry scales", she stared at him and squinted her eyes, "I imagine it must be important if you're this far out seeking me"

Kerry, "I did seek you to help answer some questions but may I ask, why didn't you remove the stitches yourself before today?"

Ari, her voice slowly returning to normal, "The curse prevented me from removing the stitching myself. I had to be offered a pair of shears"

Ari adjusted her jaw and opened and closed her mouth. She inhaled and exhaled with a smile of relief.

Kerry gave her a moment, then scratched his chin before speaking, "Um, how did you eat?" Ari looked him straight in the eye and raised her eyebrows, "I'm not your everyday average mortal. I'm surprised that whoever sent you didn't inform you of that. Now, ask me the question that sent you out here. Keep in mind that I don't want to soak in the sun all day. I can outright leave any moment because you didn't specify how long I had to stay here."

Kerry nodded, "I understand, my apologies. I truly appreciate your time"

"Now, ask what the important questions are. I will give detailed answers as It's only fair for helping me remove the wire. If it's a certain spell you seek, I can't help much. I have minimal abilities as most of my energy is locked away...and no I don't know why"

Kerry reached into his shirt. He pulled out the necklace and revealed a key, "how about we make a deal"

Ari stared at the key intently and dashed towards it.

Kerry quickly rolled out of the way, unsheathed his sword, and held it up, "Don't do anything reckless. I don't want to cause you harm. I understand you want this. Please, just hear me out". He tucked the key into his shirt with his one free hand. The blade on the other hand was pointing towards Ari, "I strongly believe that you may like my offer"

Ari intently watched the key being put away before glaring at him, "What is your offer?"

"I would like to offer you this key; in exchange, you answer all my questions without holding back any important details regarding King Hubar and Prince Dudesow. Once I'm satisfied with the information provided, I'll give you this key and you'll be free to go"

"One moment", Ari said before using her arms to lift herself over the railing and back into the water.

Kerry rushed over, then after careful consideration had decided to step back, sword out towards the water.

After a few moments, she lifted herself back onto the ledge of the boat, "I feel so much better, the dry scales were starting to irritate me." She wrung out her hair, averting his eyes for a moment while deep in thought. After a few moments, she turned to him, "How are we doing this deal, a verbal agreement?"

"Nice try, I want to do a Salvatorian blood agreement." He reached into a pocket and pulled out a vial.

Ari smiled and nodded towards the vial, "you must be one of Hubar's men to get your hands on one of those vials, made that batch myself"

"Then you know that I'm serious"

"I'm well aware of the severity of a Salvatorian blood agreement, you have yourself a deal"

Kerry sheathed his blade. He picked up the shears off the boat deck with his free hand. He poured the vial contents onto the shears. Then, she handed the shears over to Ari, who held them over her hip.

She grimaced, "So, specify the terms one more time, followed by the word 'Salva' for me to proceed in sealing the agreement."

Kerry nodded, "I want you to answer all my questions today truthfully, and you will give me all the information you know regarding King Hubar and Prince Dudesow. After that, you will have satisfied the agreement, in which you will be handed the key and will be free to leave at your leisure, Salva".

Ari slowly plunged the shears into the scales near her hip, an inch deep. Tears went down her eyes as she suppressed wailing out in pain, then handed the sheers back to Kerry.

Kerry took the sheers and cut his upper arm. He then raised the sheers. The sheers had an aurora of gold "It is done"

Ari nodded, "What are your questions?"

"Tell me about who you are, how were you involved with the King and Queen, more about these vials, and everything you know about-"

Ari raised one hand in protest, "Hush, one question at a time"

"I apologize. Ari Feirune, please tell me how you were involved with the King and Queen"

Ari looked away, her expression saddened, "I'll start from the beginning"

✳✳✳

Ari Feirune, long before she was trapped in a mermaid form, was a sorceress who mostly kept to herself in a cozy cabin within the Merry Mystic Woods. The woods offered a sense of calm and energy that practiced magic and those who are magic. Dozens of cottages can be found throughout the forest, the residents ranging from magical beings to magic users.

The sun beams cut through the tall pine trees to show the condensed dark purple grass that covered the ground. Ari, with the appearance of a young woman in her early twenties, has (as far as Ari can tell) been the longest-living resident in the woods. Ari had seen the families in cottages nearby live full lives, from generation to generation. When the neighbors would kindly ask for her age, she would always give them a smirk and remind them that it's rude to ask a woman her age.

Ari would routinely leave the safety of her cottage and make supply trips to the nearby market at the Default Kingdom. She would leave with her heavy pine green robe, keeping her warm on her travels. The robe had intricate gold constellations sewn in with care. Each star is notated with its residing overseeing god.

With time on her side, she took her time on her travels. She always looked forward to her journeys to the kingdom, waving and catching up with the neighbors on the way there.

As she traveled the path toward the Default Kingdom, she was usually offered a ride by neighbors and travelers heading that way. She respectfully declined offers every time.

She was always lost in her thoughts.

Her recent travels have shown her a shift in people's hopes, a growing unease. There was a feeling of despair in the air. It felt stronger the closer she got to the Default castle.

Ari was determined to continue her trips to the market, she shrugged off her intuition and continued her usual trips to the market.

When she arrived at the market, she spoke with the locals with genuine interest and kindness, regardless of whether they responded kindly. The majority of townsfolk found her kind soul contagious, even in the Kingdom's dark times.

Ari would usually frequent certain merchant booths. With time, the buyer and seller conversations went from mundane business pleasantries to more deep, meaningful conversations and grew to ones of genuine interest. Ari would always ask the merchants how they and their families were doing. Whenever the seller had expressed grief about a loved one being wounded or a loved one failing health, Ari would offer air that ranged from medicine to doing minor healing. Spellcasters, especially ones with healing abilities, were rare. So word had spread throughout the kingdom of the kind Ari and of her healing abilities. Ari had a track record of saving individuals who were near death's door. Ari often provided the healing free of charge, as she didn't desire coin. If anything, she'd always appreciate a book when offered.

Ari had never envisioned herself as a healer, but with her ability to craft magic by drawing from the energy within, she can be creative on how to apply that power. The kingdom in despair and most healers being too expensive for most of the townsfolk, Ari found herself spending more time away from her cozy cabin, spending days tending to the ill and creating elixirs. As the townsfolk asked for healing elixirs, Ari had found herself unable to find time to return home; the demand was too high, and she didn't have enough time. She often requested a room to rest, often sleeping long hours to regain strength. Ari found that direct healing had drained her strength and power faster, in comparison to elixirs. So she decided to focus on creating elixirs, as they use up less energy from within and can help more people easily by handing them out. One day, leaving her room, the innkeeper handed Ari a set of keys, stating it was for the gift outside. Ari asked who it was from, and the innkeeper shrugged.

Ari headed outside and found a merchant wagon outside. It was a decently sized mobile merchant cart, it had an intricate wood carving design. Ari walked around the cart and noticed a shop window on one side and a padlocked door on the back. There was a note on the door:

"Thank you, Ari, for everything. We appreciate all you've done. We all pitched in to get this for you. Please accept this cozy cart as your home away from home.

-A gratefully anonymous supporter of what you do"

Ari found herself smiling as a tear fell from her eye, as she never expected anything in return for efforts, but a gift is always a welcome surprise. Ari took out the key and opened the padlocked door.

✳✳✳

For the next few months, Ari created elixirs with nothing but mixing in her energy and the ingredients she purchased from the market. She felt like she was making a real difference, people would make donations in exchange for elixirs. The first month of opening the cart on the market street was an exhausting time for the sorceress who was used to taking her time, finding it difficult to meet the demand. As time passed, finding a rhythm of quicker elixirs and seeing the gratitude of the locals, Ari found it got easier. As her elixirs helped the majority of those in need, the demand started to decrease. There were finally excess elixirs on the shelves.

Ari was feeling a turmoil of satisfaction with what she accomplished, to overall physical and mental exhaustion. The usual restore time it took to regain her magical stamina was concerning. As it was taking longer than usual. Ari was bitterly thankful that the demand for elixirs decreased, as she knew that she'd pass out if she pushed herself any harder.

Ari closed up the shutters to prepare for a nap when a rampant knock was done on the shop window shutters.

"We're closed" Ari bellowed back.

"Ari Feirune, I have a message for you, from King Hubar"

Ari, taken back from this, returned to the window and opened the shutters.

Ari as she looked out the window, there stood a court nobleman, escorted by two guards. The nobleman bowed before continuing, "King Hubar requests your presence at once, for an urgent matter of most importance." The noblemen paused for a moment, then continued, The King has heard of your good deeds and would only like a word with you."

Ari was curious about what the King had to say, so she accepted the invitation and was led to a horse-drawn carriage. As she watched from the window on the side of the carriage, Ari felt her good spirits diminish quickly as the passing townsfolk looking directly at her gave her grim expressions.

Kerry interrupted, "Where was I, I would've recalled this. I remember all the spellcasters and scholars who were requested by the king, for I had to -"

Ari rolled her eyes, "I don't know, don't interrupt me. I don't know where you were, perhaps you were in a bedroom, kissing a certain someone's wife"

Kerry, obviously ashamed of his recent words, said, "I apologize, Ms. Feirune "

"It's fine, and please, it's just Ari. Now, what was I saying?"

"I'm sorry, please continue"

"Anyways, as I was saying…"

✳✳✳

Ari was escorted into the throne room. One of the thrones remained vacant, while the other was occupied by a King whose face was etched with mischievous glee.

With an eagerness that surprised her, King Hubar rose from his seat and approached Ari, extending both hands to shake hers vigorously. "Welcome Ari Feirune, It's truly an honor to meet such a well-known sorceress. I've been looking forward to your arrival."

Letting go of her hand, Hubar gave a genuine smile, "I find myself in dire need of your assistance, a matter of grave importance."

Ari nodded respectfully. "I'll do what I can, Your Majesty. How may I be of service?"

"Excellent," Hubar said, motioning for her to follow him. He led Ari out of the courtroom. A few guards trailed behind her.

Hubar led her down a lengthy flight of stairs, their path illuminated by torches affixed to the stone walls. At the bottom of the stairs, a long corridor stretched out before them, its doors unmarked.

The hallway was eerily silent.

Hubar walked a few doors down, mumbling.

Ari believed he was counting the doors.

Hubar suddenly pivoted to the left towards a door, unlocking the unmarked door and ushering Ari inside. Hubar stepped in and walked ahead of her. Arms spread out, offering her a view of the area. The room was an amalgamation of various elements: a large mirror at one end, a cauldron in the center, shelves lined with books, and many jars filled with mysterious ingredients. Beneath those shelves, there was a workbench. The other side of the room was more mundane, with only a straw bed, and a bucket.

A sudden impact against the back of her head sent shockwaves of pain through her skull. As she grappled with the pain, she felt an object being pressed into the back of her head, followed by a twisting motion. She reached for the back of her head, fingers searching between her hair, and felt a deep cut at the back of her head. Her vision blurred momentarily, and when it cleared, she found herself surrounded by guards. One of them handed King Hubar a key.

Hubar dangled the key in front of Ari, a sly grin on his face. "Do you know the significance of this key?"

Ari winced, suspicion evident in her eyes. "No, but I have a feeling you're about to enlighten me."

Stepping backward, Ari bumped into a guard.

The door a few steps away behind her had abruptly slammed shut.

"You're correct," the King replied, his tone smug. "I'll be happy to explain. I've placed what's known as a 'mind safety lock' within your consciousness. That peculiar cut that is behind your head is a keyhole. If you can assist me, but only if you succeed, will I unlock it and remove it from your mind. Let me enlighten you on how it works. If I turn the key to the left, it releases the lock. My loyal Knight Archibald here, will turn the key all the way to the right, which will make you incapable of causing harm to anyone and will reduce your powers significantly. I can't have you trying to harm me, or my guards when our backs are turned. Any attempts to do so will result in a painful shock, paralyzing you temporarily. I don't advise testing it; our last visitor, a stubborn wizard, met an unfortunate end trying to break past it."

Ari's expression shifted from shock to a mix of anger and confusion. "What do you want from me?" She yelled.

The King sighed, folding his arms and pacing around the room. "I desire a better life. While the wealthy merchants and elite revel in their leisure, I'm confined to endless meetings and tedious affairs of the kingdom. It's become tiresome."

King Hubar paused, turning to face Ari directly. "I've devised a plan, a brilliant one. With your assistance, we can create a believable scenario that will allow me to depart with the kingdom's treasury. My trusted associates and I will then vanish. I, leaving behind the burdens of royalty."

Ari frowned, skepticism evident. "So you want to abscond with the kingdom's riches, without the risk of being hunted for revenge or killed for your ill-gotten wealth?"

Hubar gave a wry smile, "More or less."

"How and why did you want me? I'll do what I can so you can rid me of this mental shackle."

The King smiled confidently, ignoring her last statement. "It may sound audacious, but I'm no fool. I've prepared multiple contingencies, fail-safes, and escape routes. I have the imagination to craft an ingenious escape, but I need your magic to lend a touch of authenticity. Together, we can make this happen."

"Whatever, just….let's get this over with. The quicker the better, I want to return to my cottage"

"I admire your willingness and grand enthusiasm, but I must advise that completing this project will take some time. You can't rush perfection, so please, get comfortable. You're in for the long haul."

Dread crept into Ari's expression, and her head tilted forward.

Ari's hands curled into fists.

Hubar snapped his fingers, and a guard outside opened the door. Hubar walked out, with Archibald tailing from behind him.

Archibald slammed the door behind him.

Ari heard the mechanism of the door lock, sliding into place.

Huber spoke from the other side of the door, "Any moment you decide to disobey me hurt me or my staff, or foolishly try to run away, mock or insult me. All I have to do is break this very key, and…you die. It's that easy."

***

At this part, Kerry stood up.

He grabbed a bucket and walked over to the side of the ship.

He scooped up some ocean water. He walked over to Ari and spilled the water to cover most of the scales.

Ari smiled, "Thank you, that feels much better".

Kerry nodded and then sat down, "Please proceed".

***

Ari found herself waiting alone in the room for what seemed like hours. With no windows to gauge the passage of time, it became increasingly difficult to track how long she had been there.

Restlessly, she paced around the room, deep in thought and contemplation.

Then, a knock echoed through the room, followed by the door opening to reveal Archibald. King Hubar trailed behind him, and both entered the room.

Archibold stood guard at the door. Arms crossed. A helmet blocked any visible expression.

The King leaned casually against the cauldron and gestured towards a stool tucked beneath the workbench. "Please, have a seat. We have much to discuss"

Ari strode over to the stool, deliberately dragging it across the floor with a loud screech. She plopped onto the stool, her arms tightly folded across her chest, her eyes locked in a glare directed at Hubar.

The King acknowledged her glare with a smile and directed her attention to the massive mirror in the room. "This mirror will serve as your window to various locations. Mirror, show me Queen Stace."

The surface of the mirror rippled like a stone dropped into water, gradually revealing the image of Queen Stace. She lay backside on a bed, with a staff member standing vigil beside her, ready to provide any assistance needed.

Hubar drew nearer to the mirror, pointing toward his wife's pregnant belly with a mix of disappointment and frustration. "My beloved wife, whom I hold dear, carries a child that bears no connection to me. I possess no concrete proof, yet I feel it in my very soul. This child does not share my bloodline"

As he uttered these words, Hubar's face turned a deep shade of red, and he seemed momentarily distant. The room fell silent, save for the flickering torchlight.

After a few moments, Hubar released his grip on the cauldron and wiped his hands on his shirt. He then offered a weary smile and spoke, "I apologize; let us continue."

Approaching the mirror once more, he instructed, "Mirror, reveal to me the troops of Galgone"

The mirror responded with rippling images of hundreds of troops on the march. "I've received intelligence that our neighboring kingdom of Galgone has dispatched their forces in an attempt to invade our castle," Hubar explained. "In anticipation of this joyful news. I had Archibold kill the messenger." Kerry shrugged and continued, "I later granted most of our castle guards the night off, declaring it a celebration for my child's impending birth"

Ari looked at Hubar incredulously before turning to Archibold, questioning, "You're alright with this?"

Archibold, his arms still folded, remained silent.

Hubar snapped his fingers, refocusing Ari's attention on him. "Pay heed to me, not him," he commanded. "If you're curious, he will be rewarded for his unwavering loyalty"

Hubar continued to pace around the cauldron as he explained his plan. "I will feign surprise when the news of the invading forces reaches me. Meanwhile, your task is to make the upcoming battle as challenging as possible for my troops. Keep a close watch on updates through the mirror. Introduce unfavorable weather conditions tonight, create complications—get inventive. I'll be occupied comforting my wife. If all goes according to plan, the Kingdom will fall, and my associates and I will escape unnoticed"

With those instructions, Hubar headed out, leaving Archibald behind. "Archibald here will keep an eye on you," he added before closing the door.

Just before the door clicked shut, he threw in a parting comment. "And ensure misfortune befalls that wretched newborn tonight as well."

Once the door was sealed, Ari stood up and stood up and faced Archibold, her eyes turned a shade of light blue. She extended both her palms towards him and began chanting. Unseen yellow symbols appeared and glowed on Archibald's armor, emitting a bright radiance as she continued her incantation.

Ari shook her head in frustration and kept chanting. Confused by the delay.

In response, Archibold swiftly moved, seizing Ari by the neck and lifting her clear off the ground. "Don't try that again," he growled before flinging her forward.

Ari landed on the ground with a painful cry, writhing in discomfort. Archibold watched for a moment before crossing his arms. "Get started," he ordered sternly. "Don't make me do that again. Your attempts to harm me will do nothing, as my armor has protective wards.

Archibold returned to the door. He nodded and pointed towards the mirror before crossing his arms.

✳✳✳

Kerry rose from his seat, his face flushed with anger. "That damned brother of mine," he seethed, "he never took honor or the knight's code seriously during his training. I should have known he'd stray from the path of righteousness. I always suspected the King would resort to underhanded tactics, but I never imagined he'd be the cause of Dudesow's and everyone's suffering. I had assumed it was some external malevolence relishing in our torment"

He turned his gaze to Ari, his tone softening. "None of this was your fault. You were exploited for your abilities, and..." He trailed off, his voice filled with sympathy. "How did you end up as a mermaid? Why was your mouth sealed? I imagine most would have starved in your situation."

Ari averted her gaze. "I'm not a mere human; I don't require food and water to survive," she explained. "I'm a lower-level deity, imperfect like any other being. But let's stay on track."

Ari was about to speak once more but frowned. She appeared hesitant in what she was about to ask, "May I soak my tail in the water while I continue the story? I won't flee, per our agreement promise. The somewhat consistent pouring of water onto my scales is not ideal"

Kerry dropped the bucket he was holding and patted the key hanging under his shirt. He then gestured towards the water. "Go right ahead."

Without hesitation, Ari dived off the boat, causing Kerry to nearly lose his balance. He rushed off to the railing. He stared into the water, searching for her.

Ari swiftly resurfaced, her arms draped over the railing. Kerry startled, slipped, and landed hard on his bottom, a mild look of annoyance on his face.

Trying to hide the amusement on her face, Ari continued, "Much better! Now, where was I?"

Ari didn't need nor require a cauldron. She wasn't sure if King Hubar knew if she wasn't a witch. Perhaps this cauldron was left over from the last unfortunate resident of this room. So she leaned back against the cauldron and stared at the mirror.

Ari averted her eyes as Queen Stace was in labor.

She didn't want to cause harm to an infant, so she turned around and glanced back.

Archibald was still at the doorway. His helmet turned towards her. He uncrossed his arms for a moment to wave her away. She returned her attention to the mirror.

She was thinking about what the King said, "Make sure misfortune befalls that wretched newborn tonight…"

That left a lot of wiggle room.

He didn't specify how to kill the newborn.

Ari could work with that. She just had to get creative.

She walked over to the shelf of books. Glancing over them, one title on a spine caught her attention. She headed over, and reached over for a book that was between the books "Curses for Beginners" and "Revenge for the Unimaginative." She wiped the dust off the cover with her sleeve.

She read the title in her mind, "Finding Success with Mischief: Using Minimal Invested Magic and Receiving Maximum Return." This looks promising she murmured to herself.

✹✹✹

Thankfully for Ari, but not for Queen Stace, the labor lasted for several hours. Ari, reading the book with intense interest, found herself grinning. Reading advice from finding loopholes in deals to satisfying bargains by doing nothing at all. She didn't know why this book was there, but she thanked the probably dead previous resident for leaving it there. She smiled as she knew how to proceed. Ari never saw herself as malevolent, and she didn't plan to go down that path anytime soon.

When the prince Dudesow was born. She picked up a wand she had obtained on the workbench. She pointed the wand at the mirror and made a show of it. Archibald didn't need to know that the want was redundant, but this needed to appear genuine. She focused on causing a scene, careful now to harm the child.

She managed to stifle her laughter as Prince Dudesow flew feet-first into King Hubar's face. She caused some staff to slip and stumble, but nothing that would cause major harm. When the infant was steady and safely held, the room's door swung open, smacking King Dudesow in the face. Ari wished she could take credit for that, because, like, it hurt.

Ari redirected her focus to another location in the mirror, changing the scene to the front of the castle where a few guards patrolled the battlements of the city's exterior walls. She began to circle her arms, her eyes clouding over as her powers surged.

The clear sky began to fill with dark clouds, and a light drizzle started to fall on the guards' faces. In the distance, a man on horseback raced toward the gate, yelling on repeat, "Open the gate!"

The guards recognized their scout and quickly raised the gate. When the gate was fully open and right before the gate guard was about to release the lever, Ari unleashed a lightning bolt directly at the crank. There was a deafening crackle, the guards screamed as they witnessed the mighty flash. The chains and cranking mechanism melted into a misshapen mass of metal and mud.

Ari couldn't help but smile. This should satisfy Hubar's request to assist the enemy troops in gaining access to the city. She hoped that the guards would use their blades to break the chain to drop the gate when the time came. She had focused on creating minor disruptions to the kingdom's troops, ones that would be more of a nuisance than a threat. Ari didn't want to be responsible for causing harm to the townspeople. Her natural pacifist nature made her wish no harm would befall others. However, she would be an exception for the King's life, if she was able to. She quickly pushed that thought aside, as a quick pang from that thought gave her a headache.

Hours later, Ari watched the battle unfold, occasionally increasing the rain. The muddy ground seemed to be most of the work for her. Many on the battlefield were slipping and stumbling. The enemy was advancing and had overwhelming numbers. She changed the scene to view the commander's tent. A table set in the center had a map and tokens of two different colors. King Hubar was scolding Kerry. Ari couldn't hear what they were saying, but it looked like things weren't going as King Hubar had planned. Huber pointed the finger at Kerry and stormed off. Ari imagined that Hubar expected the enemy troops would have made their way into the city, but Kerry was tactical, and his well-trained troops prevented the enemy from advancing into the city.

✳✳✳

Kerry looked away, his cheeks red. "Flattery won't make me give you this key any sooner"

Ari shrugged, "That wasn't my intention. What I say is true though. Any other leader would have given up with those cards dealt. Most of your guards were not ready, with half of your assigned troops told to take the day off early. Even if you had every one of your troops ready, you were still outnumbered. You had a tactical and home advantage when the enemy relied on numbers"

"Thank you, Ari, I appreciate that. I must ask that we continue this story forward. I believe you have almost answered all my questions and more with your tale"

"May I ask you a question?"

"Go right ahead, throw the question"

"Where did you hear about me and the key?"

Kerry's face filled with sorrow, "It was given to me by Queen Stace, she told me where to find you and ask for the truth. She said you'd want this key. I was unaware of its purpose before, but now I see its importance"

Ari frowned, "I imagine she stole the key from Hubar at some point. I imagine Hubar tells her nearly everything from when I overlooked their activities in the mirror. From what I saw, they were close but were physically distant." She paused, then raised an eyebrow, "The queen was often rather close to you, from what I could see.

Kerry blushed, "Please, don't judge the Queen harshly. It was an arranged marriage. She saw Hubar as more of a friend than a lover. Stace, the Queen, we have fallen for each other long before Stace had been set up to marry Hubar by her parents. I know what we had wasn't-"

Ari held up a hand, "Say no more, for I don't have any negative impression of either you or the queen. We went off on a tangent, let me continue the tale"

✳✳✳

Ari stared deeply into the moving images in the mirror. With the wave of her hand, the image on the image changed to a different area overlooking the kingdom. The surviving townsfolk made their way back into the city. Carts carrying the wounded and dead. A tear dropped down from Ari's eyes, she deeply wished she could be out there providing medical assistance. She was running low on power. She needed to rest. She made her way to the bed.

The door started to unlock and Archibald stepped aside.

King Hubar kicked the door open and pointed at Ari. His face was red with rage, words stammering to the point his teeth were audibly tapping; "you! I gave you an easy assignment. Let the enemy troops conquer the land and have the prince die. You've failed at both.

Hubar turned and nodded in the direction of Archibald. He snapped his finger and pointed at Ari, "Reward her for her utter incompetence"

Archibald stormed over to Ari.

Ari turned, and before she had a moment to react, a gauntlet swung into her face. She lost her footing, and her shoulder hit the ground.

The King spat, "Continue"

Ari tried to get up but Archibald put a hand on her shoulder, he held her down. With his free fist, he pummeled her stomach.

The King, red-faced, ranted, "For sure, I thought with my military vastly outnumbered and drafting in untrained farm folk, that this damned kingdom would fall. I was gravely mistaken, for I had a commander who is too perfect at his job and a pathetic weak witch who is incompetent at her job"

The King walked up and shoved Archibald aside, kicked her hard in the face, and she blacked out.

✳✳✳

Kerry stood up. He turned to face away from Ari, "That's unforgivable, what my brother has done to you. Regardless of whether it was the King's orders"

Ari was taken aback, "Your brother?"

"I've trained him since he was a mere squire. No matter how much I've tried to improve his character, he would always return to being a troublemaker amongst the ranks. He would've been removed for being dishonorable sooner if he didn't have the king's blessing. Now I know why, he was secretly the King's lapdog"

"His actions are not your fault""I should've tried harder to remove him from the ranks. Someday m'lady. I swear, he'll pay for his actions"

"I appreciate the sentiment, but I'll be the first to make the King and his minions pay for their actions. Once I'm back on my own two feet"

Kerry turned back to face Ari, "I apologize if you find offense if you don't mind me asking. You're a magic user, why didn't you defend yourself?"

Ari sighed, "I have very limited power, enough for minor magic. If I don't use magic for a while, I may be able to build up internally to cast a more powerful spell, but not by much. I've had a cap placed upon me. For the last century, someone has been draining my powers, I'm not sure how"

"Who?"

"Let me get back to my story, to answer your original question before I sway too far off in some tangent. I need to fulfill my end of the deal"

※※※

Ari woke up on the floor. Archibald guarding the door, with his usual stance of arms being folded. He said nothing. She sat up.

Ari felt pain all over. Her tongue felt dry blood along her teeth. She limped her way over to the mirror. She looked terrible. Two black eyes, a broken nose. Dry blood all over her face. She made her way over to the workbench and began to review the supplies to make a remedy.

Archibald knocked on the door once and then stepped aside. A guard from outside brought in a buck in one hand and a tray in the other. The guard placed them on the floor next to Ari's feet and then quickly walked out. Archibald closed the door and then stood in front of the door. The tray had stale bread and a cup of wine. The bucket had water.

Ari reached down and gulped down the bitter wine. She picked up a bucket and placed it on the table. She mixed different ingredients into the bucket and stirred the top with her finger. She started chanting.

Archibald glanced at his armor, it didn't glow so he didn't take action.

Ari finished chanting and lifted the bucket over her head, she tipped it over. The water fell and evaporated right before it touched her skin.

The bruises slowly fade away. The dry blood disappeared. Her clothes and skin were still dry.

A few hours later, Ari assumed it was a few hours later. The King opened the door and barged into the room. He was taken aback by her completely healed state, "Wow. If only you were as good at helping me as you are at taking care of your appearance".

Ari glared at him, shooting daggers from her eyes.

She said nothing.

"The battle was a disaster, but the madness you've created during Dudesow's birth turned out much better than I expected. The staff and their love for spilled brew had them spreading rumors that there was something wrong with the prince, due to such a peculiar birth. Phenomenal work, I can work with that and go from there. Archibald, follow me. I've got a Prince to deal with"

They both left. Bolting the door closed on the way out.

The torch in the room started to dim as Ari rushed over to the mirror on the wall.

Ari asked the mirror to show her the newborn prince. The prince was being cradled by his mother. The mirror didn't produce sound, but Ari could make out from the scene that the mother appeared to be singing the prince a lullaby, occasionally giving loving kisses to the newborn's forehead.

Archibald and a castle guard stormed into the room, followed by the King. The mother looked concerned. Hubar appeared to be shouting something and pointed towards the mother and child.

A guard went up and snatched the baby away from Queen Stace. Archibald blocked the path as the guard holding the infant and the King left the room. Archibald appeared to be shouting something that held the Queen back.

Archibald closed the door on the way out. Stacie appeared to be screaming and wailing, pounding her fists on the door.

"Mirror, just reflect"

The mirror showed her solemn expression. Ari turned away and slowly laid down on her straw bed, deep in thought.

✳✳✳

She started to doze off when she heard the door unlock. Archibald stormed in through the doorway first, and a guard followed from behind. The guard that followed had cautiously strolled in as he carried a small infant in his arms.

The baby looked ever so miserable, its mouth gagged with a cloth, and it wailed a muffled cry as tears streamed down its eyes.

Ari rushed over and took the baby from the guard, in dismay, yelled, "What's wrong with you people?!". She took the gag right off and began to console the wailing infant.

King Hubar strolled in. A smug expression on his face.

She glared at him, "What are you planning to do with this child?"

"I need to keep him away from the public eye for a while. When he's older, he'll be allowed to roam around the castle grounds so people know he's alive. For now, I need you to keep an eye on him"

"I'm no mother"

"You'll act as one because doing so will keep him alive"

"What, why? Why me?"

"I'll assign one of the castle's guest suites to him, that door will be locked. From here, I want you to cause some show of bad luck to anyone who so happens to walk by that room. Cause them to trip, something like that"

"I don't understand this new elaborate ruse"

Hubar turned and leaned forward towards Sir Archibald, his thumb pointing at the guard who brought in the prince, "is that guard with us?"

Before the guard could react, Archibald unsheathed his blade, swung around, and plunged the blade into the unsuspecting guard's chest. Archibald pulled out the blade, and the guard fell to his knees, then topped over.

Archibald dragged the dead man's ankles out of the room.

Hubar shook his head, "I can't take any chances of word getting out about this"

Archibald returned, "The guards outside are ours"

Hubar smiled, "Thank you." He returned his attention to Ari, and his smile faded. "Don't fail me, or I'll give you a fate worse than death"

Ari patted the prince on the back as she watched the King leave.

She kissed Dudesow on the forehead and whispered into his eye, "I'll protect you for as long as I can"

✳✳✳

Ari kept busy the next six years raising Dudesow. In her free time, she studied each book intently, stocking her concoctions into vials and placing them onto a shelf. She found the spell books rather enjoyable, learning new types of spells that she wouldn't have bothered to learn in her past life. She kept the outside of Dudesow's door in constant view in the mirror. Dudesow's future room was empty, but the castle staff didn't know that. She kept watch for any staff that walked by it. Causing them to slip or trip, to continue the ruse.

Archibald no longer monitored the room. She was often alone with Dudesow, bonding with him. She taught him essentials like how to walk and how to use the bucket. She experienced tears of joy when his first word was "air". It was close enough to him ever saying her name.

The following day, Archibald took Dudesow away.

Ari watched the mirror as Archibald put Dudesow into his new room and locked the door.

It was fortunate that Ari didn't need to require food and water. As no one would check up on her for days at a time.

Hubar told her to make a scene the day that they invited the called experts from across the land. She believed she found the opportune moment for the chandelier to fall. She recoiled as one of the men was dragged away after the chandelier fell. She shook her head and turned away from the mirror.

✳✳✳

King Hubar would order Ari to intervene with local trade, crops, and whatever else he could think of. Ari would put a minimal effort. Hubar would return later at some point and have Archibald punch and kick her until she passed out. A recurring discipline for failing to cause the kingdom to fall into ruin.

She was unhappy and alone.

The only joy she felt was watching Dudesow grow up into a smart young man. She started to view him as her own son. Ari noticed and took a mental note of the only man who cared for him while she was trapped in the dungeon. For everything she wasn't able to teach the boy, the noble and wise Sir Knight Kerry taught Dudesow everything else a child should know.

✳✳✳

Kerry raised his eyebrows, "so, you do know who I am"

Ari looked back at him smugly, "Of course, once you asked about the King and Dudesow, it didn't take long for me to figure out who you are. From there, I decided to be more cooperative. Before the days I was a prisoner, I've heard quite a lot about you, all good things"

"I'm glad to hear that. I promise you, those stories are exaggerated, but my honorable upbringing and virtuous actions are always true to my character. I mean, you have no harm and no vile intentions. When you're ready, please continue your tale"

Ari continued, "My sad tale is almost done"

✳✳✳

Hubar burst in one day, "It's time, I've tried everything, and you've left me with no choice. If you had executed my plans as instructed, you wouldn't have had to follow your final order. You must kill the prince. You didn't do it before, but you will do it now"

Ari looked away. "No"

Hubar pulled out the key from his shirt and threw it to the ground. He promptly stomped it.

Ari passed out.

***

Ari awoke, being shaken by the collar by Archibald's firm grip, "wake up" He said sternly. Once he saw Ari's eyes open, he released his grip and she fell back.

Hobar hovered over her. "That was a warning. I will make you regret any further objections hurt"

Ari's eyes watered up, "I will not"

Hubar, his face enraged, observed the room. He spotted the vials, "open her mouth"

Archibald, his armored hands, roughly opened her mouth.

Hubar picked a random vial from the shelf and poured its contents into her mouth.

She started to have a seizure.

Hubar stared in amusement, keeping his eyes on her. He called out, "Bring in the other two guards."

The guards rushed in. One of them spoke, "Yes, my lord?"

If she survives this, tie her up. Seal her mouth shut, and dump her body into the sea.

"Yes my lord"

The guards pinned her to the ground.

King Hubar, picked up the empty water bucket and carefully placed the remaining vials into it. "Thanks for these"

The King headed towards the door, bucket in hand. He pointed at Ari with his free hand, "Assist these too, make sure this final farewell is done correctly. Tomorrow, you will take the dinner tray and serve Dudesow his final meal. No witnesses"

Archibold nodded, "Yes my lord"

Ari's teeth clattered, and a barely audible "no" cried out.

Hubar left. Archibald pushed one of the guards aside. He went over her torso and put his knees on her arms. The other guard held down her legs.

Archibold looked back over his shoulder at the soldier who stood confused. "Don't just stand there; grab some rope and some wire"

"Yes sir", the guard ran off.

Archibold took off his helmet and placed it on his side. A smile reached his eyes. "I always look forward to this, it's a shame it's the last time"

Archibold began to punch her face relentlessly.

***

Hours later, the guards carried Ari down the hall, in the opposite direction of the stairs. Ari's mouth was sewn shut with wire. She was tightly bound with rope. Her legs were trembling as they were slowly merging into one. Ari compared the sensation being like your legs fell asleep while thousands of ants bit your legs at the same time.

At the end of the hall, the door opened to reveal an ocean cave with a tiny dock and a small paddle boat tied to it.

They tossed her into the boat and then stepped into it.

The two guards took the oars while Archibold stood and placed his foot on Ari's forehead, "I find it amusing that the vial contents I forced you to drink earlier had transformed your legs into some sort of fish-like tail. I suppose you are destined to spend the final moments in the ocean. The King hired some mage to magically wire your lips shut, something about dead men tells no tales. Does that include women? I don't know, but hey, if you're spirit haunts me, please let me know"

Ari gave up struggling and just tried to stare at the moon. This was her first time at sea and she wondered if it would be the last.

Once Archibold determined they were far enough out in the sea, he tied a large stone and connected the rope to Ari's restraints. volunteered to dump Ari into the sea all by himself.

Ari quickly plummeted.

She sank deeper into the depths, farther and farther from the light.

***

She hit the sand, unable to move. The restraints and heavy stone anchor keep her in place.

Days passed, she discovered that she didn't need food or water, and she also didn't need air.

Terror took hold of her at the realization that she may spend eternity in darkness.

As She lay there in the darkness. Closing her eyes, she focused on dreaming to pass the time. Ari didn't know how long she was down there. She was too far down to see the sun's or moon's light.

She just laid there. Dreaming.

As the years passed, the rope loosened as bacteria ate away in the rope.

The rope binding her finally eroded enough that her body slowly floated to the surface.

The surface light burned through her eyelids, instantly waking her up.

She tried to cheer but her sealed mouth prevented her from doing so.

She tried and failed to remove the wire, as it hurt to remove it. She placed a hand on the wire. She could feel the curse bound onto the wire. It cannot be removed unless someone offers her sheers.

Frustrated, she dove back into the water.

She swam for countless hours, alone with only her thoughts.

✳✳✳

Ari clapped her hands. "And that's it. I've been swimming alone, unable to find anything or anyone who can help me with transformation. I'm just trying to figure out how to get back home. I have no other useful information to share"

Tears escaped her eyes.

Kerry gently placed a hand on her shoulder, "I'm sorry".

Ari looked solemn, "No need to be sorry. It's not your fault or your concern. This is my life now"

"Thank you for raising and caring for Dudesow at such a young age. You've told me more than enough, here-take this." He offered the key.

Ari, with both her hands, separated the hair at the back of her head. She then eagerly took the key. With one hand, she carefully placed the key into the keyhole at the back of her head. She turned it, and her suspicion was correct. After turning the key to the left twice. The lockbox slowly phased out the back of her head. She caught it before it fell into the water, and then tossed it onto the boat, "I've had that lock long enough. You keep it. Perhaps you can put it into the back of King's wrinkled fat head"

Kerry shrugged, "He deserves no less from what you've told me".

Ari dropped into the water.

Kerry waited awhile. Enough time had passed that he sensed that she wouldn't return. He unwrapped his wound. It was gone. His questions were answered, and the agreement was fulfilled.

Kerry stared out into the horizon. He decided to sail back tomorrow and return to his old estate. He hoped Dudesow would forgive him. At sunset, he lay on his weather blanket and blew out the light of a lone candle.

Kerry said a silent prayer. The same prayer that he said every night before bed, he prayed that Dudesow was alive and well and that the King would never find him.

The next morning, he awoke to find a bucket next to his face. He peeked inside, and several crabs were trying but failing to climb out. Kerry was surprised to see Ari nearby, reading one of his books.

"Thanks for the breakfast, I've never expected in my lifetime that a mermaid would be giving me crabs"

Ari smirked, placing the book down while shaking her head with lighthearted disapproval. She sat on the railing, her tail dipping in the water. Kerry noticed that today, she proudly wore a crown made entirely of coral.

"I can see where Dudesow got his obsession with books from", He pointed towards the coral headpiece, "I like the crown"

"Thank you," She said jovially.

"I found it underwater a few years ago. I thought it looked pretty, so I wear it occasionally on a good day, like today." She blinked at him with an amused expression, "I like to call this crown my coral wreath."

Kerry flashed a smile before he regarded her skeptically, "Why did you return?"

Ari's cheery expression waned from her face.

She took off the coral wreath and placed it onto the deck, spinning it slowly with her finger, "After raising Dudesow during the earliest years of his life, I grew rather fond of him." She turned away, a pained expression on her face, "I think about him all the time. I've never had children, and raising Dudesow during his youngest years had placed a maternal bond in my heart. I wish to know what happened the night the king had ordered Dudesow's assassination"

Kerry's face grimaced, "Does it matter? I saved that boy's life"

"It matters to me. So, I ask again, how? I brought you a morning meal. I believe that's a fair exchange for this information"

"I appreciate the food you've served me in this...this silver bucket. It's only fair that I share with you my own story about why I'm here. When the Queen handed me a key, she told me that King Hubars had a secret experiment chamber, I scavenged it before heading out..."

✳✳✳

Kerry swiftly left the experiment chamber and silently moved through the castle, heading towards Dudesow's room. He kept an eye on the window, ensuring that the moon had not yet risen. As long as the moon remained hidden, he still had time. Kerry moved cautiously, avoiding any potential witnesses.

About halfway there, he glanced out another window and saw the moon beginning to rise. Panic surged through him, and he abandoned stealth, dashing down the corridor. Time was running out. He needed to reach Dudesow's room before the dinner staff, whoever had been hired to assassinate him, arrived. He suspected that the food they brought would be poisoned, as nobody dared to approach the young man closely.

Kerry turned a corner and was horrified to see a knight stabbing a man outside Dudesow's room. The tray clattered to the ground, but the knight swiftly grabbed it to prevent any noise. Kerry recognized the knight—it was his own younger brother, Archibold.

Kerry was the first to speak, his voice trembling with shock, "Is that—"

Before he could finish his sentence, Archibold charged at him, wielding his sword with both hands. Kerry drew his blade just in time to defend himself as Archibold relentlessly swung his sword.

"Brother, what is the meaning of this?" Kerry demanded.

"It's nothing personal, brother. These are the King's orders," Archibold replied grimly. "I can't have any witnesses"

They continued to parry and clash, the sound of swords clashing echoing through the corridor.

After blocking another strike from Archibold, Archibold paused.

Kerry stepped back, staying in a defensive stance. "What is it?"

Archibold hesitated, his expression conflicted. "As much as I despise you, I also respect your achievements, and you're the only family I have. I'm torn."

"Is there another way?" Kerry asked urgently.

Archibold sighed, lowering his sword slightly. "There might be. The man out there can be the scapegoat. I'll tell the King that you've him after he killed the prince, I arrived late, being the only witness"

Kerry nodded, "Let me escape with the prince, and we'll leave this land behind, never to return. Tell the King that you disposed of Dudesow's body for the safety of others, to prevent lingering misfortune"

Archibold considered this for a moment. "Fine by me, brother. But know that if I ever see you again, I will have to kill you"

"Understood, thank you, brother"

Archibold stepped aside to allow Kerry to proceed. Archibold placed a small blade in the dead man's hand, creating a false scene. Then he nodded at his brother before walking away.

Kerry whispered a heartfelt "Thank you, brother" before returning to Dudesow's room to inform him of their escape plan.

***

Ari rubbed her eyes, "I hate your brother, but at least he did something minor to redeem himself. Don't be mistaken, I will never forgive him, and when I see him again, I will kill him"

"That's fair, from what you've told me, I can never forgive him for his actions. For he has done too many irredeemable things, killed too many innocents"

Kerry continued the tale of how Dudesow and himself escaped by horseback. Leaving Dudesow at his estate, and how he's been searching for Ari for all these years.

***

"Wow", Ari, raised her eyebrows. She ran a hand through her hair, "Now, that you've completed your personal quest when you found me, and you've heard my side of the story. Now what will you do now?"

Kerry turned away. Half listening. Thinking about his brother, the Prince, and The Queen he's left behind, "I'm going back. I need to check up on Dudesow, and then...I'll confront the King"

Ari kicked her tail fin up, to get Kerry's full attention. "If you don't mind, may I tag along? I want to see Dudesow, it's been so long."

"You're more than welcome too"

"I humbly ask for your assistance, temporarily, to help set up a form of transport for me for land travel. I feel weak, I feel as if my power has not yet fully returned. I cannot create a transformation spell at my current state"

Kerry turned away for a moment then looked back at Ari, "Our interests align, If we are going to settle our business back at Default Castle, we will need you at full power. I will assist in creating you suitable transportation"

Ari's smile turned into a frown and she pointed into the sky behind Kerry.

Kerry turned and focused in the direction of where she was pointing.

A dragon was high above them, circling the boat.

"Get down", Ari ordered.

Kerry ducked as she put her left arm into the air. She moved her arm in a circular motion. The water rose up, it cased around and over the boat, creating a protective barrier.

Kerry stared in amazement at the sudden protective sphere. Miraculously, they were in a bubble, protected by water, while the boat floated on the water. It was quite the spectacle.

Kerry blinked, in awe at Ari's power ... and then the water dropped.

It hit Kerry hard, and now he was soaked. He blinked a few times before turning his astonished gaze towards Ari.

She spun and gasped at Kerry, her eyes wide in embarrassment. "I'm so sorry, I couldn't hold the water barrier for long. You see, it's easy for me to wave water around, but right as the spell ends...it always lands, hard with a splash, " she said sheepishly.

Before the stunned Kerry could respond, she interrupted, "You'll be happy to know that the dragon is leaving"

Chapter 10

Dude and Adam were walking up the slope towards the castle gates when Adam stopped abruptly.

Adam quickly spun around and stared up at the sky.

Carrot flew towards the castle at full speed.

"Carrot spotted a boat heading this way"

"A boat? Did he say anything else?"

"No"

Dude started jogging back towards the beach. He stared out into the horizon.

Adam walked up to him, "Do you have an idea who it is?"

Dude shrugged, "I haven't seen any boats around these waters surprisingly. The last time I saw a boat…..it was many years ago"

"Someone you knew?"

"An old friend"

"I'm sorry to hear that, I imagine they must've had a good reason to leave you."Dude looked distant, "I hope so"

Carrot descended gracefully. Blowing out steam from her nostrils, she turned her head and stared at Dude.

Adam nudged Dude, "She says it's the old man that fed her that peculiar carrot that one night. If that makes any sense"

Dude stood up, "It is him, I need to see him." Dude looked at Adam, "Could you stay here and watch the fort?"

"I don't see why not, I have nothing better to do-wait! Are you?"

"I'm not waiting. I'm going to him"

Carrot lowered herself, Dude climbed onto the saddle. "Today, I'll fly. I put it off for far too long. I can do this." Dude leaned forward and pointed up.

Carrot shot up.

Adam could hear Dude's screaming as the dragon shot up the sky. He frowned, "I hope those are screams of joy"

***

Kerry sat back against the railing. Relaxing as the wind pressed against the sails, moving the ship forward toward the land on the horizon. He stared out with a squint. Mentally preparing for the moment his eyes would see the shores of his old family estate.

Kerry could hear Ari swimming by the vessel's side.

He reached up and scratched underneath the coral wreath on his head.

Ari had joked that he, as a captain of the vessel, needed a captain's hat and promptly placed it onto his head. He didn't want to be rude, so he kept it there ever since they started the return journey.

Kerry pondered about what he should say to Dudesow, after being gone for all these years. He wondered if an apology and the blunt truth behind his non-existent curse would be enough to make up for his long journey away from the prince. He wondered if Dudesow, who'd been on his own for so long, was even alive.

His mind was distant, he didn't see the dragon flying far above.

Kerry imagined Dudesow in trouble, he envisioned him screaming for help, alone, surrounded by bandits.

The scream, faint at first, had gradually gotten louder.

It sounded like it was closing in.

Something impacted into the water with a loud splash.

The boat bobbled from the impact.

Kerry rushed to the side, scanning over the surface of the water, while he leaned over the railing.

He didn't see Ari.

Kerry rushed over to the other side of the boat, seeing nothing, he turned and opened a storage compartment.

He pulled out a bundle of cloth.

Unwrapping it, he pulled out his sword.

Kerry stood, now fully alert and battle-ready.

***

Ari was swimming along the boat, humming a song she knew that was long forgotten by humanity generations ago.

Well, except for two other people, she thought.

She frowned, the last time she hummed that song was to Dudesow when he was just an infant.

Ari wished she could hold him again-

There was a splash as something dropped fast into the water on the other side of the boat.

She dove, and she noticed something vaguely human that was going into the depths quickly. They appeared unresponsive.

She dived closer, who appeared to be a man. She kicked her tail hard to increase speed.

She swam under the man and caught him. Carrying him upwards with both arms, moving as fast as she could towards the surface.

Ari picked up the speed and then-

She flew out of the water and onto the boat deck, landing hard on her back while still holding onto the man. She slid the man onto the floor next to her.

Ari looked up at Kerry and scoffed, "Put that damn sword away and help me"

Kerry dropped the sword onto the desk and rushed over, "How can I help?"

Ari gestured, "Hold open his mouth and hold him down. This will startle him and probably be painful, but it should save him if we hurry"

Kerry nodded and used his two thumbs on the stranger's mandibles to pry the mouth open.

Ari put her arms straight out, hovering over the man. She mumbled a mantra that gradually became more clear and louder. A glow radiated from her hands.

Water was rushing out the man's mouth like a cyclone. Ari guided the water with her hands to go directly from the man's lungs, into the ocean.

Ari, without losing focus, "I'm doing great so far, I believe this should work"

Kerry looked in awe, "I can see that. Wait does that mean…"

Ari, without losing her focus, nodded, "Yes, this is the first time I've attempted this, wait, I believe that's all"

The cyclone ended, and Ari closed her left hand into a fist. She swung the fist towards the man's mouth. Before her fist made an impact, she opened her hand, covering her mouth. Then she quickly retracted her hand.

The man gasped. Eyes open.

Ari, Kerry, and Carrot sighed in relief in unison.

Kerry and Ari looked up, and immediately fell back, startled by the dragon hovering overhead. They were so distracted in the moment of saving the man, they didn't notice the dragon hovering over their shoulder.

Carrot leaned forward and nudged the man. The young man coughed, patting the dragon's head, "I'm okay, I'm okay! I must say, that really hurt. Don't you ever do that again, stopping abruptly in the sky like that? I flew right off the saddle!"

The young man looked up, noticing the two strangers staring at him. The man looked unsure of how to respond, with a mermaid and an old man looking back at him. He blinked twice in a double take, "Wait a moment, is that…..Sir Kerry?"

Kerry smiled awkwardly, "Yes, you are correct. I am retired. Please, just Kerry. Are you feeling well, did you break any bones?"

Dude jumped up and hugged him, "I thought I'd never see you again"

Kerry relaxed and returned the hug. Before Kerry could save the moment, Carrot, still hovering above the boat, leaned down to nudge Kerry.

Kerry turned his head, facing the dragon, "is this-"

Carrot whined with a happy neigh.

Kerry nodded towards Ari, 'It's great to see you too, I believe you should be taking a moment to be thanking the one who saved you"

Dude slowly let go and turned his attention to Ari, "Thank you", he bowed, "I am forever in your debt"

Ari gave a warm smile, "I'm happy to help, and it's great to see you again"

Dude gave a befuddled look, glancing back and forth between Kerry and Ari, "again?"

"There's a lot you need to know"

Chapter 11

The boat slowly sailed back, the sun setting. Carrot followed them from high above. Ari is relaxing with her arms on the ledge of the boat. Kerry, Ari, and Dude sharing stories.

Ari shared her memories of raising Dude in his younger infantile and toddler years that had made her imprisonment at the castle more bearable, "raising you had kept me sane, as you brought me happiness in my darkest days"

Dude was feeling a joy he'd never felt before, "I admit, Sir Kerry, that I was a little bitter for you leaving after we've escaped the castle, but introducing me to Ari somewhat makes up for it."Kerry grimaced, "I apologize. Many people recognize me, and little to none have seen your face. I felt it was best to have you wait at the castle while I seek the mage your mother told me to find. The journey took a lot longer than I anticipated-"

Dude turned towards Ari, "I'm grateful for you to care for me when my birth mother couldn't even bother to do so"

Kerry spoke up, "That's not entirely true"

Dude's appearance turned to one of annoyance, "It's true to me. My mother was never there for me. I don't care for her or my father. I rather not speak of them. I'm more upset that Ari was taken away while I was at a young age. I vaguely remember your face, but at that age, it's all such a blur. I hate that your kindness to me was never recognized sooner-"

Ari spoke with sadness in her voice, "I'm not a saint. I was forced to help enable the King's elaborate facade that you were cursed, which caused you years of misery I imagine. Saving your life today, I believe, would still not be enough to make up for what I've done"

"Don't be saddened; you were imprisoned and under my father's orders. From what you've told me today, you've been more of a mother to me, than my actual mother."

Ari smiled.

Kerry sounded disheartened, "I assure you, your mother loved you. She just wasn't allowed to see or talk to you"

Dude, dismissed the statement, "I can't say I believe that. Also, I don't know why you're defending the Queen"

Before Kerry could speak, Dude stood up and walked to the bow of the ship. "I see the castle. When we get there, you'll meet Adam. He was camping at the castle while I was away"

Kerry raised an eyebrow, "Do you trust this Adam?"

"Not entirely, I just met him when he tried to invade my home two days ago. After interrogating him, I decided he was trustful enough. He's just down on his luck." Dude looked uncertain, "I left unexpectedly and was gone a lot longer than I usually am when I'm away with Carrot. Even then, I'm sure he doesn't want to be on the bad side of the guy who has a dragon, I'm sure everything is good at Kerry's Keep"

Ari and Kerry exchanged quizzical glances.

Chapter 12

Kerry tied the boat to the dock. The old wooden pier creaked as the waves pressed against it.

Carrot flew down gracefully, landing on the field, seeking a good spot to graze.

Kerry and Dude stood at the edge of the pier, looking at Ari.

Ari looked at them from the water.

Kerry coughed, "So..."

Dude scratched the back of his head, "Since it's safe to assume you can't walk on land, are you going to wait for us here, or are we parting ways?"

Ari pondered for a moment, "Kerry, do you have any vials left over?"

"None. I'm sorry to say that the few I had left are gone. I...was often bored at sea. The vials I had with me had faded labels. I found some entertainment by taking a fish I caught and pouring the contents of the vial into the fish's mouth. It was somewhat exciting to what animal the fish would transform into. It would turn the fish into. I found that waiting until the fish died would be easier to eat after it transformed, instead of trying to catch a wild animal. I learned this the hard way. My first attempt was on a live fish. My folly as I found myself chasing a live goat around my ship. The chase lasted a little too long I'm embarrassed to admit. I can't say I didn't know the risk, I could've had a fish transform into an elephant or a whale, right on my boat. It was worth the risk though, I've tried a lot of exotic animals that I would've never thought I'd try. Have you ever tasted Kirit?"

Ari shook her head, "Anyways, with the vials all gone, I'm open to any ideas on travel accommodations. I want to join you both on your travels. Please don't leave me behind, I don't want to be in this ocean any longer"

"We could travel close to the coastline, or travel by boat, Ari could tail us back to the castle", said Kerry.

Dude grinned, "Kerry, did you say that on porpoise?"

"Yes my bouy"

Ari pinched the bridge of her nose, "Those are awful puns but Kerry, that's actually...not a terrible idea. I was just hoping to be on land. Any other ideas? My mind drawing a blank right now"

Kerry cut in, "I wasn't trying to make a pun, I swear"

"Are you able to create a transformation spell with fruits and vegetables? I've got some growing in my garden", asked Dude.

Ari swam to the shore, sitting on the sand, "You know what, bring me whatever ingredients you have, and I'll take it from there. I'll experiment with the idea of trying to make a substitute. It's dangerous but I'm taking the risk"

Dude thumbed towards the castle, "I should have plenty of ingredients Do you need anything in particular?"

Ari pondered for a moment before speaking, "Bring what your arms can carry, the more of an assortment, the better".

Kerry and Dude acknowledged with a nod, "Let's go". They walked up the incline towards the castle.

Ari stared at the landscape with a melancholy expression.

❋❋❋

Dude and Kerry walked up the slope towards the castle. The entry gate was wide open, with no source of light emanating from inside.

Dude held up his hand. Kerry held still.

"Something is off; be ready for anything," Dude unsheathed his sword.

Kerry smiled proudly, then got into a defensive stance, unsheathed his sword, and whispered, "I finally get to see your training in action, make me proud".

Dude rolled his eyes and moved forward.

They put their backs against the wall. Dude peeked around the corner of the entranceway.

Dude frowned and stormed in, tossing his blade to the ground, "That dirtbag stole everything"

The garden was harvested.

Dude, infuriated, rushed to his tower.

The tower door was wide open. Dude stepped inside and noticed the crates and barrels of his supplies that were once stacked against the walls were gone.

Kerry walked up behind him, still in battle-ready posture, observing the surroundings, "How long were you gone?"

"I left early this afternoon." Dude stepped back outside. Kerry followed.

"Do you believe Adam took all your supplies while you were away?"

"It's unlikely. He didn't have transport. He had to have outside help. It must've been someone he knew because I don't see any signs of a scuffle, but the garden's current condition tells us that it was picked in a hurry"

Kerry investigated the ground, "I do see fresh tracks of hooves and a cart that rode through here. There does appear to be bootprints of different sizes as well"

"I'm going to look and see what little remains in the garden," Dude said with disgust, then walked off.

Dude picked up a discarded potato sack on the ground. He then proceeded to pick up scraps of fruits and vegetables that had fallen to the ground in the thieves' rush and placed them in the sack.

Kerry kept watch on their surroundings.

Dude reviewed his haul inside the sack. Looking agitated, he strode over to Kerry and handed him the potato sack, "Could you hand these ingredients over to Ari, I'm going to stay here. I need some time to decompress"

Kerry nodded, "Take as much time as you need"

Kerry walked off in the opposite direction as Dude walked off towards the tower to climb up to his room.

Dude examined the room. It lay bare, only a straw mattress left. Everything in the room was taken from him.

Dude lay down on the straw mattress, staring at the ceiling.

There was a loud munching sound by Dude's foot.

Dude turned over to see Carrot, sticking her head through the window to munch away at the mattress. Dude was about to scold his dragon when he paused. Dude decided he just didn't care at this point, it was only straw.

Dude contemplated if he should bother caring for the garden anymore, let alone call this small castle home. He decided that he had lived there long enough, it was time to move on. Dude sat up, "Kerry is back, and he can have this old run-down castle back. Carrot-"

Carrot looked up.

Dude scratched behind the dragon's ears, "I believe I'm ready to try the jump, one more time before we leave this place for good"

***

Dude stood on the window still. He glanced down, seeing Carrot waiting below. He positioned himself to be aligned with the saddle for when he jumped down.

This part used to make Dude's knees shake and make him feel lightheaded.

Not today though. Dude felt determined to get it done right today.

Carrot, was in position at the bottom of the tower, ready for take off.

Dude took a deep breath before he leaped.

He landed perfectly onto the saddle, grabbing the reins tightly. He whistled and Carrot flew into the air gracefully.

Dude cheered and Carrot neighed with glee.

The wind, stronger up in the sky, blew through Dude's air. He was smiling instead of screaming this time, he finally accomplished his goal of jumping off the tower and landing on the saddle with his eyes fully open this time.

Dude leaned forward and shouted loud to be heard, "Towards the boat!"

Carrot decelerated, and Dude held onto the reins with a firm grip.

Down below, as they descended closer to the pier. Dude saw Kerry leaning over Ari, as Ari was working on something with a bucket.

Carrot landed gracefully onto the sand next to the pier.

Dude unmounted and walked over to observe what Ari was working on. Dude was amused to see a coral crown placed on Kerry's head. Dude stood by Kerry's side in silence.

Kerry and Dude leaned in close to watch Ari's process, she was spinning her finger above the bucket. Its water and contents spun in the counterclockwise direction, while Ari's index fingers moved in a clockwise circular direction.

There appeared to be cut-up chunks of the scraps Dude picked up earlier, seaweed, shells, fish chum, and some other unrecognizable ingredients added in.

Dude was about to speak when Ari lifted her other index finger to silence him.

Ari's eye lit up orange, then she put her palm out and stated, "Reef"

Kerry and Dude exchanged glances.

Ari held out the palm of her free hand.

"Oh! Sorry! Here, take it" Kerry took off the coral crown of his noggin and handed it over to Ari.

Ari dropped the crown into the bucket. There was a sound of a splash, but no liquid had sprayed out. Ari reached into the bucket and pulled out the coral crown, which started to glitter like orange diamonds. Ari closed her eyes and placed the crown on her head.

The glittering stopped.

Ari's eyes remained closed, and they didn't say anything.

Kerry and Dude resisted the urge to speak, but after a few moments that felt like an eternity, Dude spoke, "What's supposed to happen now?"

Ari's face went red and she gripped the crown with both hands. She opened her eyes, her iris was no longer orange but her natural eye color was pink. She slammed the crown into the bucket and turned away, arms crossed.

Dude, feeling responsible, said, "I'm sorry if I ruined the spell. Can you try the spell again?"

Kerry walked up and placed a hand on her shoulder, "I'm sorry, what's wrong? what can I do to help?"

Ari politely brushed his hand away, "I can't work with this, It doesn't matter. I know we can't get the ingredients I need here. I'm just experimenting with alternative ingredients to what is here, hoping it would work. I am a fool for expecting that to work"

Ari's eyes started to water up, "I was so ready to get my legs back and return to my cozy cottage, I was willing to try out the spell, even though my intuition told me it wasn't ready. I'm so close to getting my old life back, and here I am, unable to stay out of the water for long without being in pain. Even with the correct ingredients, I'm only somewhat certain it will work, I-"

Ari broke down, the water works unstoppable anytime soon.

Kerry reached a handout and then reframed himself from doing so, looking unsure of how to proceed.

Ari turned around and jumped into the water,

Dude rushed and drove in after her.

Ari let herself sink to the bottom and was startled when she felt Dude wrap his arms around her. To her surprise, he wasn't trying to pull her up. He was holding her tight, in a tight embrace. An underwater hug.

Ari smiled with a sense of calm rushing through her. She patted his arm, he opened his eyes and she pointed up. She gripped Dude's arm and pulled him to the surface. Once at the top, Dude gulped in some air, and Ari went up to Dude and gave a warm embrace, "I knew I raised you well"

Kerry interrupted, "I helped raise him too, you know; I hope I get a hug too"

Dude laughed, "a hug from who?"

Kerry gave a warm smile, "either will do, but let's not make this weird"

Dude slowly let go, "Will you be ok?"

Ari nodded, "I'll be fine. I've just had a lot of emotion pent up these last few years, and the crown not working was my breaking point. I'll be fine now"

"I'm happy to hear that because we're a team now, you, Kerry, Carrot, and I. We'll work on turning you back onto your old two feet as soon as we can. Right, Sir Kerry?"

"The young man is right, it would be an honor to help you return to your former two-footed self"

Ari smiled warmly, her cheeks growing a shade of red, "Thank you both, then I shall awake for your return. Please bring me an assortment of fruits and veggies, fresh ones, mushrooms, and herbs, too, if you're able. I have to experiment to get the combination just right"

Dude's expression turned sincere, "I have no intention of leaving you behind, we will get what you need, together"

Ari regarded him skeptically, "I appreciate the sentiment but I can't exactly leave the water for too long"

Dude burst out into a smile and pointed behind him, "We have all we need in the field behind me"

Kerry smirked, "It will take some time, but It can be done"

Ari glanced at them both, "is there something you're not telling me?"

Dude spoke with excitement, "We have plenty of parts to build a cart. We can build one that will hold enough water and would hold you comfortably."

Ari looked at him, unsure, "That's quite the task. Are you sure you can do that?"

Kerry smacked an arm over Dude's shoulder and rustled his hair, "this young man has read enough books; his head is practically a library. He has enough know-how to figure It out"

Dude kindly removed himself from Kerry's grasp, "Thank you thank you, I appreciate it but I don't want to have unrealistic expectations set upon me"

Ari smirked, "Too late now, I expect you to find a way. You've offered to take me with you and Kerry on this little quest, you'll find a way"

Dude had a look of determination on his face, "This challenge does sound fun"

The gears are already turning in Dude's head.

✳✳✳

Kerry looked over a sketch done by Dude, it was the blueprint for Ari's water transport.

It looked like a large wine transport carriage, with a small window on each side. Access could only be through the top, with the roof having a circular latch for access. The windows could be slid open or closed. The windows were just big enough for Ari's head and arms to fit through, but it would be rather difficult, if at all possible, for Ari to fit through the tiny window.

It took about two weeks to finalize the cart, with lots of care put in to make sure it had enough layering to prevent water from leaking out. The sides were held together tight with iron, making the carriage appear like a large wine barrel with wheels.

Kerry had Carrot set up to pull the cart. The dude sat at the stagecoach seat, turning and tapping on the window, "Are you ready?"

Ari slid open the window, "I am, it's rather dark and cold in here though"

"Try to think of it like the ocean, it should start feeling like it too as the cart gets moving"

Ari grimaced, "Please don't move too fast"

"We'll try to keep it steady, I'm started to have regrets after seeing you in there"

"Don't doubt your decision, I'm glad to have finally left the oceanside. I'm excited to view the landscape once again"

"Let us know if you need us to stop, we'll head north to a nearby town to buy all the ingredients you need"

"Thank you, Dude, this means a lot to me"

"Don't thank me yet; let's get you turned back first," Dude looked towards Kerry, "We good to go?"

Kerry, done reviewing the reins, hopped onto the vacant side of the bench, "We're good, let's go"

Carrot started to trot then suddenly started to lift off. The front wheels of the carriage started to lift off the ground.

Dude and Kerry started to shout and roughly pulled the reins, "No! No! Stop, Carrot no!" They both started to scream in unison.

Carrot neighed disapprovingly, and the cart landed hard; there was a muffled complaint from inside the barrel. Carrot didn't move.

Dude hopped off the bench and walked up to Carrot and scratched behind the ears., "Carrot, I'm sorry, please stay on land, we should've said something earlier. I promise to spoil you with apples later, I believe they are currently in season"

Carrot shook his head neighed in excitement and started to trot forward; Dude quickly hopped onto Carrot's saddle.

Dude, without reins, just leaned forwarding, laying onto the neck to remain balanced, with Kerry guiding the reins. Ari, lying in the barrel, half filled the ocean water, spun the coral crown lazily in hand, lost in thought.

Chapter 13

A few hours went by, they were crossing the yellowing grassy hills. Dude was snoring. Kerry knocked on the barrel, and Ari slid the window; Ari slid head out, glancing at the surroundings, "It appears we're still traveling through the Goldwylde Hills?"

Kerry nodded, "That's correct. I've traveled these hills a few times in my youth. I've had a few field training exercises in these hills. The area lacks trees, mostly low grassy hills for miles. Making it harder for bandits to ambush travelers out in the open. However, the hills gradually grow larger and eventually turn into mountains as we near Kleon, that's where we should be wary of bandits"

Ari laid her head on the windowsill, "It must be nice to traverse this land without marching into battle"

Kerry half-heartedly smiled, "It is, but I must remain alert. It's never good to let your guard down. It's one of the reasons I've survived this long. I do tire, though; I will be waking the young man to take over soon. We should be reaching the town of Inkberk by sundown"

Kerry yawned.

Ari smirked, "I believe it's time for you to take a break, I'll wake up the sleepyhead, as his snoring has prevented me from getting a good nap in. It's hard enough to sleep behind swished around as it is. Watch this"

Ari crisscrossed her index and middle finger on her right-hand several times and then pointed at Dude. There was a green aura that appeared around Dude's head.

Dude sat up and coughed, "Ugh, what's that smell?"

Ari and Kerry failed to withhold their smiles and Dude gave them a confused stare. The aura of an unpleasant smile around Dude started to dissipate away.

Ari smirked while ducking her head back into the barrel. " It wasn't me, " she said, sliding the window shut.

***

It was dusk, Dude pulled the reins to a stop once a town was spotted up ahead. The town was surrounded by trees and high walls. The walls were painted white but had faded, with some portions of the walls having splattered black marks. It was a dark navy blue sky. The grassy valley is gone, now replaced with trees blocking most of the view on the horizon.

Dude gently shook Kerry's shoulder, who blinked quickly awake, then knocked on the barrel window.

Ari stuck her head out, "That's odd; the wall surrounding the town is white, but the trees are painted entirely black; they are a bit odd.....wait," Ari squinted, "look at the trees; something is moving. Are they dripping something? It's too dark out to see. There are dark puddles underneath each of the trees"

Dude shrugged, "maybe it rained?"

Ari shook her head, "I doubt it, I've have yet to see any rain or rain clouds lately and I only see puddles under the trees"

Kerry leaned forward, "Something is off, I'll scope it out. Dude, stay here with Ari"

Dude was about to say something but Kerry held up a hand, and continued, "Let me scout the area, then we'll plan from there"

Kerry withdrew his blade and slowly wandered forward.

Dude turned to Ari, "We're a team, but I believe Kerry has self-appointed himself to be the leader"

Ari shrugged, "I didn't want to be leader, did you?"

Dude raised his eyebrows and sighed, "I guess not, but it would've been nice to have the option, I've never been a leader before"

Ari laid a hand on his shoulder, "You'll get the chance someday, they say the best leaders are the ones who have earned the role, not ones who are constantly seeking it."

Kerry returned, sliding his boot across the ground. "I don't like this. There are black puddles underneath the tree. They smell of ink. The liquid is slippery and slightly sticky to the touch. It's splattered on the town's walls, and it's dripping from the trees.

Dude glanced around, "We haven't eaten anything all day, and we need to search for the spell's ingredients. We'll enter town and leave if things feel off. Unless there's another town we can go to?"

Kerry shook his head, the other nearest town is two days' travel. We have no food and are short on drinking water. I am not volunteering to drink from our barrel of ocean water"

Ari, her expression grim, said, "I don't want to talk about the water situation either, for I have my concerns on that as well"

Dude waved his hand inwards towards himself, "Let's go, Kerry, I don't see any alternative"

Kerry, his face skeptical, turned to speak to Carrot, "I'm not sure it wise to bring the whole team"

Dude waved it off, "I wouldn't worry about it, why hide a dragon when people will think twice about messing with us because we have a dragon?"

They approved the town gates. The lamps at the town entrance gate were bright white.

There was a rope at the gate in rough shape. Kerry pulled it, announcing their presence as the bell rang with one loud clang.

Ari peered her head out, "Ring it again, two rings to let them know we're friendly. One ring means we're here to sell them something"

Dude shook his head, "No, ring the bell three times, so they know it's neither, as we're just passing through. We're not staying long enough to make friends, just to purchase what we need and then leave"

Ari, "No you don't understand, three rings mean that we are enemies. They'll think we're so confident that we'd overtake the town, that we ring the bell instead of breaking down the door"

Dude, "then we'll ring four times"

Ari, "No, ring the door more than three times, then you're just annoying the whole town. That's asking for an arrow to the head"

Kerry snapped, "Quiet! I feel like an arrow is in my head right now. I'm tired and hungry and neither of you is helping"

The gate slowly creaked open. Ari ducked her head in and closed the window.

When the door opened wide enough, Two guards stood there, their spears pointed at them.

Their attire was white, with black ink splatters. Their gloves and boots were soaked pitch black dry ink. One wore a black helmet with its eyes and mouth outlined with white paint. The other wore a white mask. Black ink oozed from its eyes and mouth.

Neither guard said a word. Their spears still pointed at them.

Kerry put his sword away, and put his arms up, "We mean no harm, we are simply seeking to pay for food and shelter for the night. I assure you this dragon means no harm to the town, as it is trained. As a retired knight, I give you my word"

The guards looked at each other. Not a word was spoken.

Dude smacked the barrel, "We're simply wine sellers, we mean no harm. As you can see, this carries a lot of wine. A lot of people would be tempted to rob us for this wine alone, and a dragon makes a great bandit deterrent"

The guards nodded and retracted their spears. One guard waved them in.

Kerry hopped onto the bench, and Dude guided Carrot forward with the reins.

As the cart rolled forward, there was a slick sound as the wheels rolled on the ground. Ink painted the wheels. The ground had a thin layer of ink as if there was a spill at some point that had flooded the town. The homes and merchant shops were white, with black trim. The roofs were painted. The windows were fogged and many had black window shutters. The white walls show signs of recent ink splatter.

Kerry whispered over to Dude, "I've been here before, many years ago, this was once a beautiful village. The town of Inkberk is known mostly for its' ink production and exports. It didn't look this distraught the last time I was here. It was very pristine and orderly and now... I'm not sure what happened since then"

The town was eerily quiet. The townspeople's heads turned, Everyone wore a black or white mask, wet ink, or signs of dried ink from around the eye and mouth area.

Dude turned to whisper to Kerry, "This is a prime example of bad vibes, let's leave"

None of the town folks moved; they stopped what they were doing and stood in place, their masks facing the newcomers. The only sound was the wheels moving over the inky ground and Carrot's claws walking across the inky ground, sounding like walking on wet paint with each step.

Kerry, "It may be too suspicious to leave abruptly-wait, listen"

Dude pulled the reins to halt Carrot.

There was a sound that something was getting near that sliding and slimy. The townspeople put their hands on their hips and started to bend their knees. The townspeople started to move in sync, moving up and down.

Around the corner, a large tentacle gripped the side of the house. More tentacles appeared, gripping buildings, pulling a large squid head forward.

The townsfolk stopped moving. The heads looked towards the squid, and ink spilled from their eyes and mouths. Gurgling sounds echoed. The townspeople eerily turned around and stomped into their homes.

Their footsteps sounded wet with each step.

Ari slid the window open a bit and then slammed it shut, "oooh no, we need to go"

Kerry and Dude nodded, "let's go"

The squid overlooked them, as it was taller than a two-story home, its tentacles as long as its height, started to slowly advance towards them.

Dude, pulled the reins, "Carrot, get us out of here!"

The wheels turned, but the carriage wheels just slid, the carriage stuck in place.

The squid was nearing closer, the tentacles almost in reach of Carrot.

Dude pulled the reins again, panicking in his voice "I know I said not to fly, but fly. fly now!"

Carrot flapped her wings. The Carriage lifts slowly off the ground. The bottom became heavy, with the carriage turning at a vertical angle. Carrot straining to lift upwards with all the weight.

The squid reached up, almost able to reach the bottom of the carriage.

Dude, trying to stay on the bench, quickly hit the window and shouted, "Ari open the bottom window, we need to lighten the load"

Ari slid the rear window open, water started to pour out.

The squid spoke with a wet screech, *"wAteR, pReCiouS WaTeR"*

Ari spoke, trying but failing to sound remotely nonchalant, "Oh, this isn't water, it's uh, white wine or vodka. Definitely nothing a squid on land would want. Now if you'd excuse me-"

The coral crown nearly fell off her head, Ari caught it in time and retracted her head and arm back into the window with the crown in hand. She slid the window on the barrel shut.

The squid, who saw the crown, *"mY pReCioUs CrOwN, rEtuRn It, tO mE"*

A tentacle smacked onto the bottom of the carriage. The tentacle suction stuck onto the carriage, and the squid slowly pulled the carriage down.

Kerry unsheathed his sword; he leaned over and tried to swing at the tentacle. It was out of reach. He leaned further over to try again and lost his balance. Dude reached over and grabbed onto Kerry to pull him back. It caused them both to lose their balance. Dude and Kerry started to slide off the bench. Kerry grabbed hold of the harness with one hand, and the sword with the other, Dude, holding onto Kerry's ankle.

One of the tentacles started to reach for Dude's legs, Dude tried to kick the tentacle away.

Kerry shouted, "Stop moving so much, I'm working on a plan"

Dude shrieked as a tentacle swacked at his leg, the blunt hit causing pain to shoot up Dude's leg.

Kerry looked up, "Carrot, I need you to set this squid a blaze, let me try to cut this harness"

Dude shouted at Carrot, "What are you doing!"

Kerry swung at the harness while Dude tried to climb up his leg and was failing to do so. Dude howled in pain as the tentacle hit him with blunt force on the back. The force caused Kerry to sway, having his sword miss his target. Kerry swung again right as a tentacle reached up once again. The harness was cut.

The harness ripped and tore away from Carrot, from the weight of the carriage. The carriage landed with a crash in front of the squid. Water splashed everywhere, with Ari lying unconscious in the pile of wood.

Dude and Kerry fell. A tentacle grabbed Dude around his waist.

Kerry landed on top of the squid's head, he struggled to stay balanced.

Carrot flew down, her mouth opening to prepare an eruption of flame.

Kerry's eyes went wide, he quickly jumped down to avoid being cooked along with the squid.

A tentacle hit the side of Carrot, she was thrown into the side of the building.

Kerry glanced over to Ari. She was half covered in broken debris. He called out to her, but she lay there unresponsive. Kerry rushed over and checked her pulse. Ari was alive, Kerry thought with relief. Kerry used his one free hand to pull Ari out of the wreck. Kerry searched around and found an alleyway nearby. Kerry dragged her to the Alley and leaned Ari against the wall.

Kerry glanced back and saw Dude, still trapped in a tentacle grasp, being swung around. Carrot climbed out of the rubble and flew towards the squid.

Kerry gripped his sword with both hands and ran towards the squid.

Dude yelled, "the crown!! Get the crown!"

Kerry halted and observed the area around the carriage wreck; he spotted the crown.

The tentacle-holding Dude started to move toward the squid's mouth. Dude screamed, "Give it the crown, give it the crown, hurry!"

Kerry quickly grabbed the crown and climbed down toward the squid's eye.

A tentacle hit Carrot, her flame hitting the roof of a nearby building instead of the squid.

Kerry waived the crown in front of the squid's eye, "Let them go, and I'll give this back"

The squid stared at the crown with its one eye intently, "*rEtuRn, rEtuRn, ThE CrOwn*"

Kerry gently placed the coral crown onto the ground.

Dude was let go from the tentacle's grasp. He fell but didn't hit the ground. He hovered a moment above the ground and then landed gently.

Ari was leaning forward on her side, her hand out. Dude smiled towards her, and Ari nodded.

The squid reached over with two of its tentacles to pick up the crown. The crown gradually grew in size while in the squid's tentacle grasp until it was sizable enough to fit nicely on top of the squid's head.

The squid screeched.

Doors of the homes and shops opened.

The townspeople walked out of the buildings on their hands and feet, their limbs bending into a joint-popping crabwalk. They eerily started crab-walking toward Ari.

Kerry grimaced, "Umm, let's fall back"

The squid pointed at Ari, "*ShE's ThE OnE, ShE's ThE One WhO StOLe ThE CrOwN, KiLL hEr*"

The townspeople made popping sounds as they crawled their way over to her. They occasionally slipped on the ink on the ground. Ink continuously pouring from their eyes and mouths.

The two gate guards ran up to Ari. They dropped their spears. One guard's arm turned into tentacles. The other guard's arms turned into crab-like arms with intimidating pincers for hands.

They coughed out ink before leaning forward to pick up their spears. Aiming them at Ari's head.

Kerry swung his arms, "Let's not get hasty, I returned the crown. Let's talk this out, find a solution we can all agree on"

A tentacle swung at Kerry unsuccessfully, and he quickly dodged out of the way.

Dude whistled. Carrot flew down and Dude hopped onto Carrot's back. Dude yelled as Carrot flew above the squid head, "Help Ari"

Ari had spun the wrists from both her hands, then pushed the palms outwards abruptly. The townspeople around her had been flung back.

Kerry stood beside her, "any ideas?"

Ari grimaced, "My head is bleeding, and I'm lightheaded. I'm limited in my ability right now. I can't think.... clearly right now...my brain is too fogged up for a plan"

The townsfolk started to crawl back towards them. A spear landed into the wall behind Kerry, who ducked in time.

Dude held onto Carro tight, as the dragon hovered above the squid's head. Dude yelled, "Grab it!"

Carrot grabbed the massive coral crown with her claws; the squid screeched and tried to grab it back but it wasn't quick enough.

The squid frantically tried to climb buildings to reach out to the crown, but Carrot stayed hovering out of the squid's desperate reach.

Dude yelled down at the panic-driven squid, "If you harm my friends, I will have my ferocious dragon here break your crown and melt it into a chard sad lump with her unforgiving fire. Choose your next action or words carefully"

The squid paused. Then it leaned back and gave a loud and ear-splitting sound. The towns folk fell onto their backs. Their mouths gurgled black ink. Kerry and Ari stepped back in repulsion. They remained at the ready for whatever was happening next.

The townspeople's mouths opened wide, as tiny squids slowly slimed out, pulling themselves out with their victims out with their tentacles. The little squids landed on the ground with a wet plop and then pulled themselves towards the mother squid; its victim fell motionless onto the ground after.

"My BaBiEs, rEtUrN tO mE." The gigantic squid, who must've been the mother, waved two tentacles, motioning the squids to return to her, "*wE WiLL leAvE aNd NeVeR rEtuRn*" The giant mother squid pointed one tentacle towards Ari, "*PrAy ThAt YoU'lL nEveR SeE **mE** aGaiN*"

The squid mother and her offspring slowly left. Carrot landed next to Kerry and Ari, and Dude hopped down off the saddle, "we'll, that was odd"

Kerry asked Ari, "Why did you have that squid's crown?"

Ari looked guilty, "Can we talk about this later? We have a more pressing matter," she pointed behind Kerry.

The people lying on the ground started coughing out ink. The ink in their eyes slowly reverted to their normal eyes, and they blinked and rubbed the ink out. Most were hurling out an unnatural amount of ink. Others, like the gate guards, started to wake, with their mutations still in place.

Dude, walked towards them with a weary smile, "Well, I believe it's as good a time as any to ask for a room at the inn"

Chapter 14

The Toner Tavern is a cozy establishment. The smell of wet ink still lingered in the air. An old man was mopping the floor, failing miserably. Constantly cursing he tried to clean the floor with an ink-soaked mop. An elderly woman who was working hard tried to scrub the tables. After a few scrubs, the elderly woman gave up and tossed the rag angrily into the fireplace. Kerry, Dude, and Ari sat at the corner table, near the fire. Averting their eyes to not make eye contact. The old woman stomped out the front door in frustration. The ink-stained the tables and floor, with some splattered onto the walls. was dry, on the table and chairs, so they relaxed comfortably. Dude, fell asleep, head on the table with a pitcher half empty in his right hand.

Kerry glanced over at Ari, waiting for Ari to speak first. Ari noticed and tidily returned her attention to the wooden cup in her hand, rocking it. Kerry turned away from Ari for a moment when he noticed movement. It was the old man, who abruptly stopped moping. The man had given up on trying to mop off dry ink, so he walked over to the bar and began to clean mugs.

Kerry returned his attention to Ari and continued to stare. After a few moments, he raised his eyebrows.

Ari side glanced and sighed, "I wasn't trying to cause harm I-" she whispered, "I don't want to speak too openly about this, in fear that the whole time will blame this whole thing on me, but this town's recent misfortune may have been maybe somewhat perhaps..my fault"

Kerry raised an eyebrow, "explain further, please"

Ari shoved the mug away and crossed her arms, avoiding eye contact, "I was a mermaid for far too long and I longed for my old life back. I yeared for my warm, quiet, cozy cottage in the forest in the Merry Mystic Woods. I'm a sorcerer, not a witch. I cannot easily transform myself back to my prior form with limited energy. It's not for a lack of trying. My very limited expertise in the study of witchcraft comes from creating potions that change physical form, I've read from the books found in the room I was trapped in back in the dungeon. Any hope of me turning back was futile, as the ingredients required were found on land and, even then, were hard to come by. I was limited in options. I cannot move on land easily and I'm in pain just from being out of water for an extended amount of time. I don't believe I'll die being out of water, but I will certainly grow weaker as time passes.

Kerry was about to speak but Ari raised a hand, "I digress. I had to get creative to find alternative solutions. One day, as I explored the ocean depths, I found a trench that left me to a large squid sleeping, with a glowing crown on its head. Its coral crown glowed, it glowed brightly, luring me closer. Drawing me in. I had enough wits to know that while the crown helped the squid lure food to it, It was no mere simple-minded fish. I swiped the crown to study its magical properties, hoping I could use it. After experimenting with it in my hideout, I found the crown did not affect me. Instead of giving it back to the original owner, I decided to keep it as an accessory. I should have returned it to the squid"

The bartender slammed the mug he was cleaning down onto the counter, "You may be seated at the far end of the tavern, but my old ears still hear everything that's said within this establishment of mine. I will say that I don't approve of what you've done, stealing the crown from our town's ink supplier"

Ari shifted awkwardly, trying to sit steady in the chair.

The bartender continued, "However, I can see why you'd want to do something so self-fish-" The bartender chuckled, "I imagine you are trying to get your legs back; why else would you half-fish want to be with the land folk?"

Ari spoke with caution to the bartender, "I'm sorry. I hope my actions didn't cause you and your family too much suffering,"

The bartender picked up the mug and started cleaning it with a cloth and shrugged, "I can't be mad at ye. You and your friends did resolve the ink madness. You may have irritated the squid, but you're not at fault for the squid taking his anger out on innocent townsfolk"

Ari eased up and gave a warm smile, "You have some spot-on insight, I appreciate your words because now I can ease up a bit, instead of drowning in guilt"

Kerry raised up some coins, "let's have another round, I'll pay for yours as well"

The bartender shook his head, "these on the house, just for today"

Kerry nodded, "Thank you, sir. Would it be rude to ask if you could refrain from sharing this new information you've obtained today? We only ask you to keep the information to yourself, just until we leave town?"

Bartender smirked, "I have given free food and drink to show appreciation for saving the wife and I. Anything beyond that, I will require a coin as payment for my silence"

Kerry stood, "I assure you, you will receive ample payment." Kerry stood up and slid his chair in. Before he headed over to the barkeep, he paused and placed a gentle hand on Ari's shoulder, "Don't feel bad; what happened to this town wasn't your fault. You may have taken the crown, but it was the squid's fault for overreacting and releasing its wrath onto this small village. There were casualties, but they were not by your hand. I'd compare it to stealing a bone from a wolf, and the wolf decided to lash out at other creatures in frustration for losing its favorite stick, I mean bone. You know what I mean. I assure you, that this is hardly your fault"

Ari gave him an appreciative look, "Thank you, Sir Knight"

Kerry smiled reassuringly, "It's just Kerry now. I'm glad to have made your day a little better"

Kerry headed to the bar to talk to the barkeep. Ari looked at Dude and rustled his hair.

Dude slowly lifted his head, his eyelids heavy, "How long was I asleep for.....shit". Dude quickly stood up. Dude noticed the mug in his left hand was at the wrong angle. the beer had spilled all over the top of his lap while he slept.

Ari gave him a smug response, "We didn't want to wake you. You'll forget your discomfort in a moment." Ari focused, her eyes closed. The mug on the table started to fill, while his trousers started to dry.

Dude's jaw dropped, "that is phenomenal" He held up the mug in astonishment, eyeing it before raising the rim to his lips.

Ari, using her mind, was preventing him from consuming the beer.

Dude, looking annoyed, "What gives?"

"Don't be disgusting. Please get a new mug of beer, that one has a mixture of ink and beer that was soaking on your dirty trousers"

There was a loud sliding of the chair as Dude grumbled, got up, and begrudgingly headed over to the bar. Ari caught his sleeve, giving him a pleading dopey smile, "While you up, can you please order us some mozzarella cheese swords?"

Chapter 15

Adam Yutae was tied to a pole.

The pole was close to the riverbank in the Troubled Woods. Adam recognized this camp; this was the Troubled Thieve's camp. They were deep in the forest, the thick forest in all directions. The last time Adam was here was the day the leader had rendezvoused with local thieves on attacking dragon's keep to retrieve and split the gold. Looking back on it, poor locals with thieves working together to attack a dragon to loot gold? Even if there was gold, it was still a ridiculous plan. He was ashamed that he agreed to it. To his right, he saw the camp, to his left, he saw the river. It was night, and the campfire glowed right. Drunk chatter can be heard around the fire. A group of three people stood up from around the fire and started walking towards him.

Adam grimaced. He told them immediately when they showed up that there was no gold, coins, or the rumored fair maiden. However, with the dragon gone and a castle stocked with plenty of food and essential supplies, they had their doubts that Adam was telling the full truth.

They believed that he hid the gold after conquering the dragon. The thieves believed that he was at the castle because he claimed it as his own. They believed he spent some of the gold on supplies and got comfortable at the tower. They tied him up, took all the supplies, and took him back to camp. He didn't put up a fight, he was outnumbered thirty to one. Adam knew that it was only a matter of time before they tried to torture information out of him. They wouldn't believe him, even if he told the truth.

One of the men, their leader, Hairissac. He stood between the men, a metal cattle prod in his hand, its tip bright and hot. Strood up to Adam and sighed, kneeling to meet Adam eye to eye, "Let's try this again. Where is the fair maiden?"

Harissac placed a hot branding iron next to his side, not close enough to brand him, but Adam could feel the heat.

A bead of sweat dripped down Adam's forehead, "Look, there is no fair maiden, there was only this man who-"

Hairissac pressed the iron against Adams' side, scorching a bloody X.

Adam screamed while the iron sizzled into the flesh.

Adam pulled the iron back and firmly asked again, "Where is the fair maiden?" Then, press the X brand onto another location. Adam let out a loud outcry.

"I'm telling the truth, there is no fair maiden. The dragon was controlled by a man at the tower"

Hairissac retracted the branding iron, "Now, that sounds possible but I'm still skeptical. Where are they now? Where is the gold?"

The men froze and looked into the dark woods behind, the sound of a horse approaching.

Adam was unable to see who was behind him.

Hairissac and the men stared at the newcomer, who rode on a regal horse. It was a knight.

Hairissac and the men stared as the knight descended and walked over the river. He dropped a single gold into the water and announced, "I pay the toll for I pass"

The knight dropped another gold coin, "I pay once more in advance for when I cross again in the future"

The knight climbed back onto the saddle and guided the horse across the river. The river was deep but the horse was able to cross the river safely.

The knight descended from the horse and walked up to Hairissac, "Does he know who resides in the tower"

Hairissac shook his head, "He speaks nothing of the fair maiden..."

The knight firmly took the cattle prod from Hairissac's grasp and then backhanded the thief's leader. The metal hand armor breaks the bride of Hairissac's nose, "That is not what I asked you fool"

Hairissac covered his nose, "My apologies. He speaks of a man who resides there, a man who tamed the dragon but knows not of where they are now"

The knight turned to face Adam.

Adams' eyes went wide, for it was the knight Sir Archibald.

Sir Archibald hovered the cattle prod over Adams' side and then pressed it firmly. Adam let out a sharp cry and started breathing heavily when the knight retracted the brand iron, "Who is the man who resides there? How many live there?" The knight demanded.

Tears streamed down Adams's eyes, "I don't know; there is only one man who lives there. He said he had to check on something. He hopped onto the dragon and flew off. I haven't seen him since"

The knight lowered the iron and pondered, looking into the distance. Looking at nothing in particular while he was deep in thought. Hairissac got up, his head tilted back, a thumb a finger pinching his nose closed, "Sir…"

The knight glared at the man and Hairissac immediately shut up.

Sir Archibald returned his attention to Adam, "What was the man's name, was he a knight?"

Adam avoided the knight's stare, "His-"

Sir Archibald pressed the iron against Adam's side. Adam yowled in pain.

"Look at me", The knight yelled and pressed the iron against Adam's side again.

Adam was screaming. The knight retracted the hot iron.

Adam tried to maintain his composure and stared back at the knight, "He said his name was Dude"

Sir Archibald's eyes glared intently at Adam, "Dude…Dude was his name? Are you sure?"

The knight slowly moved the branding iron, lowering it enough to almost touch the skin of Adam's shoulder.

"How did you get past the dragon? We've sent dozens of men and none have been successful. How did some pleb like you get in?"

Adam felt weak. He knew Hairissac asked a question but he couldn't make out what he said. He gave no response.

The skin on Adam's shoulder sizzled loudly as the iron pressed firmly down.

The pain spiked; Adam prayed. He prayed loudly in his mind, to no one and anyone who was listening.

The knight was saying something but all Adam could hear was ringing in his years.

His eyelids were heavy.

He yelled in his mind. Please, someone help me.

A moment passed.

A deep voice echoed in the back of his mind.

Who dares speak into my mind?

Adam looked around the best he could and saw no new bystander.

Forgive me, for I don't see you. I am Adam, I need help.

Why should I help you?

I'll make you an offer, what do you need?

Pay the toll. Pay the toll and his head will roll.

Adams' eyes went wide, and they tried to look behind him but could not see the river behind him.

Toll? I do not have gold, what else can I offer?

Gold is the usual toll, but perhaps...you could offer something new. Offer a unique offer and I shall assist you.

Adam was tensing up, trying to distract himself from the pain and think of what he could offer. As the hot iron once again prodded his skin, he tried to focus on what he could offer the voice. He bit his tongue.

Adam tried to focus. His pockets were empty, he had nothing but his clothes on his back. The thieves took his few meager belongings.

He heard the voice growl.

I am growing impatient; I will leave soon if you don't provide me with an offer.

Adam tensed. He mentally spoke to the unknown voice, how about something that weighs nothing but holds value? I can offer companionship. We can help each other out long-term or until you no longer need me.

There was only silence.

The knight slapped Adam with his backhand, "Describe the man! Did he mention anyone else?"

The voice returned to Adam's mind.

You have yourself a companion. How can I assist?

Please rid me of my captors and free me of my bindings

The iron branding pressed into Adam's stomach. Adam wailed.

The knight grabbed Adam's collar and stared directly into Adam's eyes.

Sir Archibald's face was boiling mad, "Don't ignore me, peasant, for I will find a way to get my answers. You have yet to feel any real pain. Don't-"

There was an eruption of water. The water drenched the men. The branding iron sizzled.

There was a serpent who leaned out of the water, it stood tall above the men. It had dark blue scales, and sharp white fins along its back. It had two arms that were reaching over the men. Archibald dropped the branding iron and pulled out his sword. The two thieves that stood next to Hairissac, ran towards the camp.

Hairissac turned to Sir Archibald, his eyes wide and pleading, "Kill it, save us from this foul serpent sir knight!"

Sir Archibald grabbed Hairissac with his free hand and then kicked him towards the serpent.

Hairissac stumbled back. The serpent grabbed Hairissac with one of its sharp claws and then looked Hairissac in the face. The man screamed as the serpent's mouth opened over his face.

The serpent blew a purple smoke over the man. The screaming faded and the man went limp. His eyes rolled to the back of his head. The serpent tossed the man into the river.

Hairissac did not reemerge.

The serpent reached over to a tree by the river bank. It was using its teeth to rip it out of the ground. The serpent spun in the water quickly before tossing the tree towards the camp.

The men yelled as the tree landed on the firepit. Embers and firewood flew. Nearby tents caught aflame. The camp settlers started to evacuate, and Adam could hear the sounds of horses galloping away.

The river serpent reached over towards Sir Archibald, who pointed his sword at the serpent's scowling face.

Sir Archibald shouted, "Halt serpent, for I have already paid the toll for a second safe crossing across the river. I will use that pass now. You know you can't harm those who pay the toll. Doing so will have you face the wrath of the King"

The serpent halted and retracted its teeth before slowly backing away to let the knight retreat to his horse. Sir Archibald guided his horse across the river and rode into the Troubled Woods. The serpent never left their eyes on the knight. Once the knight was out of sight, the serpent slashed the bindings wrapped around Adam with its claws.

The ropes fell. Adam slowly stood up, wincing as he did.

"Thank you", said Adam with a weary smile. "I am Adam, and may I ask the name of my new companion?"

Companion? I've never had a human companion. This will be...interesting. Human Adam, I am Riverfin, the guardian of the Teal River. It is now your turn to assist me. You will find a way to break me free of my current obligation.

Riverfin's nostrils blew out purple smoke—the thick smoke, instantly engulfing Adam. His burns and wounds suddenly felt very cold.

Adam slumped, feeling very tired.

The last thing Adam saw was Riverfin grabbing him by the waist and dragging him into the river depths.

Chapter 16

Sir Kerry, Ari, Dude, and Carrot had taken camp at a cove that was about a two-hour travel south of Inkbert. A vacant inn and merchant buildings surrounded the cove, boarded up, and were protected with dimly visible enchantments to deter thieves and intruders. The cove was a once busy port known by the locals as Inkport. It had once been a very active port with laborers and merchants who worked with deals with the Squid deity to get their mass quantity of Ink to sell across the continent. The merchants would exchange fish and crustaceans with the deity in exchange for bulk quantities of ink. Now that the Squid deity has descended from the cove and hasn't reemerged. Ink export operations have halted indefinitely. The port was mostly vacant, except for a few active fishing boats. Lanterns from the fishing boats idling in the cove left a beautiful orange glow across the water in the late evening. Ari had swam around the cove to moisturize her dry scales.

Carrot was grazing on hay piles that were left in a vacant stable nearby. Sir Kerry and Dude sat near a fire pit and were discussing how to proceed from here. Some fish sizzled on a pan set above the firepit. They gradually scooted closer to the fire pit, as the cool breeze from the cove grew unrelenting.

Dude stood up, "I'll look for some more firewood"

As Dude stood up, he noticed two individuals approaching. They walked casually towards their camp, no weapons drawn. One of them, a tall, lanky man with bushy hair, raised his hands, and the woman next to him, did the same. The man gave a kind smile and said, "We mean no harm, please let us join you around the fire."Dude gave Kerry a side glance look, and Kerry nodded and said, "We got plenty of seating around the flame, make yourself comfortable. We're about to eat soon and there's plenty to share"

The two newcomers went to an adjacent spot from where Kerry sat, they placed their travel packs onto the ground and used them as makeshift seats. They both were wearing grimy farmhand attire. The man appeared to be in his thirties, while the woman appeared to be in her late twenties. Kerry and Dude got the impression that these two had been on the move for a while, as both the newcomers appeared weary.

The man nodded at both Kerry and Dude, "Thank you for the hospitality, we've been on the foot for a while"

Kerry gave them a warm smile, "we've been on the move for a while as well. I'm Kerry and this young man here next to me is…"

Dude cut in, "Dude", taking a slight bow.

The man nodded and smiled at them both, "It's a pleasure to meet the both of you, I'm Kashmir and this", he thumbed in the direction of the woman by this side, "is my annoying little sister Brishine"

Brishine gave her brother a playful shove, "I assure you, he's more annoying"

"I'm sure you are both tired of each other's company after traveling together for so long. I'm already tired of hearing about my friend's gardening tips," said Kerry.

Dude looked appalled, "You should've told me you tire of my gardening tips. I must insist that I continue, as my passion for gardening will grow on you"

"I doubt my zero interest in gardening will change anytime soon." Kerry peered back towards the cove, unable to see Ari; he shrugged, "We have one more in our little group, I'll introduce you both to her later this evening."

Brishine glanced in the direction of Dude.

Dude averted his eyes and stammered, "I've noticed the fire is starting to die down, I'm going to go grab some more food for the fire, I'll be back"

Brishine stood up and strolled up next to Dude, "I'll help you gather"

"I appreciate it, but I'll be fine. I expect you must be tired from your long journey-"

"Yes, but It's cold and dangerous to go out on your own. Besides-", She nudged her elbow into his side playfully, "We can let the old men hang back while we collect the firewood"

Kashmir protested, "Whoa now, I'm not that much older than you"

Kerry pouted, "I'm younger in the mind and spirit"

Kashmir stood up, "I'll go help them-"

Kerry looked back with a smirk and then poked a stick at the fire, "No no, sit down, don't worry about them. They'll be fine. We'll work on preparing the food"

Dude avoided making eye contact with Brishine and yelled back towards Kerry and Kashmir, "We'll be back soon, don't share any good stories until I, um I mean we, we get back"

Brishine patted his shoulder, "I assure you, I got the farmer's strength, I can carry my weight or more in firewood. Unlike the man next to me"

Dude rolled his eyes, but he couldn't help but crack a smile, "You know what, this was originally just a mundane supply run, but now it's interesting. Now it's a competition, let's go"

Dude and Brishine walked off. Kerry tended to the fish over the fire, and Kashmir stared blankly at the fire.

The silence continued for far too long.

Kashmir glanced towards Kerry.

Kerry noticed Kashmir was staring at him. Kashmir looked away and then proceeded to rub his eyes.

Kerry sighed, "Is everything ok?"

Kashmir looked mildly embarrassed, "yes, sorry, the wind is making sure all the smoke is going right into my eyes"

Kerry raised an eyebrow, "I sense that there's also something else"

Kashmir stood up and picked up his travel gear. He moved away from the direction of the smoke before sitting down on his gear at a new location adjacent to the smoke, "you might laugh, but you look like someone I once saw in the kingdom. You even have the same name, but that wouldn't be plausible"

Kerry stopped tending to the food and stared at Kashmir.

The former knight stood up. Kerry glared with piercing eyes.

Kashmir leaned back, and raised his hands, "I Imagine I'm wrong, I meant no offense. I'm sure my mind is making false assumptions"

Kerry sat back down, his sights back on the fish, he flipped the three fish on the pan He raised an eyebrow, his eyes then glanced back at Kashmir. Under a hard tone that was trying to sound nonchalant, he asked, "Let's say you're right, what then?"

Kashmir gave a half-hearted smile, "I would ask for his assistance"

Kerry glanced up at the man, his stoic face gone, replaced with a genuine smile, "now, I wasn't expecting that"

Kashmir looked taken aback, "I'm not sure what you mean"

Kerry shook his head, "My last assignment of being a knight led to my forced retirement. The King announced to the world that I had died for reasons I care not to explain. I assumed that anyone who went seeking me had to be doing so with malicious intentions."

Kashmir's eyes went wide, "I assure you, that's not the case. This is just purely a blessing for me, and my sister to cross paths with you and your friend. I remember in my younger years. I would stand in the crowd. I recall seeing you on horseback, leading the army through the main path and out of the kingdom gates. I was there when you later returned through those very same gates as a victorious hero"

Kashmir stood up, his voice escalating, "I've heard stories of your valiant quests. Your good deeds, and kind heart. As a young lad, you brought hope to the crumbling kingdom"

He grimaced, "I was saddened the day the King announced your death. Meeting you here.... I assure you, it is a mere coincidence"

Kerry glared at him for a few moments in silence. After what felt like several minutes, he signed, "I'll honor your word but don't be mistaken. If I find out you fibbed, or have intentions that cause harm to me or my friends, I won't be afraid to cut out a liar's tongue"

Kashmir said somberly, "You have my word that I won't harm you or your party, and I have no ill intentions. I do need your assistance, even if it's just your advice"

"Kashmir, what is troubling you?" Kerry said with genuine concern.

Kashmir, his eyebrows now furrowed. He picked up a small stone and tossed it into the flame, "Brishine and I are traveling in search of our missing brother Rez. We believe he went seeking the Good Wizard Wilmar, to ask him to bring back his missing dog. He's a young, naive child who won't take no for an answer"

"What of the parents?"

"They were killed during a raid on our village. Brishine and I have been raising our little brother Rez ever since"

"Are you confident that he went to see this wizard?"

"We're hoping so, and it's our only lead. He's asked us multiple times to take him to see this so-called Good Wizard Wilmar, and each time we told him no. One morning, we found his bed empty. We assume Rez snuck out during the night. None of our neighbors or their children have seen him, so we decided to make the trek out to see if he went to Kleon Village to speak to their wizard"

"I believe it is in my good interest to join you in this journey. You see, I'm working on helping my friend Ari. We are currently looking for a spellcaster to help her in her current state. Perhaps this wizard you speak of will be able to assist us as well. I feel like I've heard that name before, but I can't quite place where I've heard the name"

There was a whistling sound. Carrot flew above them, going towards the direction of the cove. Kashmir dove to the side, crawling for cover towards a vacant merchant cart that was parked near the bonfire.

Kerry couldn't hold in his laughter.

Kashmir peeked out from under the merchant cart and looked at them with a mixture of confusion and dread on his face, "What... what in the fog moon was that?"

"That was Carrot, our noble steed. Who happens to be a dragon, who is giving a lift to our mermaid friend Ari"

Kashmir just stared at him, speechless.

Kerry smirked, "When you leave your home, you embark on an adventure. When you're on an adventure, nothing is ever mundane. That's why there are more stories with adventures than there are of life at home"

Chapter 17

Dude and Brishine walked away from the camp. He had lit up a torch. The sun had fully set, and the moon had not yet risen to provide sufficient light.

Brishine spoke, "so……Dude….that is a peculiar name. Is it a nickname or is it short for something"

Dude scratched the back of his head with his free hand, "I will admit that it is a unique name. I-," Dude thought for a moment, "I was called worse things growing up, and one of them as a joke was the name Dude, which eventually grew on me"

"So, if Dude is a nickname, what is your-"

"Enough about me, is this an interrogation?" Dude tried to sound playful, but ended up sounding awkward, "I'm not the only one with a peculiar name. Can you believe that you so happen to be the first Brishine that I've ever met? I've never heard of that name before"

"That means you don't travel out many west lands of the kingdom much because It's a fairly common name in my village of Windgnome"

"That makes sense, I've never been in that area. Um, forgive me if I'm out of line but Brishine, that's a very lovely name.

"Dude"

"Yes?"

"You're the first Dude I've ever met, and I can assure you that it's not a very common name, and I don't care if you don't forgive me when I say this, it's not a lovely name but you have lovely eyes"

Dude was taken aback and looked over at Brishine, who only then winked at him with a jovial expression.

Dude felt his face reddening, "Yes, very funny, and thank you. If you look over there, there's a woodpile over behind this collapsed building-"

"I can imagine how it must've been tough for you growing up to have children bully you. It's kind of cruel that they would give you a nickname that compares you to that compares you to that one dead prince...Dudesow"

Dude averted his eyes, "uh huh"

He stayed silent as he walked towards the woodpile. Brishine followed him close behind.

Brishine continued, "In my small village of Wind Gnome, the kids used to sing songs and make stories about all the misfortunes. At the local tavern, they would sing a drunkard's rhyme, "Prince Dudesow, who's full of woe and vertigo, he'll bring the Kingdom down you know"

Dude grimaced, "I can say that my childhood wasn't easy, but I imagine that prince had it worse"

"I imagine that it must've been a miserable childhood for the young prince to grow up with everyone blaming their problems on him."

"That does sound like a lonely and sad life." Dude, reached down and started picking up planks of wood.

"Did you know that the town folks living in the castle walls continued to gradually fare worse even after the King announced Prince Dudesow was dead?"

Dude froze, "That's unfortunate...especially when everyone in the kingdom had always hoped that the opposite would occur...."

Brishine continued, "When everyone's hopes were torched by the following days of gloomy skies and higher taxes. The once hushed whispers were now spoken out loud in the open, that perhaps the prince was indeed a scapegoat, a ruse, a face to blame. A distraction from the truth"

Dude, intentionally avoiding eye contact until this point, looked up at Brishine. She was staring directly at him. Dude was unsure what to make of her expression, "I'm glad they are starting to redirect their blame elsewhere." Brishine looked away, "Hopefully, now the prince can stop tossing and turning in his grave"

"It has been a while since I've heard any updates on the ongoing events in the kingdom, what happened after the prince passed on?"

"The reality of the Kingdom's misfortune finally stirred the fog of lies. The blame was starting to point towards the crown. The protests started to grow more violent. We stopped visiting the market inside the Kingdom's walls, it wasn't safe. It was very likely to get hit with a fist or sliced by a blade by simply being near another riot. My siblings and I stayed in our village and avoided any business near the castle. The King had ordered his knights to round up any protestors, deviants, and any innocent bystanders that even looked remotely suspicious and took them away to who knows where"

The moon was now starting to appear, providing sufficient light. He unintentionally made direct eye contact.

Dude gave her an awkward smile and turned away. He tried to ignore the sudden drumming in his chest. He went to place the torch onto a torch holder pole that was near the woodpile. He tried his best to avoid her eyes and focus his attention on picking up planks of wood. He randomly picked up a fair amount, he noticed that Brishine didn't pick up any, and he felt Brishine just staring at him, "Did you want me to hand you some, or did you change your mind on helping me out? Because...that means I can carry more than you and that would make me the victor"

Brishine shook her head and frowned, "I'm sorry, I'm just a little distracted. Let's hurry back". She picked up some planks of wood, "You challenging me had reminded me of my little brother Rez. He loved making challenges and chose to make them fun. He's my little brother my brother and I are working on getting him back. He ran away a while ago"

Dude faced her, with genuine concern in his voice, "I'm sorry to hear that. Is your bother ok?"

Brishine observed the sky, "I believe he's lost or perhaps captured. We've been working on getting back home after he ran away"

Dude stopped, "That's terrible, do you have any clues on where he's at? I can ask my friends and perhaps we can help"

Brishine stopped and had her eyes set on him, "I'd appreciate any help you can offer. We're on our way to talk to the Good Wizard Wilmar in Kleon Village. I hope the rumors are true that this wizard exists because we believe our brother went to seek him. Can you believe that he was foolish enough to just up and run away to talk to this wizard he's only heard tales about?"

Dude adjusted the pile in his arms and stepped forward. "Let's keep walking before my arms give out. I'm sorry. Why would he run off?"

Brishine picked up some dry wood from the pile, "Rez is young and not the brightest for someone his age. There are tales of a kind wizard who helps those in need. Rez believes he can ask the kind wizard Wilmar to bring his missing cat. If a pet goes missing, I would say it's safe to assume that it got devoured by some wildlife but that's just me"

"It sounds like his heart is in the right place, he must care greatly about this cat to risk going out on his own. How old is your youngest brother?"

"He's about to turn thirteen years old. He's brave but dumb and you're wrong. His heart isn't in the right place, because if he were truly so empathetic, he would've told his older siblings, who are worried about him, some sort of notice instead of where he went. We can only guess he went to find this village at Kleon. I swear, he loves his cat more than us because there he goes running off, without saying goodbye. Gone, without a trace, just like the cat!" Brishine said with exasperation. She smiled, but it didn't quite reach her eyes, "I'm worried about him". Dude turned to face the direction of the camp, "That explains why you both appeared so exhausted on arrival. I imagine you've had a long journey. I'll talk to friends and see how we can assist you on your journey, I'm sure they won't mind"

Brishine gave him an intense stare that Dude couldn't quite place. She walked a little closer to his side, "Thank you. I could tell by looking at you that you are a good person" Dude had an odd feeling but shrugged it off, "I'd be honored to help. I had some matters to attend to but I can put them aside for a time to help you and your brother out"

Brishine stared at him for some time and then smirked, "You know, you look kinda handsome when the moonlight hits you just right"

Dude suddenly felt an emotional sensation that he'd never felt before; he stammered, "I suppose, thank you. Let's hurry back; I imagine the others are worried about us by now." he began walking towards the camp. He walked faster than his normal pace, not looking back.

Dude heard Brishine give a lighthearted laugh, she was catching up to his pace. He kept eyes facing forward, he heard her steps keeping up with his brisk pace, walking behind him. Dude said nothing else on the way back, his gaze forward, but his vision lost in imagination, his mind distracted, his heart dancing like it never had before.

Chapter 18

Dude and Brishine walked up to the camp.

Once they made it to the clearing at the edge of the camp, they both dropped the wood onto the ground, both slightly out of breath from the speedy walk back. When they saw the camp, the small fire was out, and their stuff was gone. No one else was around.

Dude was staring into the sizzled fire pit, he started panicking, "This isn't good"

Dude felt a light tap on his shoulder and looked over to see Brishine pointing towards the far end of the cove.

There was a huge bonfire in the distance. Dude could see that the bone fire had a metal fence placed flat over it, and dozens of fish were cooking.

"I don't know why they relocated the camp over there. let's just go," Bri said with irritation.

They both groaned, they picked up their stockpile of wood and quickly made their way towards the new fire.

All the fishermen's boats were docked on that side of the pier next to the bonfire. All the lanterns lit up. Dude and Bri jogged awkwardly, as they tried to balance their wood stacks as they made their way down the creaking dock planks towards the activity. They saw dozens of people conversing next to the fire, some carrying bottles of wine. As they got closer, it appeared and sounded to be a gathering in good spirits. The lanterns of the pier and the giant bonfire provided the only light that fought back the intimidating darkness surrounding the cove. Dude was surprised that all this was set up while they were away to get firewood.

"Wow, I guess we were gone a lot longer than It felt". Dude felt embarrassed as he recalled the journey back felt like an eternity as he was mentally distracted by the overly intrusive thoughts of a future together with a woman he had barely met.

Dude realized that she was the first woman he had spoken to at his age. He wondered if she'd let him call her Bri.

Dude shook his head at such thoughts.

Brishine nodded towards the spectacle, "Let's go, I'm starving"

Dude blinked and felt his nose invasively overwhelmed with the smell of fish and an array of spices, and smiled, "Then, let's go"

They hustled over into the bone fire area, and Dude heard a shriek and heard the sound of wood planks dropping to the ground with a thud.

Dude turned to see Bri holding a plank of wood defensively and looked skeptically at the dragon who lay down sleeping a few steps away from the bonfire, "Is that dragon…"

Dude placed the wood planks on the ground and stood next to her, and smiled, "That's my noble steed. She's never eaten anyone that I'm aware of so I can assure you that you're safe. Probably"

Brishine looked over at him to see him winking at her with a comical smile. She shook her head, "I'm still sleeping with one eye open tonight."

Kashmir rushed up to Brishine, a fish kabob in one hand and a bottle of wine in the other, "Oh sis, you missed it! Kerry over here asked their dragon to carry a fisherman's net across the cove, and each time the dragon swooped down, it entrapped so many fish. The dragon did that several times and-" Kashmir pointed at a huge net of captured fish that took up a good portion of the back of a nearby boat, "…. look at that pile. The fisherman said they have enough fish here to sell and more than enough to feast on, so they might as well take a long holiday. They are so grateful that they offered to share their drinks with us. The dragon, I must say, was quite the sight; then leaned over the bonfire, and helped cook the fish quicker with its spectacular film," The roasting of fish was done quickly so now we can all eat and drink and celebrate!"

Kashmir tried to take a bite of his kabob and stumbled. Brishine caught Kashmir and guided him to a log on the ground, "Here, brother, lean against this log. Steady yourself, so you can enjoy the food and wine"

Kashmir gave a heavy nod, "We sure will. Soon we shall reunite with our brother and go home"

Brishine sat down next to Kashmir and patted her brother's shoulder, "We will, brother"

Dude walked away and looked around, "he saw lots of unfamiliar faces, conversing around the first. He spotted Kerry, who stood next to the pier and appeared to be talking to the water. Talking out towards Kerry, Dude saw that Kerry was speaking to Ari. Ari has her arms crossed on the pier ledge while looking up at Kerry while they spot.

Ari spotted Dude and gave a heartwarming smile. Kerry looked over at Ari's line of sight and waved him over.

Dude walked up, "I found myself surprised to return to a festival on my way back"

Kerry smirked at him, raising his eyebrows, "It took you a while to return, did you intentionally take the long route to the wood pile?"

Ari looked up at Dude and spoke in a playful tone, "A long detour? I suppose a nice long walk would be ideal for you to get to know the women who quickly volunteered to help you. It makes perfect sense. She looks around your age and that's great because you need practice talking to a woman who hasn't at one point changed your diaper cloth"

Dude, bright red in embarrassment, was torn between trying to deny it or storming away. Instead, he sighed, "I'll admit, that a part of me was interested in getting to know her, but I was wise enough to keep my distance. I didn't share my past. She mentioned that my name reminded her of the deceased Prince Dudesow. I had to be cautious"

Kerry nodded approvingly, "That is wise; we don't know them. They might be telling the truth or they might be deceiving us"

Ari gave a somber expression, "You see Kashmir over there kissing the bottle? He's in a chipper mood because when I cast a well-being spell, it informed me that his brother hadn't passed on to the land beyond. He made that statement as his brother was alive. I couldn't confirm that, but I did confirm that his brother's soul is tied to this plane. I feel guilty as I didn't have the heart to tell him that the results don't entirely mean that his brother is out there still alive. I can only see so much, and the spell reveals so little. It seemed to be enough to remove Kashmir's grim mood"

Dude sat on the ledge of the pier next to Ari, "how does that spell work?"

Ari reached out and yanked a piece of hair off of Dude's hair.

"Yo-ow!", Dude retracted, scooting away just enough to get out of Ari's reach, "What was that for?"

Ari smiled, holding up the hair. She had it pinched between her thumb and index finger. She whispered a word and the hair started to glow a shade of light green, "The color reflects the health. All I need is a piece of a person- like a strand of hair or something they wore to cast the spell. Green is for good health, whereas yellow can mean that person is unwell or in danger..."

Dude interrupted, "Red or black for death?"

Ari gave him a revolted look, "what? No. That doesn't make any sense. If they died...the cloth evaporates, to show that they are no longer part of the land of the living"

Dude exhaled an exaggerated breath, "Sorry"

Kerry glanced back towards Kashmir and Brishine, then nodded toward Ari, "Tell Dude what you saw"

Ari's smile faded, "I wasn't candid with Kashmir. I told him his brother was alive, but the torn cloth he provided had lit up a faint yellow, and then it slowly evaporated. I didn't tell him what the colors meant. Perhaps I should tell him...that in my experience, his brother is dead, but...his soul is still tied to this plane, unable or resisting the transition into the afterlife beyond"

Kerry sat down next to Ari; he spoke to her with compassion in his eyes, "It would probably be for the best that you don't. We'll make it to the Good Wizard Wilmar tomorrow. They traveled for several days with nothing on their mind but uncertainty. Their hope is keeping them going. Now they're hopeful and in good spirits. They'll talk to the wizard tomorrow to find out from him what happened to their brother. He can answer their questions. That shouldn't be your burden to tell them. If you told Kashmir the complete truth, he would've just stormed off into the night, waking up the wizard in the early morning. Demanding to know the truth. The wizard, who is probably not a morning person like us, is now upset about not getting a full night's rest. The siblings now feeling the wrath of an upset wizard, probably turned into frogs or worse as punishment. Right after that, we'll be the next in the queue to talk to him. He'll be too upset to help. I say we avoid that scenario"

Dude leaned forward, a mischievous grin obvious on his face. He winked at Ari, "The wizard turning them into frogs wouldn't be so bad. The worst thing they might get turned into is something strange and smelly, like a mermaid"

Ari gave Dude a fierce glare, "How about I turn you into some strange and smelly fish food?" She pointed her index finger at him.

Dude immediately ran.

An expression of fear and glee on his face as he ran.

Kerry laughed heartily before stopping and looking concerned: " You aren't going to really transform him, are you?"

Ari watched Dude run and then turned her attention to Kerry.

Her expression was playful, "No, of course I wouldn't. The chances of me snapping into a fit of unbridled rage and wildly using my magical unfiltered energy to cause some damage to others are unlikely"

Kerry smiled, "That's-"

"But never zero"

Kerry's smile faltered as Ari aimed her index finger at his chest.

Kerry took an offensive stance and quickly pointed his fish kabob toward Ari.

Ari and Kerry stared at one another in a tense standoff.

The silence dragged on for a few moments.

Both of them failed to keep a deadpan expression for long.

Kerry spoke, "It appears we're at a stalemate"

Ari slowly nodded, "It appears so"

"Perhaps giving you this fish kabob will deter you from turning Dude or myself into fish food?"

Ari reached out and took the kabob from Kerry's hand, "For now, yes"

She took a bite of the fish, her face lit up, "this is amazing!!"

Kerry tried to contain his smile, "just don't look at the fish"

Ari quickly laid her eyes on her meal to see ink oozing out of the meat cuts of fish. She glanced at Kerry, who flashed his teeth at her, showing a thin layer of ink stain.

She repulsed.

After a moment, the disgust faded from her mind, and she shrugged.

She took another bite.

Chapter 19

Dude awoke with a mild headache. The smell of cooked fish is strong in the air. The sun was slowly rising above the horizon. He slowly stood up, Kerry and Carrot were nowhere to be seen. Around the firepit, laid sprawled out fishing folk, passed out from a long night of drinking and socializing.

From the corner of his eye, he noticed something floating on the water near the pier.

Dude walked up to the pier and noticed Ari floating on the water, her eyes were heavy, "Were you able to get some sleep?"

Ari shook her head and groaned, "I couldn't sleep. Do you know how a mermaid sleeps? It's an inconvenient process of finding a nice cozy, safe spot first. Once I'm sure I'm not going to be an easy defenseless snack for a predator to chew while I sleep, I then proceed to get some slumber with one eye open"

"I would've thought a cove would've been somewhat more safe-"

"It's not. This is a fishing cove. I try to lie down and end up with a thousand little stabs of fishing hooks that are littered on the ground. I gave up and slept with my head in my arms at the edge of the pier"

"Will you be alright for today's travels? Perhaps we can postpone-"

"No, no, no, I'll be fine. I don't want my bottom half being part fish any longer"

"Let me know if you need any breaks during our travels"

"I appreciate the kindness, but I'll be fine, my head is just killing me this morning. Drank too much last night. If you find anyone brewing up a hot cup of clawfee, or selling a cup of Joel, whatever, just let me know"

"Clawfee? What is that?"

"You really were sheltered." She let out a soft laugh, "It's a brew that's popular with the spellcasters and academics that live within the Merry Mystic Woods and the Kingdom's market. It's a popular drink for travelers to take on their commute to and from the kingdom. I doubt there's any out this far south, but the moment I obtain some clawfee beans, I'll brew you up a cup of Joel to try"

"I'm assuming that Clawfee and Joel are the same? Why is it called a Joel?"

"It's just a nickname. Some will say its meaning is long forgotten, but I've been around long enough to know it's named after a man named Joel. Joel sold clawfee out of a corner shop, he made his clawfee stand out from the more affordable competition by marketing it as journey onward energy liquid. His descendants continued selling the clawfee under that brand name, gradually raising the cost. It's now a successful clawfee shop with several locations. It's a popular clawfee brand brew for travelers and merchants to take on the go, usually to show their elite status that they can afford it. It's dumb. I'd usually prefer to make my clawfee at home but right now I'd pay silver for a premium cup of Joel right now"

Ari pointed at a tiny merchant cart nearby, "Could you bring that over, I have a feeling we'll need that for the trip out"

Dude went over and removed some litter from the cart. It was a small cart that an individual or a single donkey could pull in tow. He grabbed the cart's two arms with a firm grip and pulled it forward towards Ari. As Dude pulled the cart close to the pier ledge, he lowered the cart's arms.

Ari pulled herself onto the pier and then put her hand out, "I'd appreciate a lift"

Dude, without hesitation, helped Ari onto the cart, "You help raise me, the least I can do is raise you off the ground"

Ari was smiling as she rolled her eyes, "Har har"

***

Before the team left Inkbert to head towards Inkport, several grateful residents gave donations of coins they could spare and rations for their travel. They purchased a carriage to accommodate Ari. They purchased a worn-down carriage that was heavy and required the strength of four horses, or at least one dragon, as it was the perfect size for a Carrot to pull comfortably. Once the team arrived at Inkport, they got comfortable. Ari dove into the cove, and Kerry and Dude set up camp. Carrot ran over, quickly destroying their new carriage as it bounced into smaller pieces as the dragon ran towards the nearest open field outside the port.

Ari sighed, recalling that carriage. It was comfortable, even if her scaled tale was drying out in the elements.

Now, Dude was pulling the small cart with her in it, towards Kerry. Kerry had just descended off the saddle on Carrot's back, "I had Carrot fly over the Kleon village. As a precaution, I believe I had Carrot fly high enough that, hopefully, we didn't get spotted. I'd hate to scare the townsfolk and ruin their afternoon"

Ari spoke, "More importantly, did it look like a nice normal village"

Kerry smiled, "From the looks of it, yes"

Dude gently placed the cart handles onto the ground, "That's a relief, I've had my fill of creepy hostile villages for one lifetime." He pointed at Carrot, "Any idea how we're gonna have Carrot pull this cart?"

Kerry shook his head, "it wouldn't work, Carrot is too big, and the cart is too small. The cart would keep tipping over"

Ari cringed, "I don't like the mental imagery of that, any other ideas?"

Dude gave a hopeful expression, "Any way you could work in some sort of magical solution?"

Ari looked vexed, "Magic can't solve all problems. If it could, the world would be a better place"

Dude, had a look of dismay, that soon quickly turned into one of curiosity, "I apologize, I'm just not sure how magic works"

Ari sighed, "It's alright. My powers are more innate, while others, like a wizard or witch, are learned. Innate magic can only go so far, while learned magic is almost limitless. My innate magic is taking power from something internal within me. While external magic is taking power from an outside source"

Dude nodded, "that makes sense. I'm just confused about the limitations."

Kerry walked up closer with visible interest, "You mentioned a while back that you were able to practice witch magic to create the transformation powers? How were you able to accomplish that?"

Ari perked up, like a student asking an instructor the right question, "I was able to use witchcraft due to having a magical external source. That source was the cauldron on site, which had a magical source of power that I could draw from. Witches and Wizards, not all but most have magical items to draw energy from to cast spells and ingredients to create the spell or potion for later use. Since the magical cauldron was available, along with books explaining the process. I was able to conduct and create the transformations. I currently don't have any of those three things to create a transformation spell or potion"

Kerry was deep in thought, "Thank you for explaining. I knew that there was a difference between sorceresses and witches, but I didn't exactly know what those differences were. I was afraid to ask, I didn't want to be rude. I'm thankful for Dude's blunt but naive question answered that for me"

Dude avoided eye contact, looking embarrassed, "What are your powers? How do they work?"

Ari appeared amused, "Thank you, Dude, I wish you could've just asked politely earlier"

Dude facepalmed, "I understand, I'll work on thinking before I speak"

Ari pointed her finger at Dude, clearly speaking a few words for her two spectators to hear: "Ooh low, emer re ci cri ci. " She then retracted her finger and closed her hand into a fist.

A gust of wind struck Dude in the right shoulder, he almost lost his balance as it startled him.

"Ooh low, emer re ci cri ci", Ari made a hard slap motion, and a gust of wind struck behind Dude's left knee.

Dude stumbled, "All right, I can see you have powers. No more demonstrations needed"

Ari looked satisfied, "I draw my power from within, I can perform a spell with a memorized or spoken spell. If I draw too much power from within, I can grow weak or pass out. I certainly can't just make up a spell to fit my desired action"

Kerry leaned over and spoke to Dude, "What to take away from this is that Ari can't use her magic to make it easier to move the cart. Perhaps she could send a small gust or two of wind to help move the cart a bit forward, but I imagine it would tire her out quickly. We'd still have to pick up the slack"

Ari nodded, "Exactly"

Kerry patted Dude's shoulder, "I'll help pull the cart. The sooner we get Ari over there, the sooner she can get her legs back"

"Let's get moving, nothing worse than dry scales. It's like an itch you can quite fully scratch"

Kerry picked up one of the cart handles, and Dude picked up the other. They started moving. Carrot ascended and flew around the cove.

Dude observed the surroundings; most of the fishermen had left the camp area, and a few were still sleeping on the ground, sleeping the afternoon away. Further around him, he noticed a few people he recognized from last night's festivities transporting crates and barrels on the dock, others packaging fish, and some movement of people on nearby boats that were still attached to the pier, "Where's...where's the two who would be joining us on this journey?".

"They are waiting for us a little up ahead, they are anxious to get going. I told them we'd meet up at the entrance area"

***

The team spotted Kashmir and Brishine waiting at the entrance. Kashmir was pacing back and forth, a walking stick in hand. Brishine sat on a tree stump, she noticed them and stood up. She said something that they couldn't hear, causing Kashmir to stop pacing. Kashmir and Brishine started to walk in their direction so they could meet halfway.

Kashmir smiled at them as they closed in, "Are we good to depart?"

Kerry nodded, "We're good to depart, we're going on foot. Carrot will fly above, keeping watch and ideally fly down to defend us if needed. At least, I'd hope so"

Kashmir stared up in awe at the dragon flying far above them, "I will say that having a somewhat reliable dragon defending the group is better than having no dragon defending our group. I imagine no thieves will dare disturb us on our journey, but nevertheless; Dude, what did I always tell you about complacency?"

Dude smiled, "Never let your guard down, or you'll be swept off your feet"

***

The group traveled southeast towards Kleon, a small village that was a day's travel south of Inkport. The path to Inkport was wide enough for caravans to travel through, but the group has yet to see any others traveling the same path. The path guided them through the lush green hills. The hills lay bare except for yellow grass, with no trees or shrubs in sight.

Kerry advised them that, even though the hills provide little to no cover for any who dare try to ambush their group. It would still be wise to not let their guard down.

Kerry, Dude, Kashmir, and Brishine took turns pulling the cart.

Ari was irritable, having to deal with the pain of dry scales.

It was currently Dude's turn to pull the cart. It was tiring, as the path was rarely a nice flat, leveled, straight path. Dude had to pull the cart upwards on an incline, "Just my luck," he muttered.

Dude felt like he was pulling the cart uphill both ways. He asked questions to keep his mind distracted from how tired he was, "Has anyone ever been to Kleon village?"

Kerry and Ari shook their heads.

Brishine looked over at Kashmir.

Kashmir shrugged, "I vaguely remember visiting there as a young child. Brishine was an infant and Rez wasn't even born yet. What I can remember is it being a nice enough village. One of the things I remember was the homes. The small homes were covered in moss and flowers, the market carts were made of twisted vines, full of bright yellow leaves. Arches of vines arched over the village streets, giving the village plenty of shade. The arches had huge flowers. It was beautiful. That's all I can really recall. My family was just passing through at that time. Beyond that, are tales of the Good Wizard Wilmar, who resides in this village. Who will help those who he feels are worthy of his help. Tales shared around the tavern are that he'll shoo those away who are selfish and help those who are truly in need. The tales were common enough that Rez must've believed he was worthy of WIlmar's help"

As the group transversed, the hills they passed were bigger than the hills before. Eventually, the hills grew into mountains. Kerry kept his eyes on the surroundings while they conversed.

The path took them to a steep incline. Dude struggled to pull up the cart, Kerry strode up to help push the cart, while Dude pulled the cart at the front. As they neared the top of the hill....

Brishrine spoke, "Look, up ahead!"

They all turned to look at the direction Brishine pointed, the view of the valley gradually became more visible as they made it up the incline. At the center of the village there was one single tall tree in the center, and there was a reason. The tree itself was enormous, as it was tall and wide as a mountain. Near the bottom of its trunk, large tree roots arched over the town. Lush think vines threaded between, through, and around the tree roots. As a result, creating a nice organic cover over the town. ginormous flowers, the size of cottages, surrounded the town of Kleon. Kashmir suddenly grabbed the cart handles from Dude, an ecstatic look on his face, "Onward! I'll happily give you a break, let's go!"

Dude wiped the sweat off his brow, "sounds good to me"

Kashmir happily hefted up and cart and took a step forward.

A look of confusion spread on Kashmir's face as he fell back. An invisible forced the cart forward, causing Kashmir's backside on top of Ari.

The back of Kashmir's head knocked into Ari's forehead, "What the-ow. I'm so sorry, I-"

Before Ari could speak, the cart sped off, as if it had a mind of its own.

It went downhill and off down the trial at a dangerous speed.

Ari and Kashmir were holding onto the sides of the cart, a look of fear and confusion on their faces as they held on with their dear lives.

It took a moment for Bri, Dude, and Kerry to process what exactly happened before they ran down the hill, chasing after the cart.

Carrot flew above, not noticing, as her mind was in the clouds.

Chapter 20

The town of Kloen village was a blur as the cart sped on through. Speeding past the market, through the alleyways, and around the pedestrians.

"Hey! Stop this thing! Help! Make this stop!?" Kashmir screamed, "Please, make this cart stop!"

Ari looked back at him with a chagrined expression, "I can't, I've tried to but whoever the power user is controlling this thing is stronger than I"

The cart was heading towards the center trunk of the tree. Huge double doors were ahead.

The doors were closed and the cart was still going at a dangerous speed. The impact was imminent.

The two of them covered their eyes, shrieking and preparing for an inevitable crash.

One of the doors flung open and the cart drove right in, just on the brink of time.

Once the cart made its way in, the cart halted. Ari and Kashmir flew awkwardly off the cart. Their screams were cut short as their bodies floated just barely above the ground right before the anticipated impact. Kashmir and Ari slowly landed on the ground.

"You're here!", a skinny old man bellowed from behind an impressive wooden desk. He peeked over with an amused grin, "Oh, there's two of you? Even better. The more I say... the merrier! I sensed a magic user in the area and I just had to meet them. I apologize for the surprise trip"

The wizard stepped around his desk and walked up to help them both up with each arm. Wilmar reached over to pull up Ari, and she waved him away, so he helped Kashmir up instead while keeping his eyes on Ari, "My my, a mermaid? Very uncommon in these parts. Especially out of water. You're living proof it's not impossible. Still, very odd. I wonder how?"

The wizard eyed them both one more time, but mostly on Ari, he had an amused on his wrinkled face, "I can spare some time for some conversation. Can you? I'd love to hear about your travels. I'll make it worth your while, perhaps over a cold glass of mead?"

✷✷✷

Wilmar pointed at two worn-down wooden stools that were vacant in front of his desk, "Please have a seat; I'll prepare some drinks." Wilmar walked over to the cabinet that was carved into the tree. The cabinet had several bottles of mead, all of which had labels featuring Wilmar's face. The words on the label were moving, circling continuously around the face, in bold text, "Wilmar's Wilder Mead". The wizard grabbed a bottle and three glasses.

Ari shifted, attempting to find a comfortable position on the worn-down wooden stool, which creaked loudly with each movement. "Would it be safe to assume that you are the Wizard Wilmar?"

The wizard did an exaggerated facepalm, "Where are my manners? I apologize. Let me introduce myself, "I'm Wilmar Wilkins, but the locals like to call me the Good Wizard Wilmar"

"I'm Ari, Ari Feirune, and this-", she pointed at Kashmir, "...this my friend."

Kashmir appeared slightly uneasy as he offered a hesitant smile and a small wave, saying, "Hi um, hello, I'm Kashmir."

Wilmar did a slight bow, "Welcome to my home." He twisted a cork off a bottle, "I would like to offer some delicious homemade mead, it's a fresh batch"

Ari spoke, "I appreciate the offer but-"

"No, no, I insist"

"Thank you but no thank you"

Kashmir eagerly raised his hand, keen to try some mead. "I'll have a glass, please," he said.

Wilmar poured him a glass, and Kashmir took a small sip. His eyes brightened. "Mmm, this is good... and it smells wonderful too."

Wilmar nodded, "I've fermented the mead myself; I'm glad you like it. If you change your mind miss...Feirune, let me know"

Kashmir carefully placed the cup down on the desk, "How did you see us? Was it with that glowing blue orb on the table?"

"Hah, no, no, no. How did I see you both? Well, a wizard like myself has his ways of knowing these things. That orb on the desk is just for decoration; it's great to stare into when I'm pondering"

Ari observed that Wizard Wilmar, appearing to be in his late fifties, was slender and slightly taller than the average human. He wore a faded green cloak and had permanent smile lines. Speaking warmly, he said, "I may need to fetch another bottle. I expect the rest of your friends will arrive soon."

A dwarf in fitted butler attire walked down a flight of stairs at the back of the room. The stairs were beautifully carved within the trunk of the tree.

Once the dwarf reached the bottom of the steps, he bowed, "Wilmar, I-"

The Good Wizard Wilmar snapped, "Don't you see I have guests? Get back upstairs".

Wilmar picked up a candelabra off the desk and tossed it at the dwarf.

The dwarf barely dodged it, "I'm sorry to disturb you, my Excellency-"

"Leave!"

The dwarf servant turned and scurried up the stairs.

Ari and Kashmir exchanged concerned glances.

Wilmar noticed their exchange and expressed his apologies: "I'm so sorry you had to see that; I can see how that can be perceived negatively. We like to have fun here. I assure you, no dwarfs are harmed within this vicinity"

Ari spoke, "What did that dwarf do to warrant such a response?"

Wilmar smiled and gave a playful shrug, "Sometimes a little playful fear teaches others to learn quickly about what can be considered inappropriate behavior"

Ari grimaced, "That's terrible. I don't agree with that, but this is your home, so I'll stop myself right there"

Wilmar grinned, "Wise woman, I appreciate you being respectful in my home "

Ari looked away, her expression unreadable

Kashmir raised a hand.

Wilmar's grin faltered, "Um, yes Kashmir, what is it?"

"I have some questions"

Wilmar squinted at Kashmir for a moment before his friendly demeanor resumed. He waved off the question dismissively, saying, "Yes, yes, I'm sure you do. Please wait until the rest of your party arrives"

✳✳✳

Dude, Kerry, and Bri just made it to the entrance of Kleon. They were panting heavily, as none of them were used to long-distance running, let alone a jog.

It took Dude the longest to recover, as it was the first time he ran in his life.

Kerry and Bri helped him up, with Kerry giving Dude some light pats on the back.

The citizens of Kleon, mainly gnomes, glanced in their direction with mild interest before continuing on with their day.

The entrance was grand, to match the unusually wide road. It was the main road, and it went towards the tree trunk. The homes were built of mainly stone, with moss growing between the gaps

The homes' roofs were covered in grass and vines. Roots from the main tree covered the road overhead. The ginormous tree trunks were easily the circumference of a single-family cottage.

Intertwined between the overhead roots that grew above the town were vines. The lively vines were full of flowers. The impossibly tall tree was almost tall enough to touch the clouds. Its wide branches and overhead roots provided a comfortable shade over the town. There were constant breezes, causing the three adventurers to have occasional chills.

They stepped onto the busy road, walking along past merchant carts. Different races waited behind their merchant carts, while the majority of shoppers appeared to be gnomes.

Dude accidentally bumped into a gnome's shoulder. Dude, looking chagrin, raised his hands, "I'm so sorry, my apologies"

The gnome glared at Dude, flashing their teeth before stomping off.

Brishine spoke in a low tone: " The local gnomes don't appear to be in a good mood today"

A gnome was arguing with a merchant nearby. Up ahead, a gnome and an elf were tumbling in a brawl. The elf's merchant was knocked over.

Dude stepped forward and Dude clasped his shoulder, "Don't. Our priority is to find our friends first. They may be in danger, worse, they may even harmed as we speak"

Dude looked torn for a moment. He removed Kerry's hand respectfully, "I'll try to make this quick"

Dude ran up ahead. Brishine followed right behind him. Kerry sighed and caught up to them.

The elf fell onto their back. The muscular gnome, who had an intimidating scar that ran between the eyes, and then curved towards their left ear., had landed on the elf's chest, their fists striking the elf's face relentlessly while the helpless elf yelled for help. The gnome smirked while swinging punches.

Dude tried to pry them apart. He caught the gnome's fist right before it was about to strike his face, "Now, now, stop; let's handle this like civilized folk."

Dude slowly let go. The gnome stepped back.

Brishine helped the elf onto their feet.

The gnome looked up at Dude, a despicable expression rippled across its face before they snapped their fingers.

Two gnomes nearby charged in. Dude, caught off guard, didn't notice the gnome with the scar run toward him, a blade now in his hand. Brishine ran up and swung a mighty kick to the scar gnome's face. The gnome landed back, their head hitting the cobblestone ground hard.

The scar-faced gnome didn't get back up.

Kerry stepped in and grabbed an attacking gnome by the collar. Once the gnome turned its head, he let go and immediately got into a fighting stance.

The gnome quickly turned to aim their fist towards Kerry's crotch, but Kerry's knee blocked it. The gnome stumbled as Kerry's fist struck them hard in the nose.

Dude swung a punch at an approaching gnome. The gnome dodged and swung at Dude's gut.

"Oof!" Dude's arms instinctively covered his gut, leaning forward enough for the gnome to land a punch at Dude's right eye.

The color of Dude's face turned bright red, "I'm done"

Dude grabbed both arms of the gnome and started lifting the gnome into the air. Dude spun around in circles, gaining speed.

The gnome shook in Dude's arms in rage.

Dude, feeling better, let go.

The red-faced gnome flew. Crashing right into the gnome fighting Kerry.

The small crowd that formed around all the commotion had cheered.

The two gnomes got up, disgruntled, and started to drag their scar-faced comrade away.

The scar-faced gnome shook them off and pointed a finger at Dude, "You better make like a tree, and get the trunk out of here before nightfall", a heavy threat in his tone.

The scar-faced gnome scowled, then turned away. Shoving through the crowd, its minions followed.

The onlookers dispersed. Dude and Kerry helped the merchant get back onto his feet.

The bruised-up merchant elf walked up to his cart, grabbing some bottles. He turned back to the group, carrying an assortment of elixir bottles in his hands, "Thank you three, I appreciate you three stepping in earlier. The local guards are never around when you need them. Please, please, take these bottles, as a token of my gratitude"

Before any of them could respond, the merchant had handed them each an assortment of health elixirs. Labels written in intricate cursive marked what they were.

Kerry spoke, "Thank you, but I must respectively offer at least some of these back to you. I would feel terrible, you do have a business to run and all this appears to be a good portion if not all of your inventory"

The merchant looked glum, "Please, keep it. It will be less for me to carry. I'm leaving town."

Dude looked at the elf with a curious expression, "Why? It looks lovely here. I'd imagine it's a great place to do business"

The merchant shook his head, "I thought the same thing myself when I set up my shop here a month ago. The entire time I've been here, running a business here has been nothing but one incommode after another. The locals have been on edge or just plain rude. They are passive-aggressive on a good day.

Dude spoke, "I'm sorry to hear that, where are you off to now?"

The elf raised an eyebrow, "I'm not used to this much interest in my well-being. I'll tell you only because I haven't had a kind conversation in quite some time. I'll probably head north towards Wetmore since Inkport has restricted entry to merchants- last I checked. If my next shop fails, I may just retire. Maybe I'm not suited for the merchant life"

Dude handed the elf some bottles back, "I won't need all this, but you certainly do. I recommend you try Inkport again. We just left there, we helped resolve the town's troubles, and from what the locals told me, they are in dire need of medical elixirs. There are many mutations there that need treatment"

The elf perked up, "Oh really, now?", He grabbed a few bottles back and then reached into his pocket pulled out a few coins and handed them over to Dude, "That's fantastic news. Inkport is a much shorter journey than Wetmore. You know what? You've inspired me. I can probably charge double and easily make back what I'm handing you now in no time"

Brishine tapped Dude's and Kerry's shoulders, "As much as I love knowing the life and business of some merchant, we really need to get going. Your friend and my brother may be in trouble"

***

Dude, Kerry, and Brishine sped and walked to the tree trunks' grand entrance doors. The double doors were unguarded. Dude looked up, really having to crane his neck up, and was still unable to see the top of the tree.

Brishine tapped on Dude's shoulder, looking impatient, "What are you waiting for, knock on the door. If you don't, I will"

"I-" Dude stammered.

Kerry stepped forward between them towards the door his voice radiating confidence, "Let me knock, I fear no door or whatever what's on the other side"

Brishine silently mocked Kerry's words, giving a stoic expression. Dude laughed in response.

Kerry glanced back at them, "What's so funny?"

Dude looked away from Brishine to regain his composure, "Nothing of importance Kerry, I thought I saw a bird trip. You can knock on the door now"

Dude whispered to Brishine, "Be nice. Kerry's a great guy, he's just a little serious at times."

Brishine shrugged, "sorry"

Kerry shook his head. He returned his attention to the door.

Right before Kerry's knuckles rapped at the door, the two doors swung inwards open.

In front of them at the doorway was an elderly man, his arms spread out in a welcoming pose, "Greetings! Step right in; It's mighty cold out there. The shade from the tree keeps this area cold. Welcome, welcome"

The three of them stepped inside.

There was an open center, an assortment of shelves, and unique decor of different cultural art and magical items displayed proudly on the walls. The room size was grand; it could easily fit 200 hundred people. Near one wall was a desk, with two vacant wooden stools in front of it.

There is so much open space, yet no Ari or Kashmir in sight, Dude thought.

Kerry spoke first, "Thank you for your hospitality. I'm sorry if were intruding-"

The wizard waved, "No, no, you're not intruding. I'm used to helping and listening to weary travelers all day, every day"

A dwarf in butler attire, startled Kerry as the dwarf just appeared in Kerry's peripheral vision, "Weapon please, there are no weapons allowed in the presence of the good wizard"

Kerry grumbled and handed the dwarf his sword, "I expect that back, that sword has sentimental value."

The butler nodded, "I assure you, I will put the sword in a secure and safe location". The dwarf firmly took the sword and walked over to a chest that was behind a desk. The dwarf placed the sword in the chest. The dwarf promptly closed the lid and locked it. He patted the chest, turning over to make eye contact with Kerry. Giving him a respectful nod.

The wizard, satisfied, gave everyone a warm smile, "Now that we have all the sharp, pointy metal jabbers away, we can now relax. Welcome!"

Dude spoke up, "Thank you, I'm Dude, this is Sir-" he pointed towards Kerry.

Kerry interrupted, "I'm Kerry, and this over here is Brishine"

Brishine spoke, "Yes, hello. It's an honor to meet you. Um, I'm looking for my brother. I heard he was seen going towards this tree, along with my brother Kashmir"

Wilmar looked disapprovingly at her. "Let me get comfortable first before you start asking for things, my goodness"

Brishine eyes went wide, "I'm so sorry, I meant no disrespect"

Wilmar shook his head, "Kids nowadays need to learn some manners. My patience has really been tested lately. Now, follow me"

Wilmar waved his arm forward, indicating for them to follow. He made his way up the wooden stairs. The hollowed trunk of the tree was cut deeper to create a staircase made out of the same tree, leading upwards. Beautiful designs were intricately cut into the tree trunk steps.

Dude leaned over to Kerry's ear and whispered, "I believe the good wizard title name may have been given sarcastically"

The three of them made their way up the stairs, Kerry taking the lead.

This room was hollowed out as well. Small Circular windows with fogged glass were randomly placed around the walls. One side of the room had stacks of crates. The other side of the room had honey fermenting machinery, a desk of tools, and, near it, several barrels of water. Wilmar walked over to the desk and sat at the edge of it, looking out towards the center of the room. At the center of the ceiling, there was a opening curving upward, into a dark unknown above.

Right below it, sat Ari in a chair, passed out.

Kashmir in a chair next to her, his expression unreadable.

Kerry was the first to see Ari when he reached the top of the stairs. His face quickly turned bright red with rage, and he rushed over to Ari's side.

Kerry turned, looking at Kashmir and then towards Wilmar, "What have you done to her?" he barked.

Dude and Brishine made their way up the steps, rushing over to the center of the room.

Brishine checked up on Kashmir, who indicated for her to stay silent. A look of concern on his face.

Wilmar smiled, "You lot took too long to get here so I offered to help her with her tail trouble. Please don't fret; I've only given her a concoction to help her fins transform into legs. It takes a lot of energy out of someone to transform, so give her time. That's why she's out cold"

Kerry stared at Wilmar skeptically.

Wilmar snapped his fingers, and three chairs appeared, "Please, have a seat"

Dude felt that Wilmar was dangerous. From what Dude could read from his friends' expressions, they appeared to have felt the same.

Wilmar picked up a bottle nearby, "would any of you like to try my famous honey mead? The locals love it"

Kashmir spoke first, "No more, please, and thank you, from the glass you gave me earlier; it's heavy stuff; I'm feeling too relaxed. It's really good"

Wilmar smiled, "I'm glad you like it, would anyone else like to try it"

There was a "no thank you" response in unison.

Wilmar shrugged a look of disappointment on his expression, "Your loss"

Dude spoke up, "I've changed my mind, I'm interested in trying out the drink. I've never had honey mead before"

Brishine gave Dude a bewildered expression. Kerry pinched the bridge of his nose. Kashmir, gave him a slow thumbs up, followed by a drunk goofy expression.

Wilmar poured a glass and started to walk forward only to suddenly transport right in front of Dude.

Dude startled, fell back off his chair.

Wilmar grinned and helped Dude back up with his one free hand, "I'm sorry, I probably should've given you a heads up before I teleported right in front of you. Here", Wilmar handed him a glass, "This is from a batch I've made recently, it'll warm your stomach up"

Dude took a sip, it had the sweetness of honey, with a fluttering reminder there was alcohol in each sip.

Dude felt the warmth in his stomach, "This is delicious, thank you!"

Kerry and Brishine watched as Dude proceeded to finish the rest of the glass. Kashmir had fallen asleep in his chair.

Wilmar, looking amused, calmly took the glass away from Dude's hand and stated, "Moving," before reappearing next to the desk. Wilmar placed the glass down on the desk, "I used to sell this mead, but the local taverns advised me of the patrons giving complaints of the temporary side effects that weren't ideal"

Dude, eyes went wide, stammered, "um, what side effects?"

Willmar put the bottle away on a shelf, "There was nothing to be concerned with. There were only issues with prolonged effects due to excess consumption. I had to temporarily halt the sale of my drinks. I'm still conducting more experiments to get the ideal results; R & D is very time-consuming"

Brishine, looking over at her sleeping sibling, "R and D?"

Wilmar rolled his eyes, "Reaction and Detriments." Wilmar turned to face them, a look of excitement in his expression, "I'm looking into making alcoholic drinks more purposeful. Why just get the same ole' inebriation when you can also obtain a special ability? I found most tavern goers found flight to be a delight." His smile suddenly waltered, "My oversight was not testing it on multiple races, instead of just one. My folly found out too late that it affects different races, but not two races experience the same reaction. Even then, the reaction may vary. It's all very frustrating"

Dude, looking concerned, "What are some of the potential side effects?"

Wilmar lifted a hand and started messing with his ear, "Well, for elves-"

Wilmar pointed towards Kashmir.

Who leaned forward, eyes went wide, honey started to drip from his nose.

Kashmir hurled, honey splattered onto the ground.

Wilmar looked disgusted, "I'm not cleaning that up." Wilmar tried not to gag, "That.....is one of the side effects for elves. Now for a human, like yourself, you're about to experience it any moment now"

Dude leaned forward, eyes wide, "My shoulders, my back, they feel like they're heating up. I think they are swelling up," the Dude cried out in pain. Dude fell forward off his chair. Kerry rushed to his side.

Dude reached behind him; his back suddenly sprouted wings. The wings look similar to those of an insect.

The wings started to flutter. Dude had lifted off the ground awkwardly at first, but gradually got the hang of it.

Kerry watched as Dude ascended, concern presented in his expression. Dude, who was on the verge of panicking, started to calm down. "This is...sort of fun"

The back of Dude's head then collided with the ceiling, "ow"

Ari didn't look amused, "That was inconsiderate and reckless of you, using my friends as test experiments"

Wilmar shook his head, "I found it fair, as they were going to ask me for something soon anyway. Now that they helped me, I can now help them with their minor problems"

Ari, looking like she wanted to stand but couldn't in her current form, raised her tone instead, "I want you to be more clear with your intentions going forward. While some of us had walked into your home by their choice, some of us were brought here into your home without consent"

Wilmar's expression went hard, "I'll remind you that I've been a good host; I've offered drinks, a place to sit, and a warm place to stay that's away from the cold breeze outside. If you want to go right to business, so be it. We'll start with you", he pointed at Kashmir, "as your side effect wasn't as pleasant as your friend's"

Kashmir is still coughing out honey. Looked to be miserable. Honey, drinking from the nose and eyes. Had been taking big gulps of air between hacking out honey.

Brishine looked lived, "I'll speak for him, as he is obviously suffering from your concoction"

Wilmar squinted his eyes, "I'd choose my next words carefully if I were you. I can understand your frustration, but I can easily remove both of you. My patience is thin but I will take your request for help, as he did test my drink"

Brishine, "I want you to cure my brother Kashmir now, for he is unwell, thanks to you"

Kashmir grabbed Brishine's shoulder and shook his head in disagreement. He spoke with a gurgled voice, "Nooo....ask....for...bro...ther"

Brishine, turned to look back towards Wilmar, "I request that you make my brother well and that you assist us with-"

Wilmar shook his finger, "It's too late to change your request; I agreed to help with one of your issues, not multiple"

Wilmar snapped a finger.

Kashmir's demeanor changed, he took a deep breath. Relief in his expression before it quickly turned to one of sadness, "Let me drink another, I will gladly consume another for another request"

Brishine spoke quickly, "I will as well-"

Wilmar sighed, "No. I already have the information now on what happens to elves drinking my concoction. I don't need to see you spitting and making a mess on my floor as well"

Brishine dashed over to Wilmar, grabbing him by the shoulders, "Please, we need your help-"

Kashmir rushed over, speaking over Brishine while trying to pull her away from Wilmar, "Let him go, we don't want to upset him!"

Wilmar snapped, "Shut up. Shut up, shut up, shut up! I've had enough"

Brishine and Kashmir stepped back, their eyes wide.

Kashmir spoke, "We're sorry-"

"I said shut up!"

Wilmar raised one hand, making a grabbing motion. Kashmir floated off the ground. Wilmar swung his right hand hard towards the wall. With his left hand, he snapped his fingers right as Kashmir hit the tree wall. Kashmir fused into the wall. His body merged with the wall. Before Kashmir could scream, he was fully integrated into the tree. His silhouette was carved into the wall, being the only sign that he was there.

Brishine stood speechless. She turned, with her hands out, ready to strangle Wilmar. Her voice was fierce, "Bring him back!". She was about to rush towards Wilmar, but a chair flew towards Wilmar's face before shattering.

To Brishine's disappointment, the chair shattered to pieces before it got too close to strike Wilmar's face. The old wizard's face was furious, he quickly swung away another chair that Ari threw towards Wilmar with her power. Ari's hands had an aura of yellow, energy flowing through them.

Ari focused, using the drive from her mind to remotely lift the last chair, her chair, remaining off the ground. Ari fell to the floor. Her expression focused as she used her fingers and hand to telepathically guide the chair. Ari spun the chair for a moment before It burst into flame. She then pulled her right arm back before pushing it forward. The chair flew forward Wilmar.

Wilmar's expression of rage shifted to annoyance. He snapped his fingers and shattered the chair, "Now, that's enough-"

Several bottles fell hard onto Wilmar's head, as Dude, from above, emptied his supply of bottles of elixirs received from the merchant earlier.

Wilmar, annoyed and rage now increasing, glared up at the Dude, flying above. Right as Wilmar glanced up, Brishine swung her fist directly into Wilmar's face.

The punch, landing successfully, caused Wilmar to stumble back. Wilmar glanced at Brishine and snapped his fingers.

Brishine vanished.

Nothing was left to mark that she was ever there.

Dude flew directly to Wilmar, extended his fist, and yelled with anguish, "Bring her back!"

Wilmar, who just glared at him. Moved one hand in a swift motion. That hand made a grasp motion that held Dude in place, "I'm not done with you-"

A bottle of honey mead levitates above Wilmar's head. It fell with a thud onto the top of the old man's head.

Wilmar let out a painful loud cry; he fell forward but caught his bearings, his right arm still extended out with a visible grasp motion that was holding Dude mid-air.

The wizard looked over and saw Ari's bright hands, radiating with yellow. His eyes "I've just had enough from you sister"

Wilmar reached out with his free hand towards Ari. Ari lifted off the ground and flew towards Wilmar, her neck now in her grasp.

A mad, gleeful expression was visibly twisting and mutating on Wilmar's face. The skin of the face twitching and slowly melting, "Now, It's about time that-"

Wilmar was suddenly cut off but a knife pressed against his neck.

Kerry, who had successfully snuck up behind Wilmar, pressed the knife firmly on Wilmar's neck and spoke with a stern tone, "Let them go, now or I'll drive this blade in"

Wilmar, through gritted teeth, "I have unfinished business. I still have my end of the deal to fulfill for the brat. Once I do, you three are free to go"

Dude's wings faded away. Wilmar released his grasp, causing Dude to fall suddenly to the ground with a thud. Dude, his chest towards the ground, slowly got up. Visibly in pain but trying to contain it.

Wilmar glanced at Dude, "What can I help you with? You helped me with my experiment, and now I'll help you. I can honor that. Just remember that you can only make one request"

Dude looked over at Kerry and Ari.

Kerry looked at him with a stoic expression and nodded towards Ari.

Ari was frantically trying to loosen the grip of the hand that tightened around her neck.

Dude, then looked over at the Kashmir silhouette of Kashmir on the wall, and then to the spot where Brishine once stood. He stood, appearing internally torn, expressing a saddened look.

Wilmar tightened his grip around Ari's neck, "Hurry, or I'll decide for you"

A small amount of blood trickled down Wilmar's neck as Kerry pressed the blade more firmly down onto his neck.

Wilmar grunted, "Don't push me, I still have a free hand. I'm currently reasonable for the moment but I can easily go back to being unreasonable, real quick"

Dude's eyes widened. "I'll have Ari make the request in my place. loosen your grip, so she can speak"

Wilmar loosened his grip and glanced directly into Ari's eyes, "I enjoy seeing my little sister struggle, but I'm curious to see what you want"

Dude spoke, "Ari, why didn't you tell us that Wilmar was your brother?"

Ari rasped, "Because he's not and-"

Wilmar cut her off, "....I'm not Wilmaaar". The old melting wizard's face completely fell off. The skull underneath showing. The jaw let out a constant cackling laughter. The old wrinkled hands exposed had melted away to reveal bones. The wizard's robe burst into flame.

Kerry fell back, startled.

The fire sizzled away suddenly, and the old wizard's bones suddenly glowed and grew a thin black coating before a sphere of darkness covered the figure for a split moment before the dark sphere dissipated away.

There, standing in front of Ari, was a woman. The bones that gripped around Ari's neck were replaced by the grip wearing white gloves.

There was a look of amusement in the woman's expression, with a look of lingering hysteria within her eyes.

She had black hair with red highlights. The ends of the hair faded to white. She wore a wine-red robe with a black, bent crooked mage hat.

Ari gasped, "Rey...."

The woman gleamed, "Rey to you, but to others who respect me, I am Reyna, the mad sorcerous. I'm rather proud of that title, I feel like I've earned it"

Dude stammered, "Reyna...I've read about you. If the tales are true, you're a fire deity whose growing desire for power drove you mad. You have done some truly unforgivable things-"

Reyna cut in, "I'd be surprised if any of the tales weren't true. I do love power but sometimes I get bored of the killing and draining others to absorb their power routine. It's nice to mix things up, so I picked up a few hobbies"

Kerry spoke, "So you decided to be a kind old wizard and make mead in your free time?"

Ari smirked, "I've killed the 'Good Wizard Wilmar.'" She spoke his name with disgust, "I heard him begging to escape his prison at Default. So I helped him out by ending his life. They took his body out of the cell at some point. Wish granted. Since he wouldn't be needing his old life, I pick up this persona from time to time for my amusement"

Kerry stomped over to her, "Your presence on his land sickens me"

Reyna swung her free hand towards Kerry. He flew across the room, crashing against the crates at the other end of the room. Mead was spilling out across the floor as Kerry groaned.

She tilted her head, looking back at Ari, "I'm still waiting to hear your request"

Ari's eyebrows furrowed, "I want my prior physical form back, I want to fight you on my own two feet"

Reyna cackled, "Thinking about yourself for once, that's a first. Instead of helping those who have perished? How amusing. No complaints from me"

Reyna, with a free hand, pointed two fingers with her free hand towards Ari's fins, then snapped her fingers. Ari's fin began to transform. Reyna let go of Ari.

Ari screamed as her legs were returning and her mermaid half faded away.

Reyna walked over to her desk and leaned onto it, "I should've mentioned the transformation process may give you some minor discomfort"

As Ari stood up, Reyna paused, looking away for a moment, with a look of excitement on her face, "I believe I hear a desperate cry of a King." Reyna patted her rob and gave a fake apologetic smile at each of them, "As much as I would love to stay and play a bit longer. I'm about to fulfill a prayer that is about to make my day a whole lot more interesting." A glimmer appeared from her hand before she waved it in a swift motion that caused Kerry and Dude to be tossed back. "I do see that there's still some fight in each of your eyes so I won't leave you disappointed." She reached down into a hidden pocket in her robe, pulled out a red flute, and began to blow out a little tune, "I would like to introduce you three to the wonderful hard workers who helped with the necessary ingredients needed for my honey concoction"

There was a buzzing sound that gradually grew louder. The buzzing was radiating from the hole in the ceiling.

Ari, Dude, and Kerry stared at the ceiling in concern.

Reyna suddenly appeared next to Ari, she leaned in to whisper into her ear. "I couldn't have imagined that you staying alive would have benefited me more than just killing you. Since you've been so generous in letting me drain your power for all these years, it's only fair that I tell you this. I wanted to thank you for giving me the extra strength I needed. I've been able to take down so many who dare defy me. Mages, nobles, gods. All begged for mercy after witnessing my power. I couldn't have done it without you. Their blood, their cries, their suffering...I couldn't have done it without you"

Ari turned to face her.

Reyna was gone.

A faint sizzle faded away from her portal

The floor trembled.

There was the sound of tools, bottles, and glasses hitting the floor.

Constant tink noises from the sound of bottles colliding within the crates.

The buzzing above them began to thunder.

Chapter 21

The face of a goblin peered out from the hole in the ceiling. Followed by several more faces of goblins. The creatures that emerged were larger than a humanoid and had the head of a goblin and the body of a bee. Their stingers were sharp and intimidating. Dozens of the goblin bee abominations were swarming out.

The goblin bees flew in circles above, some escaping out by crashing through the windows.

A goblin bee flew down, stinging out towards Dude. Ari conjured out water from the hand to splash the bee. The face of the goblin sneered and retreated.

Ari stood weakly, "I'm out of power and I'm feeling weak"

Kerry pulled on Dude and Ari's shoulders, "Let's move"

They ran down the stairs.

Kerry spotted the butler dwarf, swinging and jabbing the air with the blade that was supposed to be locked up securely.

The dwarf butler downstairs looked startled, hiding but failing to hide the sword behind him, "what's going on up there-"

The goblin bees followed close behind the trio. They began flying in circles above the ceiling. The weird bee creatures bumped and knocked things over. Many had mischievous goblin smiles and they purposely broke and smashed valuables around the office.

The dwarf grumbled, "I don't get paid enough for this" and ran towards the double doors.

Kerry ran towards the dwarf but stepped back when a goblee flew towards him, trying to sting his chest. Kerry quickly dove to the side. When the goblee dove towards him, he reached out with both hands and grabbed the stinger. Kerry pressed the goblee back with as much resistance as he could muster.

Ari ran up and punched the goblee in the face. The goblee relented.

Kerry took this opportunity to push the stinger upwards. The goblee's head now faced the ground. Kerry wrapped his legs and arms around the bee, slamming the goblees head onto the ground.

Dude ran past the dwarf and shoved open the double doors, "Sorry, excuse me, sir"

The dwarf, the moment he was standing outside the door immediately yelled, "GOBLEES! Goblees! They're back!"

A goblee grabbed the dwarf and lifted him off the ground.

The goblee, with its two goblin-looking arms, held the dwarf's armpits. The butler dwarf kicked, grumbled, and cursed, swinging but failing to hit the goblee with the sword that was too big for a dwarf to weld.

Kerry and Ari stood outside the doorway, glancing up to see what Dude was watching.

Kerry cursed, "That damned dwarf has my sword"

The goblee made a hard dive toward the trunk of the Kleon tree before suddenly turning to the left.

The dwarf hit the trunk of the tree hard, and the sword fell out of his limp hand.

Kerry, focused, caught the sword before it hit the ground.

The trio could see the goblee carry the knocked-out dwarf toward the top of the tree.

The buzzing noise was getting louder from behind them.

The trio dove to the right to take cover.

Dozens of goblin bee hybrids flew out the double doors, towards the town square.

Some of the citizens were cackling, while others were running.

The cackling citizens were convulsing. Their limbs and body were slowly transforming into goblees. Bystanders, mostly outsiders who were watching the locals transform, started to retreat.

Screams were coming from multiple directions around the marketplace.

One of the merchants nearby yelled, "From the depths of hell nah, I'm out"

Kerry turned to Dude and Ari, "We need to leave"

Dude looked up, searching the skies, "where is Carrot"

Kerry yelled, "Carrot! Carrot!"

A goblee turned and flew towards Kerry.

Kerry took out his blade and swung it widely, "Stay back, this stinger has seen more battle than you, I can guarantee that much"

The goblee growled and flew off.

Dude looked around, "I wish I had a weapon right about now"

Smoke started to spread in the area as nearby homes and shops caught fire.

Ari reached into her bag and pulled out a lone carrot. "I'm about out of power; if I pass out, please carry me." She held the carrot with one hand and then waved her other hand above it. Ari immediately dropped the carrot and stepped back.

The carrot began to multiply quickly until there were a good hundred carrots on the ground.

Ari passed out. Dude and Kerry are caught here.

There was a sudden shadow covering the three of them.

It was several goblees flying towards them, stingers out front.

Before they could get close, the goblees were engulfed in flame.

Dude cheered, "Carrot! You're here, just in time to save us"

The dragon began devouring the carrots on the ground.

Dude shook his head, "Or those goblin freaks were in the way"

Kerry spoke, "Let's go, get onto Carrot's back". Kerry and Dude lifted Ari off the ground, carrying her and placing her onto Carrot's back. She had passed out from over-exertion.

Dude and Kerry climbed onto Carrot's back next.

Carrot finished consuming the carrots and looked up. Hundreds of bees filled the sky.

Dude patted Carrot's neck, "Let's get out of here"

Carrot flew up, engulfing any bees in the way in deadly flames.

The burnt, crispy corpses of goblees fell onto the ground below.

The smell of rotten burnt honey filled the air.

Carrot flew away from Kleon, a smirk present on the dragon's face as she engulfed one more goblee in flames before ascending higher into the sky.

Chapter 22

Carrot landed right onto Dude's once vibrant garden next to Kerry's Keep.

Kerry, Dude helped Ari down. Ari assured them she was fine, and that it just took a moment for her to get used to walking back on two feet again.

Running his fingers through his hair, Dude spoke, "I don't know what, what to do, what do we do? We can't just leave there? We-"

Kerry placed a hand on Dude's shoulder, "Please, take a deep breath and find a seat-"

After several deep breaths, Dude groaned, "My chest hurts. Is anyone else having intense chest pain? I need to go for a walk"

Dude headed towards Kerry's keep.

Ari was about to follow when Kerry spoke, "Ari, please, let him be"

Ari, looked back at the man, looking both annoyed and uncertain, "What, why? He needs my support-"

"He needs space, this is the first time he's seen people he's cared about die in front of him. Give him a moment to decompress"

"That's ridiculous. I've raised him and I can't just let him go through this alone"

"I've helped raise him too. I've seen many of my good friends and family die out in combat and disease. I only ask that you give him a few moments. He's in shock and it will take a bit to"

"Alright, I get it. I'll leave him to his thoughts for now but by nightfall, I'm going to talk to him"

"Thank you"

✳✳✳

The sun had set, and the stars had not yet shown their faces.

Ari walked out of the opening of the castle and looked towards the beach. She noticed a lone figure holding a lit torch down by the pier.

Ari walked down the slope. As she approached, she noticed the boat was untied and was rocking against the pier. She observed Dude, who appeared to be examining the inner workings of the sail.

"Were you planning on leaving us behind?"

Dude frowned, avoiding eye contact, "I'm not sure. I was contemplating it but I'm still here. One reason is that I'd feel worse than I feel now if I did leave without saying goodbye. Also, I'm still getting familiar with the process of sailing the boat. I've read about it, but it's more difficult to execute the steps. Then I forgot which side is the Port and Starside. I mean Starboard. My confidence in commandeering this vessel went downhill from there." He looked at Ari, "I'm sorry. I have some thoughts to process and other thoughts to figure out." He reached down and picked up a rope that was attached to the boat, "Here, help me dock"

Dude tossed the rope, and Ari caught it with ease.

Ari tied the boat to the pier, "I was wondering if you had a moment, I have some things I would like to discuss with you"

"I've got nothing better to do, do tell". Dude hopped onto the pier. He walked to the edge of the pier and sat down, his feet dangling over the edge.

Ari walked over and sat next to him. Dude was staring at the sky, looking at nothing in particular.

Ari kicked her legs, and her toes graced the water, "A part of me will miss the tail fin. Now I gotta deal with toenail maintenance"

Dude tried but failed to contain a smile.

Ari looked into the sky, "I can tell you're not much of a talker, so I'll talk for a bit. You may want to hear what I have to say. Just in case you see Reyna again someday"

Dude slightly turned to face her, his interest piqued.

Ari continued, "Reyna is my older sister. Me, Reyna, and Deyra were infants created and sent from the mortal overseer god Glennabelle, who resides on the Darksilver star. She heard the desperate married couple's prayers for children. Glennabelle deemed the couple fit to raise three children, me and my two sisters. The couple awoke one day to find three infant daughters sleeping by their side.

The couple was grateful and feeling beyond blessed. Telling Glennabelle through prayer that they will do their best to raise them right. Little did the couple know that they were not raising mere mortal girls, but instead were raising little deities that would live long past their parents' short mortal lives.

Mom and Dad were strict but fair. Taught the value of hard work, good ethics, and everything else a child should know. We were the ideal children until the age of thirteen. Beyra and I usually behaved, we had the occasional incidents of harmless mischief and shenanigans that are expected from a young child. Reyna, on the other hand, suddenly declared herself the older sibling, even though we were all the same age. She would often run off and find amusement by setting things on fire and picking on gnomes. My parents would scold her, but she only became more careful about covering her tracks when she would sneak off to cause mischief for the locals near Wind Gnome village.

One day, the sheriff of Wind Gnome arrived, along with many of the locals, at our home doorstep, advising if they catch Reyna causing any more damage to the town, that more drastic measures will be taken, such as taking the matters to the Kingdom's court. As Reyna set the children's school building ablaze. Luckily, no one was hurt or Reyna would've faced some serious repercussions.

My parents were so mad. They had to cough up the funds to pay for the school to be rebuilt. We had to live on scraps for years.

Reyna seemed immune to any form of discipline. For the first time in years, my parents reached out to Glennabelle for guidance.

Glennabelle heard their plea and listened to my parents regarding Reyna's behavior. Glennabelle was so appalled by the behavior that she descended from the Darksilver star, onto our world to speak to my parents directly. The goddess offered them to take Reyna to the Guidance star, a star that held troubled deities. They had many gods from other stars there that enforced strict discipline on young deities who were disturbing the natural order of the mortal world, with the goal of removing their selfish and malevolent tendencies.

One day, Glennabelle knocked at my parents' door three years later, returning and presenting Reyna. Glennabelle advised that gods on the Guidance star have deemed her ready to return to the mortal world. Reyna had returned calm, collected, and respectful. Glennabelle stayed at our home for an entire week to survey Reyna's behavior. After Glennabelle felt satisfied that Reyna had changed for the better, she left our home.

It was great for the next few years, Reyna caused no trouble at all. When I looked at her, she always had this twinkle of madness lingering behind her eyes. She kept to herself, socially distant. Reyna never spoke of her time away on the Guidenace star, and My parents never asked. My sister Beyra and I would ask her to talk to us about it, but she would lash out and walk away, not wanting to talk at all. Foolish of us, maybe perhaps things could've been different if we did. I wish I tried a bit more.

During our 18th year raised by our parents, they were reaching their golden years. My sisters and I knew that it was time for us to leave the nest. But our parents asked us to wait for Glennabelle's blessing before we headed out to tackle the world and start our own stories.

As my two sisters and I stepped out with our meager belongings. Glennabelle arrived and opened a gateway to them. Telling them they have earned the right to the afterlife with her blessing. We hugged them goodbye. As they stepped through the portal, we saw them smiling proudly at us right before the portal phased out of existence.

Glennabelle then turned our attention to us. She was telling us that we have now earned the privilege to use our internal strength, which is essentially our unique powers. Through enough study, practice, trial, and error, we can harness it and make it our own. There are limitations and innovations, but with enough creativity and determination, almost anything is possible.

She asked us to stand side by side. She started with me and pressed her hand against my forehead. The moment her hand pressed against my forehead, I felt lighter, externally lighter in weight but more full of heavy energy inside. It's tough to describe this newly gained power that was surging from within me, flowing throughout my veins, just eager and screaming to be used.

Glennabelle asked to wait to finish the procedure before we tried out our powers. For she wanted to guide us.

As we each nodded our goodbye Glennabelle. She told us to strive to help others and to never hesitate to reach out if...."

Ari paused before she began wiping her eyes.

Ari stopped and just covered her eyes with her hands for a moment, trying to contain her emotion.

"I'm sorry, please just give me a moment"

Dude, immediately pulled her in, consoling her, "What's wrong? Please, take as much time as you need, I'm here to listen when you're ready"

Ari nodded, "Sorry…seeing my sister alive… it…", she went silent.

Dude waited patiently, he gazed at the stars.

There was the sound of footsteps on the pier behind them.

Dude glanced back to see Kerry walking up.

He sat down at the edge next to them. He gave a few respectful pats on Ari's back, and then he glanced at the horizon.

Kerry spoke, "There's an overseer god on every star. There are more stars than there are people. So legend has it that if you see a shooting star, it's because an overseer is bored, and to kill the boredom, they are willing to grant a lucky viewer a wish. If I see a shooting star tonight. I'll wish for someone with a big ole' pointy iron boot to kick Reyna's behind"

Ari made a sound that was somewhere between a cough and a chuckle. Dude started laughing and Kerry glanced back at them with a smile. Ari ended up coughing from all the laughter.

Dude patted her back gently, "you, okay?"

Ari wiped her eyes, "Yeah, thank you. I just haven't had a good laugh in a while."

Her smile faltered, "I've never shared this information with anyone before"

She continued, "After Glennabelle blessed me by unlocking the power within me, she unlocked Beyra's and then Reyna's inner power.

Immediately after Reyna had her power unlocked. She had this twisted smile like she was waiting for this exact moment.

Reyna had slid out a blade and stabbed Glennabelle. Reya stood over Glennabelle, anger in her eyes, "That is for sending me to that hellhole of a star. I certainly did learn a thing or two there".

Beyra and I stood in shock, trying to comprehend what just happened. As Glennabelle fell to the ground, Reyna turned and stabbed Beyra. Glennabelle lay on the ground, unresponsive. Beyra was then tackled onto the ground. Reyna pressed both her hands on the side of Beyra's head. An aura of power was being drained from Beyra's head and transferred into Reyna's hand. A look of pure bliss was present on Reyna's face.

The color drained from Beyra's eyes and she stared into the sky, lifeless.

I…felt helpless. I aimed my hands towards her.

Reyna laughed, "You don't even know what you're doing"

Reyna stood up, walked over to me, and knocked me to the ground.

I was terrified.

Reyna pressed both her hands on the side of my head. I felt power being drained from me, but not only that, I felt what can only be described as days, heartbeats, and dreams being taken from me. I felt weaker by the second. I felt like I was going to pass out before a hand grabbed my wrist.

Glennabelle had teleported us to her domain on the Darksilver Star. Glennabelle collapsed, bleeding at her side. I guided her to a seat. She told me she needed just a moment to heal. Her wound was slowly closing up before my eyes.

She told me that she didn't expect Reyna to be concerned about the darkness within her soul and truly believed that Reyna was truly a good soul. She told me that even a god can be wrong sometimes. I asked her what she could do to stop Reyna or how Reyna would pay for her crimes. She told me it's not that simple. Glennabelle told me that once a deity turns eighteen, they are their own being, and the rules are different. They are a god now, and that can only be stopped by death due to it being very rare that their character changes once they are set in their ways. She advised that it was a political thing and that it was now in the hands of mortals. It was up to the mortals on the fate of a god.

Glennabelle supported me in my grief. Once I was ready, she taught and guided me on how to use and harness my inner powers. For over a hundred years I've trained. Glennabelle told me that she senses that my powers are drained but doesn't know how Reyna is doing so. She placed a blessing on me to at least limit the power draining.

Once we both felt that I was ready to return to the mortal world. I decided that I, formerly known as Ayra, decided to change my name to Ari Feirune, for my safety in case Reyna returns.

I decided to start a new life on my own as a simple mage. I've been living life in my cozy cottage in the Merry Mystic Woods for over a hundred years with issue until...you know the rest. My once cozy life went to a complete dung pile when I got captured by King Huber, got turned into a mermaid, yada yada, and here I am now"

She wiped her eyes.

Dude spoke, "I'm sorry Ari"

" Thank you. I'll be okay. I feel better now, so much better now. It's nice to finally share my trauma with people who care. I've been alone for so long"

"Are you sure you'll be, okay?"

"I'm okay now, I promise"

"That's good", Kerry patted Ari's back before standing up, "I didn't get to hear the start of your story but I've heard enough I'm feeling inspired now to kick some ass. let's get some rest. Because in the morning, we've got some planning to do"

Chapter 23

In the morning, the three sat around a fire set in the bailey, discussing their next course of action.

Kerry wanted to have them show up on Carrot's back, having a dragon be the key advantage to being taken seriously by the King and evil powerful mage Reyna.

Ari argued that Carrot would be great if they were to intimidate the king, but it wouldn't be as effective in deterring Reyna.

Dude wanted a more stealthy approach, to scope out and then meet up afterward to plan their next course of action. He argued they needed more information.

Kerry didn't like the idea of sneaking around, but Dude argued that if he dressed up in full knight get-up, he'd be able to blend in.

Kerry recommended that Ari dress up as a chambermaid, as the guards don't question or interact with the chambermaids.

Ari's only concern is crossing paths with the King or Sir Archibald, who would recognize her face.

"Can you change your appearance by chance, or any of our appearances?" Dude asked, indicating that ideas were already forming in his head.

Ari shook her head, "I can, at best, change hair color; my power is still very limited. Convincing disguises, such as face or body transformations, would require a lot of power"

The three of them stared into the fire, which shifted quickly from left to right as the wind grew stronger.

Dude raised his eyebrows, "The wind is strong today, a perfect day to sail a boat"

Kerry turned to look at him. "Sailing the boat while a storm is brewing. It's dangerous and reckless," he gleamed. It's bold; I like it; what did you have in mind?"

"What if we used the boat to enter the castle? Ari, you spoke of a dungeon where there was a doorway that led to a hidden coastal cave. We take the boat there; we get entry into the dungeon, and separate from there. We stay scout for information, then at midnight, we meet at the cove and leave. We make our final plan back here with our new intel"

Ari and Kerry pondered for a moment, a soft drizzle began to fall.

Kerry, rubbing his chin, spoke, "What about if one of us doesn't show up at the cave at midnight? If they were captured or worse. It would be only a matter of time before the guards investigate and find our boat"

Dude stood up, "I'm not sure." He started pacing.

Ari looked over at Kerry, "Do you have any alliances with other knights?"

Kerry looked grim, "I've been away far too long to know who is left to trust. They are loyal to the king, and I would be asking them to turn a blind eye. I'd be asking them to commit treason. Keep in mind, the knights believe I died an honorable death defending the prince. I don't know how they react to seeing me back"

Dude placed another log into the fire, "Also, there's that magic mirror that Ari used back in the dungeon; we don't know if someone is using it to survey the kingdom. Ari, can someone ask the mirror to view anyone anytime?"

Ari shook her head, "Thankfully not, they couldn't ask to see us right now. Its reach can only view activity mostly within the castle walls. It is possible to view activity outside the castle walls, but not so much to be concerned with. You have to ask to see certain rooms or people individually. It can only show one scene at a time"

"That's good to know. We need more hands-" Dude turned to look at Kerry with a look of hope and excitement, "How about the funds we got from helping Inkbert? Can we use what coin we have left to hire help?"

Kerry shook his head, "We don't have enough coin to hire help to compensate for the level of risk we're taking. The penalty for getting caught is being thrown in the dungeon, long hours of torture, or execution. Perhaps all three".

Ari looked over to Kerry, "We are taking a big risk here; I want to go back and confront my sister and the King, but why are you taking such a big risk, Kerry and Dude? Why wouldn't you want to stay here, in safety and solitude"

Kerry sternly spoke, "Don't be ridiculous. I will not go into this alone, after everything we've been through." Kerry tossed a log into the fire, "I will admit that it isn't entirely selfless reasons; I am looking forward to confronting my brother and the King for their wrongdoings"

Dude spoke, "I don't care for the Kingdom, the King or Queen, but-" He looked at them both, "Anywhere I get to support my friends is more ideal than staying safe and alone in a tower"

The wind picked up.

The rain, no longer a sprinkle, had quickly extinguished the flame.

Kerry smiled, and bellowed out, "Well friends, what are we waiting for? Let's prepare the boat. This quest isn't going to get any safer"

The three of them walked out of the castle's entryway. They saw at the bottom of the slope towards the beach that Carrot was devouring apples from another cart that was commandeered from some poor merchant.

Dude rushed down, "I see a merchant hiding underneath the cart"

Kerry and Ari rushed down after him.

There was an elf, whimpering underneath the cart, seeing them yelled, "Help! Save me from this dragon!"

Dude looked up towards Carrot, "Carrot, could you give us a moment?"

The dragon exhaled some steam from its nostrils. Carrot opened her maw to take one more mouthful of apples before flying off.

Kerry helped the elf up, "Are you ok?"

The elf, soaked and covered in mud, tried but failed to wipe the mud away, "No, yes, I mean no. Is that dragon yours?" He looked equally annoyed and skeptical toward Dude.

Dude gave an apologetic expression, "I"m sorry. Please forgive my noble steed"

The elf eyes went wide in realization, "Wait, you're the lad and you," he looked at Kerry, "are the two who helped me back in Kleon"

The elf kicked the totaled cart in frustration, "There goes my new business of selling apples. I spent everything I had earned from Inkbert to buy that transport cart and apples. Not to mention the horse I borrowed, that got left behind. I'm going to have to pay them for the lost horse. This is a terrible terrible day".Dude, recalling that day, remembered that coin pouch in his shirt pocket, "I'm sorry, here are the coins you handed me that day we first met. I hope this covers it"

Kerry facepalmed, "I totally forgot about that, maybe we could've hired help if-"

The elf's eyes lit up, "That's more than enough." He reached out and took back the coin pouch eagerly; he smiled at Dude, now in better spirits, "It looks like the stars aligned, and it was meant for us to meet again. Let me introduce myself, "I'm Verse. Verse Baldree". He put a hand out in front of him.

Dude shook his hand, "I'm Dude-" he paused, looking around, before looking at Ari, "I'm Dude Feirune. This is my-" He pointed towards Ari, "sister, Ari Feirune"

Ari and Kerry gave Dude a quick quizzical look.

Verse stuck out his hand, and Ari shook his hand, "We haven't met, It's nice to meet you"

Ari nodded, "It's nice to meet you; as you can tell by the field of broken food carts out in the field, Dude's dragon has quite the appetite."

Dude shrugged, "It can't be helped. Perhaps you could someday start an insurance business for traveling merchants to have coverage if their cart were to be taken or inventory was consumed by a dragon without permission. Could be promising"

Verse looked thoughtful, "I like the sound of that, sounds promising."

Dude looked at him, "I may have to ask my dragon to disturb only merchants who don't have your coverage so you can actually make a profit"

Verses rushed over and patted Dude on the shoulder with glee. "I like this, Dude already; we'll have to set something up later." He glanced at Kerry and smiled, "I didn't forget about you, I promise." He stuck out a hand towards Kerry.

Kerry shook it, "I'm Kerry....just Kerry"

Verses nodded, "I can appreciate a man with only one name, makes it much easier for me to remember it"

Dude looked out towards the water, the waves growing in size, and the sky darkening, "Let's head inside the tower"

Kerry nodded, "The storm is not relenting. We'll start our journey tomorrow"

Verses jumped in, "You're heading out? May I join you, I'd rather not walk back on foot to Wetmore alone in these dangerous times"

"We'll discuss it once we're out of the rain"

Thunder erupted as the four of them headed up the hill towards the castle.

Chapter 24

"Have you ever ridden a horse?"

At the top of the tower, the four of them leaned against different crates around the room that weren't under a leaky part of the roof.

Verse looked back at Dude, "Yes, why do you ask?"

"If you can ride a horse, you can basically ride a dragon"

"What?"

"We need someone on standby to be with Carrot while the three of us run some errands at the castle"

"Why me?"

"Why not you? It's an experience. How often do you get to travel by dragon?"

"No, ok, let me rephrase the question. Why? Why me?"

"If someone doesn't keep an eye on Carrot, she might wander off and scoop up another helpless merchant's food cart. If someone is on the saddle, she's suddenly on her best behavior"

Kerry said, "All we ask, while each of us has our own tasks to take care of, is that you just watch Carrot. When we're each done with our task, Ari will give the signal. Your job is to keep an eye out for that signal, and then swoop in the get us once you see it" He pointed towards Ari, who closed her hand into a fist and then opened it. The palm of her hand flashed a bright white light. She closed her hand into a fist once more, and the light disappeared.

Ari looked at Verse, "I can only shine the light for a few minutes at most, so please pay attention from the skies"

Verse's face went pale, "...the skies? you want me to keep an eye on Carrot while riding a saddle on Carrot's back. While keeping an eye from the sky, high above Default castle, for Ari's signal to fly down for an unknown amount of time?"

"Pretty much and it's only till Midnight...ideally"

"What happens if I never see the signal"

Kerry, who was trying to close the window shutters correctly as they opened and constantly closed from the wind, grunted with annoyance as the shutters didn't cooperate; "We'll be entering the castle by boat. Carrot will be tailing the boat from the sky. Once the boat is out of sight when it enters the cave, Carrot will be circling the sky above the castle. All you need to do is ask Carrot to descend when you see the signal. Easy. If it's midnight, and there's no signal, Carrot will descend. She gets tired around that time; you'll be fine"

Verse stood up, looking done with the conversation, "I'd rather walk on foot alone back in town, I don't want to partake in this request. You're asking for quite a lot"

Kerry rubbed his temples for a moment before exhaling. He looked at Verse, "I'll make it worth the trouble"

Verse lifted an eyebrow, "I'm listening"

"Do you own a castle?"

"Um, no?"Kerry opened his arms, looking around in exaggeration, "I have the title to this very castle and a good portion of the land around it. I have no use for it." He looked directly at Verse, "If you do this, you have my word that this castle and the land it's on...is yours"

Verse looked at the leaking ceiling, "Hmm, It's a bit of a fixer-upper; it would take quite a bit of money for repairs, maintenance..."

Kerry smirked, "Take this into perspective, next time you see a cutie at the tavern, you can brag about owning a castle"

Verse's eyes went wide; he rushed over and rapidly shook Kerry's hand, "You, sir, have got yourself a deal"

***

The sky was clear the following day.

A sign that Dude, Kerry, and Ari found to be a good omen.

The boat sailed north, at a promising pace.

Up above in the clouds, Carrot tailed the vessel with ease.

Verse's eyes closed, and he clung to the dragon with his dear life. He held on in silence because his vocal cords had finally given out from the constant screaming since the moment Carrot bolted off the ground earlier that morning. His legs were clamped onto the sides of the saddle, and his arms held onto the dragon's neck tightly.

Carrot, unable to relay his thoughts, was relieved the elf finally ceased screaming. The dragon resisted the urge to buck off the passenger, as she knew it would disappoint her companions.

✳✳✳

On the boat, Kerry was guiding Dude on the fundamentals of sailing.

Dude, looked at Kerry for feedback after the necessary adjustments to get them back on course.

Kerry, nodded with approval, "Good work, you're getting the hang of this quickly"

Dude, smiling from the praise, "Thanks. I read a book about sailing back in the day. It just takes a moment to reflect on the information and then apply it. It's easier read than done"

Kerry sat down and unsheathed his sword. He took a cloth out to start cleaning the blade, "Perhaps we should change your alias worm"

"What? Why's that?"

Kerry chuckled. He looked satisfied at the sword's level of cleanliness, and began to apply oil to the blade, "I'll give you a moment to ponder that"

Ari, "Hey Dude, I have a question for you"

He looked over, "what did you want to know?"

"I was wondering why you introduced yourself to Verse with the surname Feirune"

Dude ran a hand through his hair, and a flush of embarrassment crossed his face. "I meant no disrespect. It's just that, I realized a while ago..." His eyes went distant for a moment.

Ari went up and placed a hand on his shoulder, "are you alright?" He shook his head, "Yes, I apologize. I just. I needed a moment" He turned to face Ari, "Thank you. I...I realized that my name can remind others of the name Dudesow. My folly for not changing my name entirely. So I figured when I introduce myself again, I'll give a surname. When said time happened, I didn't prepare a surname. So I quickly choose yours."

"That is fine, I was just startled when you introduced me as your sister"

"Oh, um. I said that for a reason. It was more said on the spot to sound legitimate. For a moment, I was going to say mother, but I didn't want to say mother because you don't look old enough to be my mother, but it was mostly just...I don't see you as my mother...more like, I see you like an older sister."

Ari stared at him for a moment in silence.

Dude continued, "I didn't mean to make things awkward between us-"

Ari went up and hugged him, "I assure you, Dudesow, you didn't"

Kerry looked away, he had an indescribable expression.

In the distance, the hazy silhouette of the Default Kingdom peaked over the horizon.

Chapter 25

As the boat neared the cliffside of the castle, the water was calm and the area was clear of other boats. They glanced around the bottom of the cliff for the entryway of the coastal cave.

Ari pointed out a jagged opening, "I believe that one is it"

The boat neared closer, and Kerry and Dude, the sail, hit the cliffside wall as it was taller than the entryway.

With an apologetic expression on her face, "I forgot to mention it's low and narrow. They took me away by rowboat"

Dude and Kerry lowered the sail and paddled toward the entryway. The three of them lowered their heads as they made their way in.

Once inside, the cave became more spacious. There was a pier, only a half-submerged row boat tied to it.

Dude tied the boat to the pier, while Kerry and Ari made their way towards the door. It was a rusted metal door. Locked from the other side.

Kerry turned to Ari, "Can your magic open this door?"

Ari placed a palm on the door and closed her eyes, "This door has no magical trap, I can try to open the door"

Dude walked up and peeked over, "Have either of you tried to turn the handle yet?"

They both looked at him speechless for a moment.

Ari shook her head, "I assumed it was locked"

"As did I." Kerry turned the handle. The door opened with a groan.

Dude smirked.

Kerry walked in, quietly unsheathing his blade.

The hall was long; the wall had several torches, but only a few were lit.

There appeared to be no guards.

Kerry whispered back, "All clear"

The three of them made their way quietly down the hall. The only sound was the sound of water dripping somewhere in the distance.

They walked for several minutes in silence.

"Wait"

Kerry and Dude turned, and they saw Ari standing in front of a door. She had a sullen expression.

"This is....where I held captive"

Dude grabbed the handle, "Kerry"

Kerry nodded.

Dude opened the door, and Kerry quickly stepped in.

Kerry poked his head out, "all clear"

"I'll keep watching," Dude reassured them as he closed the door after them.

Ari glanced around the room. There was one lone lit torch. Most of what she expected to be in the room was gone. The caldron, the desk, the books, the potions, the mirror, all gone. What was left was just a bed and a bucket. "They cleared out the room of anything usual"

Kerry leaned against the wall, "At the end of the hall, what should we expect?"

"If I can recall correctly, it leads into a dusty storage room. From there, it leads to a hallway on the first floor"

"I can work with that. Once we get to the storage room, I'll check the main hallway. If the main hallway is clear from there, we'll separate from there"

The two of them left the room. Dude spoke in a lower tone, "Nothing to report while you two were in there. Ari, was it always this quiet down here?"

Ari shrugged, "Most of the time, but I would've expected at least one or two guards"

Kerry spoke, "I wouldn't overthink it; I recall last I was here that a good majority of knights and castle guards were ordered to be stationed outside to handle the constant riots and protesters. We were short-staffed then, and it could be the same now"

They made their way to the storage room. It was full of neglected empty crates. Thick layers of dust on everything, with many cobwebs in the nooks and crannies. The floor from the dungeon's door to the storage door had left a clear path between the dust on the ground from foot traffic.

Kerry turned to them and whispered, "Stay here until I give them all clear. If things go sour, I need both of you to bolt to the boat and retreat. Understood?"

Ari and Dude looked like they wanted to protest, but silently stared at them with an intense glare that told them he wasn't going to argue. Ari and Dude reluctantly nodded. Kerry went to the door and pressed his ear against it.

He opened the door slowly with one hand, a sword in the other, and stepped out.

After what felt like an eternity in the dim storage room, with only the light from under the doors to radiate light. Ari and Dude exchanged worried glances.

Kerry opened the door, using his foot to keep it open, keeping his tone low, "Clear"

Ari and Dude walked out. The main hallway was empty.

The hallway boasted stone walls adorned with numerous pillars, each interspersed with expansive stained glass windows that allowed beams of light to filter through. The hallway stood devoid of any visible occupants in both directions. Toward one end lay the entrance to the grand foyer room. In the opposite direction led to a staircase. Descending the stairs led to the throne room directions. To the left and right of the throne room entrance, there were two adjacent doors, one leading to the east wing, while the other led to the west wing of the castle. Ascending the stairs would lead to the guest rooms and royal bedrooms"

Dude whispered, "I don't like this; where is everyone?"

Kerry spoke, "We don't deter from the plan; we split off here.. Dude and Ari, you scout the activity on the first floor. Ari will search the King's research room in the east wing as well as gather intel from the other castle staff. You will need to enter the first door you see to your left in the east wing. Locate an outfit in the servant's quarters. Dude, you check the throne room and the west wing, stay out of sight. I'll check the activity on the second floor."

Kerry sheathed his blade. Kerry recommended that The three of them walked casually to the stairs and around the castle, to not stand out.

At the stairs, Kerry whispered, "If you are questioned, use your wits. Be creative." He went up the stairs. Ari and Dude descended the stairs. Ari carefully opened the door to the right and quietly closed the door behind her.

Dude stepped forward towards the throne room doors.

✳✳✳

Dude took a deep breath. Dude contemplated slowly or confidently opening one of the throne room doors. He knew if he slightly opened it, it may raise suspicion if others were on the other side. If there were others there when he confidently opened it, he'd have to be prepared for what he'd say.

Dude felt a pain in his chest; his hands started to shake. He took a step back and sat at the bottom of the stairs.

He took several deep breaths to clear his mind.

In the distance, there was a sound of footsteps coming from the other end of the main hall. There were clanking noises from each step, Dude assumed it was a royal knight. He stood up and rushed to the door leading to the west side of the castle.

He quietly opened the door and stepped in, closing the door with care behind him.

Dude nearly jumped. A guard stood by the door.

There was the sound of light snores emitting from the guard. Who fell asleep on the post?

Dude sighed in relief.

He remembered this hall from his youth. He used to sometimes sneak down here as a young child, and use the servants door that led to the back of the throne room. From here, he would listen in to the King and Queen talk to visitors that ranged from nobility to advisors. They would never see him, and it was the closest he could get to them without them panicking.

Dude made his way to the throne room servant's entrance door. Opening it slowly, it was silent on the other side. He closed the door slowly behind him and crouched. Up ahead, he expected to see the backside of the two thrones.

Dude did a double-take. He only saw one throne.

Dude pondered if one of his parents died.

A realization hit him.

Dude suddenly thought back on Reyna's words that she heard the desperate cry of the King.

He dwelled on the thought of the Queen dying.

Dude wondered if he'd be saddened, he wasn't sure.

He pushed the thought aside. Dude was determined to find out what was going on.

He slowly walked up behind the throne.

Listening in.

He heard munching.

Every so carefully, he peaked around the corner.

There were no guards anywhere in sight.

The throne room door opened.

Sir Archibald stood at the doorway, "Permission to enter, my queen."

After a moment, a voice spoke from whoever sat on the throne, "You may"

The knight strode in and then took a knee near the throne. Tilting his head down in respect, "I've ordered all available guards and knights in the castle to head out to handle the protestors"

"So, the floggings aren't enough to calm them down. So be it, I want all the troublemakers gathered and thrown into the dungeon. We'll have them hanged tomorrow to make an example. First, find me a jester. I want to be amused. Put the noose around the jester's neck. We'll have the jester tell a joke, and then clunk, kick the stool from his feet. The jester won't be able to give us the punchline. Leaving us hanging"

The knight looked up, staying silent. His helmet hid his expression.

"Archie, I'll get you to laugh someday"

"I'll relay your order. Were you serious about the jester?"

The speaker on the throne casually threw a turkey leg, it bounced off the knight's helmet.

"You heard my orders. Get to it"

The knight stood, "As you wish, my liege". He turned and left the room. Closing the throne room door behind him.

Dude slowly peered over to see who was sitting on the throne.

It was Reyna, dabbing her mouth with a golden cloth napkin.

She wore a wine-red dress with a black corset. She had elbow-length black lace gloves. Her hands were decorated with several rings.

A spiked crown sat proudly on her head. The crown was black with red opals that raged fire inside them at the tip of each spike.

She smirked and snapped her finger.

Dude instantly transported in front of her.

"I didn't hear you come in, but it's hard to miss that big head of yours peaking around the side of my throne"

Dude, startled, was speechless.

Dude didn't know what to say. He expected the odds of bumping into Reyna alone to be low. He thought back on that old manta Kerry always had him recite when he was a young child.

That didn't apply here.

Dude's chest started to ache. He didn't plan for this. He felt prepared to confront his parents, but nowhere near prepared to confront a demigod. He immediately regretted scouting the throne room.

Dude's mind was racing. Ponding what to do, what to say.

Reyna waved her hand from side to side, "Hello, you there? Does my power intimidate you?"

Dude didn't respond.

She picked up a loaf of bread off her platter and threw it at him. It smacked him right between the eyes.

Dude came back to his surroundings and gulped.

Reyna stood up.

Reyna stomped over to him, jabbing her finger into his forehead, a slight pause between each word, "Don't.You.Ever.Ignore.Me.Again"

She glared at him, waiting for a response.

Dude was taken aback; he had never in his life been confronted in such a disrespectful manner before.

He felt an anger growing inside, but he kept it in check.

Dude decided it was best for now to play nice and cater to Reyna's ego.

He nodded, "I understand. I'm sorry. You're just...intimidating. Such power. I didn't know how to respond respectfully. What is your title?"

Reyna placed her hand on her chest, "I'm flattered. I don't care if you're serious or sarcastic, the words bring me joy. I'm the Queen, appointed by yours truly."

Reyna turned and pressed the front of her boot into a stone near the side of the throne.

The throne started to rise before shifting to the side. Revealing a descending stairway.

Reyna turned and pointed her index finger toward the stairs, "Would you like to see your parents?"

Dude stood there and gulped. He was contemplating whether he should run but immediately shook away that thought when he looked at Reyna's expression.

Reyna gave him a knowing look, "You can try to run, you won't go very far." She descended the steps, "Follow me if you want to see the former King and Queen"

Dude smacked his tongue against his teeth, looking around for a moment before following Reyna down the steps.

At the bottom of the steps, there was a vast open space with a rock ceiling and brick walls. The floor was ancient tile. In the middle of the river, was a large pool of glimmering water. At the back wall, There was a smashed mirror. To the right of the mirror was a large locked cell. The cell was overflowing with coins, gems, and other items of value. Standing on top of that pile of treasures, was a woman, trying to console a crying infant.

As Dude reached the bottom of the stairs, he got a better look at the woman.

It was the former queen Stace.

His mother.

He ran up to the cell door. The woman, Stace, looked over at him. Giving him a quizzical expression, "Who are you?"

Dude wasn't sure what to say. He couldn't remember the last time he had spoken directly to his mother. The only interactions he had with her were clandestine moments when he sneaked out of his room. He vividly recalled the swift reprimands and days spent locked away as a consequence of wanting to speak and see his own mother. He pondered whether he should feel sympathy for her.

Stace's eyes went wide in realization, "Wait...are you..." Her eyes started to water, "I'm so sorry. I wish I could explain. Please, just get far away from here" She turned away, trying to hide her tears.

Dude, startled as Reyna appeared to the right side of to him, "You're here, a lovely family reunion. You see your mother...and, what do you think of your father?"

Dude stepped back, stepping back from Reyna, "You've...turned my father into a baby? Why?"

Reya shrugged, "He was desperate. He spent his life despising his role as King. He did everything he could to get out of his royal responsibility, to sneak away from the kingdom to start a new life. It was one failed scheme after another. Did you know that he's one of the few lucky ones to have two pleas granted by me? The last one was the day you were born. He had this terrible idea of giving his knights the day off and forcing a militia to handle an enemy attack he knew of in advance. He wanted to sneak away on a boat with his riches in the night. Your premature birth right before the enemy attack had taken a piss on his plans. All the royal staff and guards were overwhelming your father with questions and updates. Your mother wasn't aware of the plan. His lapdog Archibald waited for him on the boat when your father Hubar never showed up; he left the dungeon too late to be of any help to salvage the plan. As his noble brother and several other knights dragged him into battle."

"Why are you telling me this?"

"Because it gets better! While the battle was over. He went to his bedroom alone. Praying, and begging for help. He was out of plans, and he was out of ideas." I appeared right in front of him, "Listening to him complain, I offered him an option. Let me place a beacon at the top of the castle, that lets me feed off the misery of the Kingdom. I only needed a good year of feeding to get to the level of power I needed to really take on people who I find potential threats. Anyway, I told him that if he could continue the overall misery of his people for a decade and then seal the deal by making a grand sacrifice, he'd have to kill a family member.

After that, I'd fulfill my end of the bargain. I'll grant him a new life away from royal responsibility while still having all his riches. What I didn't expect was the cruelty of gossip to really help in your father's favor. The rumors of your eventful birth had the townsfolk believing that you are a bad omen, bringing bad luck to the kingdom…your dad just agreed with it. He escalated it and worked on making sure the people truly believed that you were the problem. He raised taxes and whatever else it took to increase misery in the land"

Reyna picked up a coin off the ground and flicked it into the cell, "He had the Good Wizard Wilmar in the dungeon for a while, helping with the ruse. I was unaware he had my sister for a while. That surprised me when he told me. I held a slight grudge for a while because of that. But I digress, back to the subject of you. Your parents didn't want to look or interact with you, as it would make them feel guilty. Your father told your mother the lie that you were truly a cursed and she eventually believed it. When the King put the order in the have you killed, she turned a blind eye. The King was furious when he found out his own wife conspired to have Kerry sneak the prince out.

Their marriage went downhill from there. They avoided each other. The King, hating everyone, ordered Archibald to seek and kill you and Kerry, determined to have his long overdue wishes fulfilled that he's been waiting over a decade for.

Years passed, and The King was in desperate need of locating the Dudesow or Kerry; he started to become reckless, and he started becoming a little mad in the head.

I decided it would be more fun to make it more difficult for him, and just catch you before he did. From there, I'd either hide or kill you. I imagine how much fun it would've been to watch him go mad trying to search for you for the rest of his life, unable to fulfill his dream. It would've been amazing. The sheer joy I could've had just to make the hunt for you indefinitely. As you can tell, the opportunity for that has passed, for you see…."

She leaned over and whispered in his ear,

"Your father, to my surprise, killed another family member instead of you. So you can relax"

Dude's eyes went wide.

Reyna walked around, smiling at his reaction.

She continued, "When your father pleaded to speak to me, I returned to Hubar and heard what he had to offer. What he offered was a dead Stace in his arms, he backstabbed her. I don't even think he held back, I was impressed. He was finally a completely broken man, nothing more than a weeping shell of a man.. So I then granted his wish. I reverted him to an infant age and brought back the spirit of his dead wife. Let me remind you, your mother. I'm now forcing her to raise and console the man who just killed her. I love it!"

Reyna looked over at him, pure glee in her expression.

She stared at him for a reaction.

Dude took a step back...a mixture of emotions growing inside him.

She tilted her head, "do you not find it all amusing?"

He looked around the cell and one thing on the pile caught his eye.

There, half buried in the pile of treasure, was the leatherbound bundle containing the sword his father gave him at a child. The sword he rejected. The same sword that Kerry offered to the river serpent as payment to cross the Teal River long ago.

"I see why you do what you do". He slowly stepped closer toward the cell.

His mother looked at Dude quizzically as he slowly made his way over, but said nothing.

Reynas' face lit up with amusement, "You do? Please enlighten me"

"You punish those who you deem deserve pain and loss. You then reward them in a way that hurts them and benefits you. You see it as justice served"

Reyna looked away for a moment, with a curious expression, "I never thought anyone would try to make sense of my actions. It's a nice feeling."

Dude looked into the cell, pretending to look at the overall treasure with interest. He ran his hand over the coins, "Your sister told me that when a demi god has a sufficient amount of people that believe and pray to them, they will eventually earn their own permanent star in the sky. To become one of the great overseers." He paused. His hand placed near the hilt of the sword, "Out of curiosity. Are you doing all this to eventually get back at the overseers who wronged you back on the Guidance star? You live a long time, so I imagine you get creative along the way to stay entertained"

Reyna looked at him in a new light, "You think you've figured me out? You sure are confident for someone whose always been a royal reject"

Dude reached down to casually grab the leatherbound bundle, "Not quite, there's only one thing I couldn't quite figure out"

Reyna placed her hand on her hip and waved the other hand, "Curious, and what may that be?"

"What type of god would you represent? Karma, mischief, justice?" Dude opened the bundle and pulled out a sword. He spun the handle, doing a test swing in the air. Truly admiring the intricate blade for the first time.

Reyna laughed, "If you're asking that, then you truly don't understand me at all"

She teleported in right front of him.

Dude turned the blade towards her chest. Instead of stepping back, Reyna stepped into the blade, barely pressing into it, "Wanna know something wild? If you kill me, you kill my sister. I have a good portion of her demisol linked to me. Which means I have a part of her soul. It's the direct link that lets me drain her inner power over time, a power siphon. But the link also links our livelihood. If you kill me, we'll both cease to exist"

A twinkle in her eyes begged him to try.

Dude stepped back.

Reyna shrugged, "If you're not going to kill me, then you must be wanting to make a deal"

Dude looked between her and the blade for a moment. He turned, and he heard heavy steps making their way down the stairs. The knight Archibald made his way down the stairs. Behind him, was a woman in chambermaid attire, slowly making her way down in shackles. Behind her, two guards followed her close behind.

When they made it to the base of the stairs. The two guards stood at each side of the prisoner, with Archibald in front, taking a bow. "We've found her snooping around and asking other house staff questions. She fits the description of the one you seek named Ayra, but she argues that is not Ayre. She claims to be the mage Ari Feirune"

"That's her you idiot, one of the same. Now give me a moment, I'm in the middle of securing a deal"

The pool of water in the center of the room erupted. A man jumped out of the water, gripping a leather bag in his hand. A large serpent emerged soon after him- the river serpent from the Teal River, Riverfin.

"Hello my Queen, This is the weekly haul from this week's river toll"

Reyna rolled her eyes. She grabbed the bag from the man and dumped the contents onto the ground, coins and scrolls fell to the ground. She tossed the empty back, "I'm in the middle of a deal, I really don't care about your haul. Leave me be"

"But my queen, I need to discuss-"

"What is so important that it can't wait till tomorrow?" Reyna screeched at him.

Dude looked at the man. He recognized the man to be Adam. He glared at him.

Adam, just now noticing Dude glaring at him, did a double take, "Oh, hey you! Dude, I'm so sorry. I know you're probably mad at me. Someday I'll tell you about-"

Reyna clapped her hands loudly, several times, her eyes daggers, looking into Adam's eyes, "Don't look at him, look at me. You had something so vitally important that you had to tell me right now, that warranted interrupting me. Now, you're disrespecting me?"

Adam looked down in defeat, speaking softly, "I believe, after careful consideration, that I may have misjudged the importance of the question. I can truly wait until tomorrow. I'm sorry, my Queen"

Reyna pushed out both hands, and a burst of force shot out that sent Adam flying.

Adams' body slammed against the bars of the cell.

She glared at the serpent, who raised his serpent hands back in defense.

Reyna turned to face Archibald, "I expect silence from you as well, until I speak to you"

Sir Archibald and the guards didn't make a sound. Ari kept her head down, appearing to be deep in thought.

Dude held the blade tightly as Reyna turned towards him, her face still bright red, "Now, amuse me, what do you desire and I'll tell you the price to pay"

Dudes squinted his eyes, he tried to contain the anger in his tone, "What is the cost to get Bri and Kashmir back, alive and well?"

Reyna's anger shifted, and she broke into a smile, "You want to save those who lied to you and your friends?"

Dude's eyes went wide, "what do you mean?"

"In my free time, I like to take the form of one of the souls I've claimed. One of my favorites is the sweet, kind ol' man you may know as the Good Wizard Wilmar. One day, two exhausted and weary siblings show up, asking ol' Wilmar for help. They couldn't find their little brother. I told them, if they could locate you or Sir Kerry, and then bring them to me, I'd tell them where their missing brother was. They were gone for quite some time, several months without giving me any updates. I kept a mental note of that. Then one day, as I was experimenting with my honey concoction, I felt the demisol link strengthen.

I felt Ayra was near. Like it did again today. I poofed to branch high above the Kleon tree. Overseeing the town. I saw the two siblings walking along with three others. One of which caught my attention. My very own sister Ayra, being carried by cart by the taller sibling, Kash was his name, I think. Whatever, I was eager to see Ayra, so I rushed her cart over to me. I decided to keep the form a bit longer, as I wanted to see the look on her face when I revealed myself"

"I don't understand why you had to kill Bri and Kashmir. They convinced us to travel with them to Kleon. They fulfilled their end of the deal"

"I accomplished my end of the deal as well, just with a bit of spite since they didn't keep me updated. They wanted to know where their brother was, so while they were away, I did some searching and found him. I found out from Riverkin that the foolish child died trying to sneak across the Teal River without paying the toll. His soul was taken as a payment, forever in the river serpent's possession. Instead of telling the two siblings the terrible news and letting them leave in tears. I did something better, after they served their purpose, I sent them out to see their brother in the end. I do admit was a little rushed, they did rush at me after all. What matters is that they are all together in whatever afterlife mortals go to"

Dude gripped the sword with both hands. His head was down, and the veins on his forehead were bulging out.

"Ari, forgive me; I will find a way to save you someday. This fiend this beyond redeemable"

Dude rushed forward. Sword out, the aim true to cut Reyna in two.

Sir Archibald bolted to cut him off.

Their blades clashed.

Dude, backstepping, was rusty in the art of the duel and struggled to keep pace.

Reyna folded her arms, watching the combat with an expression of absolute delight.

There was a loud thud, along with the sound of a pole clank hitting the ground.

Behind Reyna, a guard lay on the ground while the other guard removed the shackles from Ari.

Ari had one palm out, facing toward Reyna.

Reyna turned, only to be blinded by a beam of light that shot out of Ari's hand.

The guard who removed Ari's shackle removed his helmet. He took the opportunity to stab Reyna in the side, while she was temporarily blinded.

She screamed as Kerry stabbed the blade into her ribcage. He quickly gave the blade a good twist.

Ari was concentrating on keeping Reyna blinded.

Sir Archibald gave Dude a swift kick to the chest, before bolting off towards Kerry.

Dude stumbled back. His foot slipping, he fell back first into the pool of water. Adam rushed after, diving into the water. The serpent Riverin quickly submerged into the water after them.

Kerry withdrew his blade, and he quickly dodged the swing of Sir Archibald's blade.

Ari spoke through gritted teeth, "Hurry up Kerry, I can't keep her blinded much longer"

Reyna, blinded and furious, pointed her index finger, shooting out balls of fire in random directions.

In the pool of water, Dude was sinking. From the outside of the pool, it was calm water, but from the instead, it was vibrant freezing of moving motion. There was no bottom of this pool, it appeared to go down indefinitely. The walls looked like a spinning vortex of different shades of blue and green. Dude was getting lightheaded, he tried to swim up, but he felt the spinning vortex pulling him down.

Dude resisted the urge to breathe. He didn't get a large gulp of air before he fell in.

He started to panic.

Moving his arms frantically, he tried to move up to the surface. The surface was getting farther away. The more he moved, the faster he felt his body sinking further down.

He had overexerted himself. He was contemplating letting go of the sword. His mind felt foggy. His lungs were burning.

Dude felt the certainty of death creeping in.

He slowly exhaled and closed his eyes.

A hand firmly grabbed onto his arm, pulling him up. It was Adam, who with his other arm, held onto the river serpent Riverfin.

Dude's eyes shot open, and he grabbed hold of the serpent's scales. He was only a few seconds away from passing out. Riverkin swam upwards with tremendous speed. Dude wasn't aware he was this far out into the vortex.

The serpent emerged. Adam jumped off Riverin, pulling Dude with him to the tile surface.

Adam patted Dude's back as the prince coughed a storm. The prince was hacking as he was trying to breathe. He helped Dude stand, "I'm glad you're okay. Not many survive the vortex long without Riverfin's protective blessing."

Dude turned to see Kerry in a tense battle against his brother. Ari, hunched over, getting weaker by the second trying to keep Reyna blinded. The walls around the room had scorch marks.

Turning to Adam, Dude whispered, "Can you ask your friend, um-Riverkin, to assist us?"

Adam gave him a glum expression, "No, because of some ancient agreement, his not allowed to harm the ruler of the Default kingdom"

"So, what you're saying is, anyone who isn't Reyna is free game?"

Adam looked at him. After a moment, smiled in realization but then looked at him quizzically, "Who are we asking him to strike? A certain someone or everyone except the Queen?"

"What? No. See that intimidating-looking knight wearing all black? Please ask Riverkin to strike him down. If we can get him down, we can then focus on taking out the Queen while she's blinded"

Adam nodded, He turned to face Riverkin, speaking telepathically, "I believe we can shift the tide of battle and on fin swim closer to freedom if you can take out that knight in the all-black armor"

Riverkin sideglanced Adam, "Are you certain you want to take that risk, for once I attack, there is no going back. If this will get me closer to my freedom, then I will do so"

"I'm certain of it. Make haste"

Riverkin leaned over and bit down on Sir Archibald, not to eat him, but to hold him. The knight was kicking and screaming. His arms were pinned by the teeth. Riverkin descended into the water, "I will keep him from reemerging. His soul will be mine. I expect you to take it from here"

Adam turned to face Dude, "That knight will soon become one of Riverkin's spirit servants. That knight won't bother us anymore."

That was all Dude needed to hear. He had his blade pointed forward as he ran towards Reyna.

Reyna, no longer blinded, snarled and glared at Ari, "I'm not done with you yet", She snapped her fingers.

Ari had been relocated into the cell. She landed hard onto the pile of treasure. Queen Stace leaned over and offered a hand to help Ari up.

Kerry rushed over to impale the sword into Reyna.

Reyna caught Kerry off guard when the sword disappeared from Kerry's grasp. The sword suddenly reappeared in Reyna's hand. She pointed the sword towards Kerry, whose momentum had him run straight into the blade. The blade quickly slid into his gut. Kerry looked down in shock.

Ari and Stace screamed.

Adam spoke to Riverkin, "I'm sure that knight has drowned by now; get up here. You can't kill the Queen, but I'm sure you can help defend"

Dude, furious, ran. His eyes were dead set on slicing off the neck.

Reyna looked into Kerry's eyes, "So this is how the Kingdom's most honorable knight dies. By his own trusted blade"

Kerry, his hands grasped the blade, wincing.

Reyna stared at Kerry, observing Kerry's suffering with mild interest.

Kerry weakly smiled, "Do you want to hear a joke?"

A smile reached Reyna's eyes, "You want to use your final words to tell a joke? I'd love to hear it".

Reyna's eyes went wide, as a blade sliced through her neck.

"I'd tell you, but it looks like you're heading out"

✳✳✳

Reynas' head landed with a thud, before rolling away.

Her body fell limp to the floor.

Kerry searched the pockets and found a key to the cell door. As Kerry limped, the blade still in his gut, was about to head to the cell door.

The head on the floor started to laugh.

Dude turned the decapitated head with his foot. The eyes stared back at him, Reyna's face looking bemused, "You thought that would stop me; I don't need my old body; I'll regenerate eventually. When I do, you will all suffer a fate worse than death"

Dude gave the Reyna's head a look of disgust, "Uh-huh. Well, I'm keeping your gross head away from your body just in case." He glanced at Riverkin, holding the head out by the hair, "As you can clearly see, the Queen isn't dead. If you don't mind hiding this somewhere in the depths, you wouldn't be breaking your ancient agreement or whatever..."

Riverkin, in one quick swoop, gulped down Reyna's head.

"Well...that works too"

Riverkin grimaced, "I fear my stomach will feel rather upset later tonight"

Kerry landed on his knees and fell to his side on the floor. Dude and Adam rushed over to his side.

Kerry lifted his hand, dangling a key, "Get them out."

Adam took the key and headed over to the cell.

Dude held Kerry's hand, "You need to stay strong, stay with me. Ari will heal you"

As Adam opened up the cell door, Ari rushed out towards Kerry.

When Stace stepped out, she quickly placed the baby Hubar into Adam's arms before dashing over to Kerry's side, ignoring Adam's complaints.

Ari leaned over the former knight and jabbed a finger at Kerry's chest, "Don't die on me; just give me a moment." She turned, heading over to Reyna's headless body.

Stace got on her knees, gripping Kerry's hand with both hands. Tears were rolling down from her eyes, "My dearest Kerry, you're so cold. Please hold on a bit longer."

Kerry coughed, "Your hands are just as cold; let me pass my love. We can be eternally cold together"

Stace gave a warm smile, "As much as I would love that, you are still breathing. I am not. I'll always be waiting on the other side. I won't be on this plane much longer. Kerry, the kingdom needs you...but more importantly-" She glanced at Dude with a hurt expression, "Dudesow needs you"

Kerry turned, a pained expression on his face, his voice weak; "Dudesow...there's something I need to tell you."

Dude, felt a pang of emotion, "what is it?"

Kerry rasped, "Stace is your mother, but Hubar is not your father..."

It took Dudesow a moment to understand. Dude stared at them both, at a loss for words.

Stace looked at him with sorrow, "I'm sorry my son, I-we couldn't have told you sooner. Hubar had his suspicions but he was never certain. I believe that uncertainty led to Hubar's dislike of you"

Kerry looked over at his son, his eyelids heavy, "I'm sorry I couldn't have told you sooner. It was a risk and I...felt it was even more difficult to tell you as time went on"

Dude, let his emotions win, "I forgive you, just please....don't go"

Kerry, "I'll try...just...remember that...I'm proud of you"

Dude stood up, wiping his eyes. "nope, you're not dying" He glanced over at Ari, "What are you doing? I, we, need you!"Ari, slammed her fists on the ground, "I'm trying to figure out how to break the link that Reyna had on me. Once that link is broken, I'll have enough energy to heal him"

"Can your friend Glennabelle help?"

"She could, but it would take a bit of time for her to hear and notice my lone prayer. She is constantly distracted by prayers....we would need to notice us quicker"

"Got it. Ok, we'll need to be loud. How about if we...."

He kneeled back by Kerry's side. His chest was slowly moving, and his eyes closed, "Ari get over here with haste"

Ari rushed over, "What's the plan?"

The little infant Hubar, started to cry behind them."Grab a hand, don't make this weird. we're all friends here right?" He looked up, "Adam, get over here, and you, um, Riverkin right? Lean forward. Grab a hand."

Adam, looking unsure what to do with the fussy infant, "What do I do with this baby?"

Stace, without breaking her sights on Kerry, yelled back, "Give him a coin to hold, that cheers him up"

Adam picked up a gold coin and handed it to the child. Little Hubar immediately ceased crying. His face was full of joy as he waved the coin in his hand.

Adam rushed over, and sat on the ground near the others, leaving baby Hubar onto the ground in front of him.

Dude looked around, "OK, everyone, grab a hand. I've read in a true story, that if a group of people believe in something hard enough, and then they announce out loud what they want, that it helps make the impossible possible. This may work"

Adam looked at him skeptically, "what was the book called?"Dude, looked sheepish, "The Many Tales of the Remarkable Use of The Power of Friendship"

There was an audible groan.

Dude leaned in, "Now, now, I know those are children's fables but unless anyone else has any better ideas, we're doing this. I need everyone to think of the overseer Glennabelle. Chat her name, reach out to her, call out to hear. Ask for her help"

Everyone closed their eyes, praying for Glennabelle to descend from her star, to guide them on how to proceed, to give them strength. To help them save Kerry.

Except for Ari, her eyes open, she was smiling the moment she saw Glennabelle appear.

Glennabelle leaned over Reyna's body, then she waved Ari over.

Ari stood by her side, giving her a puzzled expression, "Please attend to Kerry first-"

Glennabelle gave Ari a momentary glace that quickly hushed Ari. Glennabelle then placed one hand over Reyna's heart while having her other hand pressed over Ari's heart.

There was a visible transfer of energy. The transfer pulsed a faint glow, not bright enough to catch the other's attention.

The irises in Ari's eyes disappeared as her eyes glowed a fierce white. Her hands glowed with silver energy.

She smiled back toward Glennabelle, nodding towards the others, "Should I tell them to stop?"

Glennabelle smirked, "You can let them pray a bit longer. Let them boost my ego a little bit." Her face went stoic as she stared directly at Kerry, "Now hurry; he's running out of time"

Ari rushed over to Kerry's side. She placed two hands on the hilt of the blade. The blade, glowed a silver aura as the blade slid out.

Kerry gasped. Blood pooling out from the wound. Stace's eyes opened, seeing Ari tend to Kerry's wounds, she gripped Kerry's cold hand tighter.

Ari tossed the blade to the side, she quickly pressed her two hands onto the opening of the wound. The ground around him halted their prayers from the sound and opened their eyes, and their jaws dropped, as they watched a bright silver energy radiate from Ari's hands.

The onlookers stared In awe as a silver aura filled the air around them.

Kerry screamed.

Stace placed a free hand on Ari's shoulders, "Stop, please, you're hurting him!'

Kerry spoke, catching Stace's attention, "No...Stace"

Stace nodded and grasped both her hands over Kerry's left hand.

Kerry looked at Stace, giving her a weary smile, "I feel my strength returning"

The pure white in Ari's eyes faded away, and the pink irises returned to both her eyes. She lifted her hands. The wound was sealed, and all that remained was a faint scar line.

Glennabelle headed over, "I appreciate you all reaching out to me, I meant a lot, especially since some of you never reached out before." She looked directly at Ari, putting her hands on her hips, "I heard you the first time; I was finishing up answering someone else's prayer, and I was going to respond. You know I'm busy"

Ari got up, "I didn't know if you heard me. Sorry, it was getting intense for a moment there. I asked for help"

"It's alright, It's nice to hear from you again." She raised one palm faced upwards, and a ball of red energy appeared, "This here is Reyna's energy. I need to lock this up far away on some deserted star. Hopefully, that will give me enough time to prepare something before Reyna tries anything again." She frowned, "Why does the energy keep growing?"

Ari's eyes went wide with realization, "I almost forgot about her beacon at the top of the castle. She is still drawing energy from the people's misery. We need to get to the roof"

Glennabelle teleported them all to the roof.

Rivian flopped around, his arms waving, visually panicking, "Send me back. Send me back"

Glennabelle gasped, "Oh, I'm so sorry!" She quickly snapped him back to the pool.

Ari glanced around, and after a moment, she spotted a large ruby-red gem glimmering at the top of the flagpole. Its aura, in the shape of a flame, engulfed it.

"We can't have that up there any longer" Ari lifted a palm, facing the sky. A power beam of light shot from her hand.

Dude rushed over, a land covering his eyes, "If that doesn't get their attention, nothing will"

A scream, first faint, gradually getting louder, could be heard as Carrot drove down. She flew down, her tail hitting the steel pole. The pole broke off, landing with a cling to the ground.

Dude looked up, the elf still clinging to Carrot's back with his dear life. "Carrot, will you do the honor of stomping on this gem here?"

Ari looked at him, "What? No. Let me examine it first-"

Carrot stomped down hard onto the gem. Shattering it into pieces.

As Carrot lifted her claws, the aura around the gem faded away.

Ari picked up the pieces, "We'll, I'm examining what's left"

Kerry walked over, his arm over Stace.

Adam walked over, cradling Hubar in his arms, and pleaded, "Will someone please take this baby?

Verse got Carrot's back, then began stretching. Adam tried to pass the infant to him.

Verse shook his head, "No thanks"

Kerry, Stace, Dude, and Ari looked at each other. None of them wanted to volunteer.

Glennabelle reached over and carefully took the baby from Adam; she kissed the baby's forehead and then gently pinched the baby's cheek, "I'll find him a loving home, one that will raise him right."

Adam sighed in relief, "Thank you. I was afraid I was stuck with him"

She turned and looked at everyone, "It was great to see you again, Ari, and it was wonderful to meet you all. I must be going, but before I do…" The headless body of Reyna suddenly appeared at her feet. It was dissipating slowly. "Her body will disappear, and when it does, so will her." She pointed toward Stace, "Please say your goodbyes to the spirit; she won't be in this realm for much longer." She hugged Ari, "Farewell."

Glennabelle faded away.

Stace and Kerry held each other in a loving embrace.

Kerry whispered, "I don't know if I can continue on, knowing you're gone"

Stace kissed him, "We'll be together again. I'll be there waiting for you after your last breath."

Dude went up and gave them both a loving embrace.

Kerry kissed her forehead, "Hopefully, you'll be warmer on the other side; it's like I'm kissing ice."

She smiled. Slowly fading away, "It will be heaven once you are there"

Dude hugged her, "I'm looking forward to spending time with you someday"

"We'll have plenty of time together when the time comes. Till we meet again"

She smiled at them.

Kerry pulled Dude in by the shoulder, they waved goodbye.

Stace was gone.

✸✸✸

Dude told Kerry that he didn't want to return to a life of luxury. His past as Prince Dudesow was over; it was dead to him. He wanted to be forever known as Dudesow Feirune.

During the evening of Reyna's downfall, he gave everyone his goodbyes. He promised them that he would visit them all someday; he wanted to travel the continent, then, from there, the world. Dude told him that he craved adventure. He climbed onto the saddle and waved them goodbye. He held tightly to the reins, then tapped his heels against Carrot.

When Carrot shot up into the sky, Dude cheered as they flew above the clouds.

✸✸✸

The following day, Kerry made a royal announcement, in front of the people. He declared himself King.

The royal knights were surprised that Kerry was alive. They had welcomed his return with no complaint. They were honored to serve him.

The people of the kingdom cheered. He told them that the crimes of King Hubars and Queen Reyna were unforgivable. He promised that he would strive to be a great King for the people and he would work on making the Kingdoms' days brighter. He stated that the last King and Queen had taxed them unfairly. His first order, he declared, was to decrease taxes. He would announce the new tax cut tomorrow, as for today, the kingdom must celebrate.

The townsfolk roared in excitement, they began to chant his name.

Kerry ordered the staff to retrieve all the King's wine from the castle cellar and give it freely to the people to celebrate this momentous occasion.

The cheers and the chanting of King Kerry's name increased.

Music could be heard from all over the Kingdom.

People danced in the streets.

The sky was clear of clouds for the first time in over a century.

✳✳✳

Verse Baldree got his Kerry's Keep, as Kerry promised him. Verse remaining it to Castle Baldree. He spends his nights flirting with the ladies at the Black Spot Tavern at Inkbert, bragging about his castle. No one believes him.

✳✳✳

Per Adams' request, Kerry had the royal scholar locate the spellbound contract that held Riverkin's obligation to follow the Kingdom ruler's orders. He tore the contract, breaking the spell, Which set Riverkin free.

Adam requested to be the mayor of his hometown Wetmore, which Kerry approved. Adam was determined to make his hometown a better place.

✳✳✳

Riverkin released the souls he collected. For he had no use for them, for he was not a creature of malice.

One soul stayed by his side, by the soul's choice.

Sir Archibald offered to serve him of his own free will.

When Riverkin asked, "Why do you want to anchor yourself here, why don't you want your spirit to cross into the afterlife?"

"I am not ready to enter the afterlife, for I may have to answer for past actions. I wish to serve you until I'm ready to face judgment"

Riverkin nodded, "perhaps someday you will find a way to earn redemption. Until then, you may work as my guardian"

Sir Archibald's spirit form solidified, matching the shade of teal of Riverkin's scales.

A spear formed in Archibald's hands, and he spoke clearly with his diaphragm, "I will serve you, Riverkin, honorably. What are your orders?".

Riverkin nodded, "I seek to swim out to explore the many other rivers of the world, to try each of the rivers' unique fish. I do not like the ocean, for it is dangerous and unforgiving. We will travel through it, for I tire of the Teal River. I only ask that you use that spear well and provide protection in my travels"

A saddle materialized on Riverkin's back. Archibald climbed onto the saddle. He held the reins with one hand, a spear in the other. He held on tight as the serpent jumped over the estuaries, going from the river to the sea.

✳✳✳

Ari Feirune shot a spark from her index finger that Ignited the fire in the dusty fireplace. She sat in her favorite broken-in rocking chair, holding a comfort book in one hand, and a warm cup of tea in the other.

The wind chimes on the window moved from the soft breeze.

Ari smiled.

She was finally home.

About The Author

Christian R Scrolls

Christian, who currently resides in Arizona, is an avid fan of sci-fi, paranormal, horror comedy, and fantasy adventures.

Here's how you can say hi, ask questions, view socials, etc.
https://beacons.ai/christianrscrolls
Wanna buy me a coffee?
https://www.buymeacoffee.com/christianrscrolls